Sagusto

Cecil Roberts

Novels

SCISSORS
SAILS OF SUNSET
THE LOVE RACK
LITTLE MRS. MANINGTON
SAGUSTO
DAVID AND DIANA
INDIANA JANE
PAMELA'S SPRING SONG
HAVANA BOUND
BARGAIN BASEMENT
SPEARS AGAINST US
PILGRIM COTTAGE
THE GUESTS ARRIVE
VOLCANO
VICTORIA FOUR-THIRTY
THEY WANTED TO LIVE
ONE SMALL CANDLE
SO IMMORTAL A FLOWER
EIGHT FOR ETERNITY
A TERRACE IN THE SUN

and

THE PILGRIM COTTAGE OMNIBUS

Miscellaneous

GONE RUSTIC
GONE RAMBLING
GONE AFIELD
GONE SUNWARDS
AND SO TO BATH
AND SO TO AMERICA
AND SO TO ROME
THE DIARY OF RUSSELL BERESFORD
ALFRED FRIPP: A BIOGRAPHY
HALF WAY: AN AUTOBIOGRAPHY
A MAN AROSE

Cecil Roberts

Sagusto

London HODDER & STOUGHTON Limited

*The characters of this book are
entirely imaginary and have no
relation to any living person*

FIRST PUBLISHED	AUGUST 1927
SECOND IMPRESSION	OCTOBER 1927
THIRD IMPRESSION	NOVEMBER 1927
FOURTH IMPRESSION	MARCH 1929
FIFTH IMPRESSION	NOVEMBER 1929
SIXTH IMPRESSION	OCTOBER 1934
SEVENTH IMPRESSION	SEPTEMBER 1935
EIGHTH IMPRESSION	NOVEMBER 1936
NINTH IMPRESSION	JANUARY 1941
TENTH IMPRESSION	MAY 1942
ELEVENTH IMPRESSION (reset)	APRIL 1952

*Printed in Great Britain
for Hodder and Stoughton, Ltd.
by Richard Clay and Company, Ltd.
Bungay, Suffolk*

CHAPTER I

MAJOR CAMERON, looking out of his hotel window across the Venetian lagoon towards the Church and campanile of San Giorgio Maggiore, realised he had made a mistake. He had just seen the S.Y. *Rover* weigh anchor and leave the basin of San Marco, on her way to the Adriatic, carrying aboard his companions of the last five weeks. They had accomplished, the three of them, a delightful excursion down the Danube, to Galatz, journeying thence by rail to Trieste. Jack Cartwright's uncle, Sir Reginald Durose, the Admiral commanding the Mediterranean Fleet, had picked them up there, conveying them to Venice. A further invitation to take them to Brindisi had been accepted, save by Cameron.

He was now wondering whether he had been wise. Of all the cities of the earth, this Venice, the most lovely, could be the most melancholy for a lonely man. Denis Cameron knew it well, knew it in those penurious Sandhurst days when he had visited it, in the company of a friend, equipped only with a Baedeker, a spare pair of shoes and flannel trousers, and a determination to avoid the first-class hotels.

And now, to-day, he was comfortably situated, and famous. An incredible stroke of luck, the mere act of doing the sane thing in the right place at the precise moment, during that difficult affair at Addis Ababa, had carried his name from the wastes of Abyssinia to the archives of the Foreign Office, and the typographical megaphones of Fleet Street. An ovation awaited him in England, and later, perhaps, a Governorship in Africa. He was not a shy hero, he was young enough and egotistical enough to relish publicity, but these were not his reasons for not going down to Brindisi on the *Rover*. He wanted to get home to see his mother, his one possession in the world. Perhaps on Wednesday, perhaps on Thursday he would go. Alas, in Venice he was always in peril of *domani*—to-morrow. To end this he took his hat, walked down the stairs of the Hotel Danieli, out on to the Riva, and went direct to the office of the Compagnie des Wagon-Lits, where he definitely booked his berth for Friday.

Crossing the Piazza, with its pigeon-feeding tourists, he glanced up at the white pyramid crowning the Campanile. The Italian dusk darkened the blue of a cloudless August evening. Thrusting his way through the crowd perambulating the Piazza, he gained the Post Office, to find it shut. So he did not wire to his mother of his arrival in England on Saturday, and here again Fate, which had a strange way of interfering with the intentions of Major Denis Cameron, D.S.O., sometime political officer to His Serenity the Sultan Ibrahim Saud, once more changed his path.

Annoyed, as are all human beings to find any place shut when self-convenience requires it to be open, he turned through the archway, past the scintillating glass shops, into the long arcade of the Procuratie, and for no reason at all he suddenly felt an aversion from dining at his hotel. A Balkan monarch had filled it with uniforms and deputations, for which fact he had felt gratified when he discovered that the " Illustrissimo Major Camroon, the hero of the Abyssinian incident," had been submerged in five lines footing a column of the *Gazzettino*, describing the splendours of the Balkan entourage. In his contemptuous English mind he could not help associating the Balkan suite with the bad smell coming from the side canal.

The decision not to dine at his hotel made another decision necessary. Desultorily he turned off under a narrow portico to seek a quiet restaurant in the back streets. He suddenly found himself emerge upon a dark, gondola-ridden basin, hotel-bordered. He was hesitating, when a refreshing vista of green caught his eye. It consisted of a trellis-work, with festive lights among the leafy creeper, set up as a screen from the adjacent canal. It looked cheerful and sufficiently retired. Declining various invitations to visit a glass works, inspect lace, or take a gondola for a " serenata," he crossed a small bridge and gained the few steps leading to the al-fresco restaurant, roofed and embowered in a greenery festooned with coloured lights. The head waiter made a swift examination of the young Englishman hesitating before the tables, and deftly revolving his disc-like vocabulary of Italian, French, German, Dutch and English, emitted " Good-evening, sir ! " in an accent acquired from two years at the Berkeley.

The place was cosmopolitan enough, in speech, in style, in race. Two slim American students read the *Carte* in despair, and settled on the fixed *Díner* as less hazardous. " It'll be veal in any case," said one, with a Harvard indifference. In a corner an Austrian smiled over his pince-nez at a handsome Italian youth who ordered expensive dishes, which he translated into Milanese French. They were both mahogany-tanned with Lido bathing. A French cinema actress—Cameron gave her the benefit of a profession—shrilled over her champagne like a parrot, while a doting Dutchman rested his heavy eyes on her plumage.

Nearer, Cameron watched an Italian family gaily feasting. A brown-legged boy in white shorts, and shirt with Schiller collar, all on the verge of splitting, as if he resented his silken chrysalis; a velvet-eyed little girl whose black head balanced an enormous bow; the father, grizzled and walnut wrinkled; the mother, sallow, much ringed, with fingers the sole legacy of slimness long lost in oleaginous living; an elder son, leonine-headed, elegant and adventurous-eyed—they were all eating, all talking, all inquisitively examining the company around them. Cameron delighted in this salad of nations. In search of a new type, his eye went afield, roved and was suddenly checked. There was no passing her. Nowhere in the world would that woman let herself be passed over.

He saw she was not young, she was not beautiful. Forty, perhaps fifty summers had been buried in her complexion, and a lifetime of lines wiped out in her face-cream. Nobody, even in youth, could upkeep such an expensive colour in hair. Its bronze had a defiant lustre, set like a shining helmet over her white brow. She wore her make-up like a somebody, proclaimed it to a world that must admire her throat, superbly set upon a bosom weighted with pearls. Also the master-jewellers of Paris had incrusted with their gems hands in which nature had triumphed—Latin hands, Medusa-like in their tenuous fascination.

Who was she? asked Cameron. Countess, Brazilian heiress—hence the diamonds—or—— No, he would be wrong to hazard that; adventuress she might be. But courtesan? No. She was a woman with a purpose, and the adventure must offer more than seduction. Cameron was a young man, but he was well-travelled and knew the types. Here was a woman he could not place, except that she expressed in her personality, even more than her setting, a commanding strength to achieve such ends as she sought.

And then a ludicrous incident shattered his imaginative speculation. Was it possible? The head waiter stood over her, suspicion mingling with suavity. She was explaining something he was slow to understand. Their closeness, her protesting loudness, conveyed the whole situation to Cameron. The lady had lost her chatelaine and could not pay the bill. No, she could not send to her hotel, she was staying on her yacht.

Hang the fellow's suspicion! thought Cameron. Why, those diamonds alone were—— He half rose, hesitated, and sat down. Head waiters knew the cities of the world and the citizens therein. But even so. If the diamonds were not real, if the woman had no money, if—— Cameron rose again. It was absurd that a woman of so much character, so assuredly stamped with victories, should be arguing a dinner out of a suspicious head waiter!

He approached the table, and bowed, with a horrible thought that he was Continentalising himself. He asked madame if she would honour him by accepting his help.

"Perhaps the fact of an adjacent table and my seeing your difficulty will excuse me," he added.

She threw up her head with a quick glance of appraisal, then smiled on him, not eagerly, but assuredly.

"You are kind, m'sieur—otherwise I must sit here while someone goes to my yacht," she replied.

"No, no, madame!" cried the head waiter. "It is sufficient that you have been unfortunate——"

"Your assurance is late," she retorted, quickly. Then, to Cameron: "I thank you, m'sieur."

Cameron placed some notes on the tray. The disconcerted waiter withdrew. He, too, would have retreated, his service rendered, but she detained him with a jewelled hand on his sleeve.

"You must let me repay you, m'sieur. I have left my chatelaine in a gondola. I do not forget usually—kindness never."

She smiled at him, and he found himself fascinated by the whole background of her personality. It had been dramatic, surely. She was pivotal, events had moved about her, as about Helen or Circe; men had gone down in wreckage to serve her whims. She might be evil or good, but she was significant in any case.

"You'll let me give you something for your return—you'll need a gondola to reach the yacht?" he asked. "Please do not trouble to repay me."

The waiter returned with the change. She rose.

"I am Donna Soudaikos," she said, "and you must let me know to whom I am indebted—I will send your money to-morrow, m'sieur."

"Oh, no, no!" he replied, hurriedly. Then, seeing she was ready, "May I get you a gondola?"

Her eyes rested on his for a moment.

" You are English? " she said, quietly, more in statement than question.

" Yes—my name's Cameron."

There was a brief flicker in her eyes, speedily checked by the smile that lit them.

" Major Denis Cameron? " she asked, as they walked from the restaurant towards the canal.

" Yes. But how do—how can you know my name? "

She laughed easily, her white hands flitting over the pearls that roped her.

" There are such things as newspapers, m'sieur."

" Dash it—yes. I hadn't thought of that. But you must have a good memory," he added.

" Brave men are memorable," said Donna Soudaikos, looking down at the gondola at her feet. There was a gravity in her voice that made him regard her more acutely. But he saw nothing, save her profile—certainly beautiful thus seen, with its clear line of the eyebrow, the long-lashed eye, the straight, perhaps Hellenic line of brow and nose.

The gondolier held his craft by the step, the Donna seated herself, silver-grey against the black cushions, so that she seemed a part of the bright reflections on the dark water. Like a swan's head a hand rose to receive Cameron's salute.

" Adieu, m'sieur—I shall not forget! " she said.

" Adieu, madame," he replied, gravely, his lips to her cool fingers. Even in the act a sense of the bizarre troubled him. It was so like a painting on a fan. It could only happen in Venice. The gondola glided away, rocking slightly in graceful progress. He watched it a moment, the bronze hair glinting, then the gondolier obscured her.

" Good heavens—I haven't had any dinner yet! " exclaimed Cameron. Characteristically, it was his first thought. Then, the restaurant regained, the dinner ordered, he fell to thinking upon the strange episode of this evening. Not strange really.

Ladies did lose purses.   But this lady was not as others who lost
purses or anything else.   She was—she was——

But what was she? Donna Soudaikos.   Greek, probably—
that was all he knew.   And then suddenly it occurred to him
that this was all he would ever know.   He had omitted to name
his hotel and she could not find him if she wished.   For some
reason he regretted it, but all through dinner he found himself
unable to analyse the reason.   It should have been carnival-time
in Venice, period *settecento*, himself in a cloak and three-cornered
hat.   As for the Donna, assuredly that was her period, full of
intrigue, of covert adventure.

Then another recollection assailed him.   He had forgotten to
lend the Donna some money for the gondola.

No—he would have been a miserable failure in the *settecento*
setting, and, in gallantry with dames, cut out by any barber's
apprentice.

CHAPTER II

At one o'clock in the morning, following the episode with the
Donna, Cameron leisurely strolled back to his hotel from the
Fenice Theatre, where, from a golden box in those tiers of
golden boxes, he had witnessed Puccini's last work, *Turandot*.
He had looked down, not upon the élite of Venice, for it
avoided the tourist season, but upon what was perhaps the
most bizarre conglomeration in Europe.   He had not been
alone for long.

" Major Cameron ! " called a gentle voice, as he ascended the
staircase from the foyer.

He paused, pleased to be recognised by so beautiful a creature
as the Contessa Trevisan, whose luncheon guest he had been the
previous day at her small but exquisite palace on the Grand

Canal. She had united the vivacity of Washington with the blue blood of Venice. Three children, studies in blond hair and velvet eyes, had spread the fame of the mother across the picture-galleries of Europe. The Trevisan children, with lovely necks and faces, aureoled with curls, were a tradition. Cameron had played with the originals, Mario, Enrico and Elizabetta, on a marble floor where a hundred gallants had once danced a *toccata*.

"This is delightful! You must join our party," said the Contessa. "I thought you had left Venice to-day!"

"I've been leaving every day!" he laughed.

"So you are learning—in Spain *mañana*, in Italy *domani*!" she cried, playfully touching his arm with her ivory fan. What a splendid head he had! like Giorgione's Francesco at Castel-franco.

"And what is it in America?" he asked.

"Do it now!" she said quickly.

At this moment she found her party, to whom Cameron was introduced. The Contessa's cosmopolitan taste was well represented, for the company included an English peer's daughter who had turned a gift for vulgarity into money, a Greek millionaire, an Egyptian Pasha, and the Baroness D'Ermonstein, so wealthy that she studded the earth with villas and the sea with yachts.

And there was Madame de la Tourestier, so poor that she had to live by her wits. These sufficed to support a villa at Nice, an *appartement* in Paris, and a ceaseless procession of gowns. The spiteful declared that she was a Lido mannequin for a famous Paris modiste; the more spiteful that the gowns were not an end in themselves. Whatever the truth, Cameron liked her. She had sensibility and jade-green eyes. He liked her as much as he disliked her brother Henri, a feline young exquisite who had passed through an astonishing number of secretaryships in his twenty-two years. Madame de la Tourestier complained to Cameron that Henri had just deserted a most considerate German patron in order to run a cocktail bar in Vienna.

" But I can't endure a man who spits while he dictates letters—the interruption is neither polite nor hygienic!" said Henri, desperately epigrammatic.

A few minutes later the curtain rose, but not before Cameron had managed to ask the Greek millionaire a question. At first there was suspicion in the grey face of the financier.

" Donna Soudaikos?—no, I do not know her. Soudaikos? —I seem somehow to have heard the name. But Donna— why Donna?"

" I don't know—we met casually at dinner to-night," said Cameron.

The Greek detected something withheld.

" Why do you ask? Where did you meet her?" he pressed, his little eyes glittering in the light reflected from the stage.

" Her yacht's in the San Marco basin now," said Cameron, evasively. He wished he had not mentioned the encounter. After all, Donna Soudaikos had every right to her existence, and the payment of a dinner bill did not justify him in becoming an inquiry agent. Ashamed of his curiosity, he sat back in his chair as the music rose through the hushed theatre. But the Greek was not going to release him thus easily. At the end of the first act the Contessa turned to Cameron.

" I hear you've met the mysterious yacht-owner!" she cried. " Tell me—what is the lady like?"

" But why mysterious?—there is nothing mysterious about her yacht," asked Cameron, trying to mask his growing interest in Donna Soudaikos. Really, it was most ungallant of him to have put these gossips on the trail of a woman who, after all, had not sought his aid.

" Ah—you don't know all," added the Greek. " I've just told the Contessa, strictly *entre-nous*, of course." And then, in proof of his conception of a confidence, " The Greek Consul tells me the yacht's papers are not in order and she has no right to fly the Greek flag."

Suddenly from the corner of the box, came the husky voice of the peer's daughter:

" Are you discussing that Donna something?"

Cameron nodded. Lord, it was like throwing a fox to the hounds! The poor woman would not have a shred left on her bones soon.

" You don't mean to say you've met her, Major Cameron!" she cried, breathlessly. " I've thought of boarding that boat. A naval man told me she's suspected of gun-running."

" Whatever for?" asked the Baroness. " Since fighting's out of fashion, who wants guns?"

" There's always the Balkans," suggested Henri.

" Now I feel I'm in the centre of a stupendous intrigue," declared Madame de la Tourestier. " Major Cameron, you would look so well on a throne—crowns suit your particular shape of head!"

They all laughed noisily at this sally. The men rose to go to the bar. The Conte, a silent and obscured person in the scintillating presence of his wife, took Cameron by the arm.

" You will see the Fenice lives up to its ancient reputation as the gossip-exchange of Europe," he said, quietly. " We still live in such an atmosphere of incredible romance that the truth is stifled. By now, the strange Donna is probably a queen in disguise!"

The Conte had not heeded the little Greek, who followed close behind.

" It's a clumsy disguise to fly a flag to which your ship's papers don't entitle you," he said, with a flicker of his beady eyes.

" I don't believe it," retorted Cameron, sharply. " In any case, it's no affair of mine."

" It may become so," answered the Greek, quietly.

Cameron suppressed his annoyance with the hateful little man.

" I shall never see the lady again. It was by the merest accident we met," said Cameron, forcefully and ordered drinks. The topic of the strange Donna was then dropped, and, to Cameron's relief, it was not revived throughout the evening.

But it still remained in his head. In the dark theatre he retained a vivid vision of that extraordinary woman at the restaurant. Her face at once repelled and attracted him. It had such power, with a kind of beauty that retained no softness and had no element of the alluring feminine. Now, as he walked home along the Riva towards his hotel, the thought of her, of the gossip at the theatre, impelled him, foolishly, to search the moon-flecked lagoon.

Away there, towards the impressive pile of the church of Santa Maria della Salute and the low flat buildings of the customs house at the mouth of the Grand Canal, he could discern a number of ships : a liner calling on a cruise, the Trieste boat, some large schooners, and a forest of spidery ships' masts netting the moonlight. Near them rode the red and yellow lanterns on the boats of the " serenata " parties. It was past midnight, but he could hear their voices in those desperately premeditated renderings of Verdi. But of the particular yacht he sought there was no sure sight.

Crossing the first bridge beyond the Doge's Palace, he hurried on. People could not help making simple things fantastic in Venice. The whole setting was so absurdly dramatic. The gondolas, the marble fretwork of palaces, bridges and pavements —they did not belong to a workaday world. The libertines of Europe had once played here, now the tourists Kodaked it, sure of picturesque results. Why, that very moon, hung near the grey campanile of San Giorgio, was a theatrical one, its size and brilliance pantomimic !

Cameron stood a moment on the threshold of his room, held by the black-and-silver silhouette of a Gothic–Byzantine window overlooking the lagoon. Then he switched on the light and entered. Upon his writing-table lay a long mauve envelope, addressed to him in bold lettering. He opened it, glanced at the head, and then swiftly at the foot. Its contents were brief, and when he had read it he laughed quietly to himself at the ridiculous fulfilment of a half-suppressed desire. It was from the Donna Soudaikos.

> Let me repay you in person, and renew an acquaintance so curiously made. My age allows me to presume upon your kindness and express the hope you will dine with me to-morrow, Thursday night, at eight. My servant will call in the morning for your answer.

He read the letter twice. He would decline, of course. He had no wish to dine out on the eve of his departure. Besides which, there was the gossip at the Fenice.

And then, angry with himself for heeding the tittle-tattle of a beady-eyed vulture and a bevy of thistledown beauties, he perversely decided he would go. For one thing was certain: be what she may, Donna Soudaikos was a woman of decided character. For the rest, all the unknown part of her, it was an attraction. It would not be a dull evening, that much was certain.

Cameron undressed, whistling *Quando la bella luna*. A strange place, Venice! One always went to bed excited. But then, at twenty-eight, excitement is still a tonic.

CHAPTER III

IN the morning the Donna's messenger called at the hotel for Cameron's answer. He had left a note accepting the invitation to dine at eight o'clock on board the ship, whose name was the *Lucciola*. He had observed the yacht that morning from the piazzetta, a twin-masted, auxiliary-engined schooner, with a long bowsprit and clean lines that promised speed and sea-worthiness. She was painted white from bow to stern with gold rimming, altogether a substantial ship, probably requiring a crew of at least ten. The Donna must obviously be a rich woman.

Cameron did not see her messenger. He was out when his reply was fetched. After lunch, he leisurely packed, in readiness for his departure on the morrow, leaving out only such things as were essential in the interval before his departure. At seven o'clock he began to dress, and was annoyed with himself to find he was in a state of suppressed excitement. The remarks of the little Greek at the Fenice the previous night kept recurring. One simply could not be matter of fact in Venice, and at the bottom of his resentment of the Greek's gossip was a hope of excitement. In that, of course, he was doomed to disappointment. What could possibly happen? He was going to dine with a lady to whom he had rendered slight assistance, and of whom he knew nothing, except what was based on gossip. True, it was said the *Lucciola's* papers were not in order, she was not a Greek boat, and was not entitled to the Greek flag she was flying. That might be truth or gossip. It was certainly no concern of his. He would be the Donna's guest for an hour or so, and there the matter would end, despite his foolish hope that it would not be the end. For Major Cameron still liked to regard the world as a sphere of adventure. Under his quiet demeanour he was a soldier of fortune, in spirit an incurable romantic.

With a last critical survey in the mirror, in confirmation of the knowledge that he was youthful in line and worthy of immaculate dressing, he left his room and went, hatless, out on to the Riva. For no reason at all, save perhaps that an Englishman never knows what to do with his hands, he carried a raincoat. The beauty of the night mocked this burden. A mellow half-moon, the colour of August corn, rose beyond the light-jewelled line of the distant Lido. Choosing a gondola, as it took him out from the crowded piazzetta and the broad pavement and bridges of the Riva, he observed yet again the dove-grey beauty of the Doge's Palace, the two columns, the marvellous fretwork of stone and marble, the glimmering colonnade and pyramid crowning the high campanile, the jet and silver of gondola and light-flecked water— all the beauty, in fact, that rendered Venice a wordless fantasy beyond the incessant snaring of poets and artists.

"Do you know the *Lucciola*?" asked Cameron.

"*Si si*, signore!" answered the gondolier, sailor-bloused and felt-slippered.

"It is a Greek ship?"

"They say so, signore."

Cameron was silent a moment at this. Surely the gossip had not extended to the gondoliers.

"What makes you answer, 'They say so'?" he pressed.

The man propelled his black craft a few strokes before answering. It rocked across the wake of a motor launch, with the chop-chop of water so familiar in this wheelless city.

"I do not know, signore. But the crew is not Greek," said the gondolier, at last.

"Then you have been to the ship?" asked Cameron. "She looks very fine."

The white barque, resting swan-like on that black flood, with the slender masts rising against the net of stars that backed her, and the line of her portholes patterning the water with gold, gave her such beauty that she might have ridden out of Spenser's "Faëry Queen."

"*Multa bella*," assented the gondolier. "I've not been to her, signore. Her boat comes ashore for supplies. They are Slavs, not Greeks."

"Suspicious old beggar," thought Cameron. Here was the beginning of the gossip. As they neared the ship his excitement was intense, yet he knew well how ridiculous it was.

When the gondola touched the lowered gangway he saw he was expected. A young sailor, in a white jersey, hurried down, a bronzed youth of seventeen or so. He stood silently waiting while Cameron paid off the gondolier. Then, as the gondola slid away:

"Major Cameron? Will you follow me, m'sieur?" said the youth.

To Cameron's surprise the lad spoke French, a good French. He was not dressed as a common sailor. A valet, conjectured Cameron. Yet there seemed no purpose for a valet on board the Donna's yacht. Perhaps a secretary or a steward. The youth had an air of breeding, of self-possession.

Cameron followed him up the gangway, across the deserted deck, with its glimmer of polished brasswork, to a companion-way shining golden in the gloom. The youth descended the few steps, walked down a short corridor of cabins, and holding aside the curtain covering an open door, stood back for Cameron to enter. To his surprise, Cameron found himself, not in the presence of Donna Soudaikos, but in a small cabin, with a sleeping berth and the usual ship's accommodation. At a glance he saw brushes and toilet requisites spread out on the small dressing-table.

The youth smiled at him sedately, took the major's coat, and hanging it up, said:

"Madame Soudaikos will receive you in a few minutes, m'sieur."

With a courtly little bow he withdrew, closing the door quietly. Was that boy a Slav or a Greek? wondered Cameron. He could not be a Slav, the features were too clear-cut, without the broad Slavonic nose. He might be Greek or Italian, or even southern French—but with those blue eyes and fair sleek hair? French probably; his accent was perfect.

Cameron looked at himself in the mirror, brushed a vagrant wisp of hair, scanned the dressing-table, adjusted his bow. The porthole was shut and the cabin stuffy. He hoped the Donna would not be long in receiving him. As he waited he heard the campanile bells toll eight. Then footsteps sounded in the corridor. The youth was returning.

Cameron gave his dress waistcoat a final tug. He was going to find the Donna interesting. Then the footsteps passed away. Two, three minutes went. A little impatiently he sat down on the carpet chair. He greatly disliked people who deliberately kept one waiting in order to heighten the effect of reception.

But at that moment something happened that drove all impatience out of his head. Following a pattering of feet on the deck overhead, a confused medley of thumps, and a clanking of iron, he felt the ship give a little shiver and then fall into a rhythmic vibration. Was she changing her mooring? This surmise was followed by a certainty. There was something familiar in this quivering of the boat. All at once he recognised its cause. It was from the engine, which had started!

In that moment of realisation he felt a vague shock. Then he dismissed his apprehension. The yacht was changing her mooring for some reason. But scarcely had he satisfied himself with this explanation when another sound, arousing all the attendant whisperings so familiar aboard ship, informed him that the propeller was revolving at half-speed.

Swiftly he went to the porthole. It was screwed down, but he could see through it a moving line of lights on the shore. In that moment his curiosity passed into a vivid sense of trickery. He went to the cabin door. One turn of the handle confirmed his surmise. It was locked. He was a prisoner in a ship putting out to sea!

CHAPTER IV

I

AT first he was inclined to laugh at the absurdity of the thing. It had a childishness characteristic of these hare-brained foreigners. If he had really been kidnapped, the attempt would collapse disastrously. You could not, in these days, lock up an Englishman on board a ship and put out to sea, as in the swashbuckling days of old. And even so, what was at the back of it all? A ransom?

No, it could not be that. There was such a thing as a British Fleet in the Mediterranean. There was also, he reflected, a maze of islands down the Dalmatian coast, and it would take a devil of a time hunting him out. Could that be the game? This woman, with her fine presence, her smart yacht, her diamonds, and all the accoutrements of wealth, was merely a pirate?

No, the thing was ridiculous. But it was also a complete mystery.

He looked round the cabin that had become a cell. It was quite an ordinary well-equipped cabin, with a single berth, electric light, revolving fan, etc. Then, on the table under the porthole, he noticed something covered with a large white cloth. Lifting it, he was amazed to find, on a tray, a complete dinner laid out, as if in anticipation of his coming. Near a plate lay an envelope, addressed to him in the same bold writing as the note sent to his hotel. He tore it open.

> For reasons I will explain later, I must ask you to dine alone. At nine-thirty we shall meet. Forgive this temporary failure of my hospitality.
>
> > ROSA SOUDAIKOS.

That was all. The briefness, the insolent assurance, filled him with swift anger. At nine-thirty she would see him! Who on earth did the woman think she was? Perhaps that suave young villain who had locked him in would come and fetter him at the appointed time. They had a very poor opinion of their victim if they thought he was to be marched about at their pleasure.

Cameron looked at the dinner. One could fight better on a full stomach than on an empty one. A large bottle of Asti

had been included. Perhaps it was drugged. He uncorked it
with the corkscrew thoughtfully provided and cautiously sipped
the amber liquid. It was not likely they would drug him before
an interview obviously desired by this melodramatic donna.

No, not melodramatic—damn silly would be more applic-
able to her conduct. Sitting down, Cameron began to eat
heartily. After all, it was a unique thing these days to be kidnapped. He was so constituted that the unique always appealed
to him. Nevertheless, that Donna woman was going to have
an unpleasant interview. For the moment the excitement of
discovering her motive overcame his indignation. It in no way
impaired his appetite, however.

II

Punctually at half-past nine, as Cameron lay smoking in his
berth, listening to the sea-noises of a ship going full speed ahead,
there came a tap on his door. This futile politeness amused
him, and he shouted " Enter ! " as though his valet had knocked.
Into the cabin, after unlocking, stepped the same youth. He
halted in the doorway, perhaps a little apprehensive of violence,
then, seeing Cameron on the bed, gave him a smile that had no
insolence in it, but simple youthful charm.

" Donna Soudaikos would be pleased if you would see her
now, m'sieur," said the youth blandly.

Cameron sat up and knocked the ash off his cigarette.

" That's kind of the Donna," he replied. " I suppose if I
don't go at once, in all gratitude for this little farce of yours, I
shall be taken in chains? "

The lad shook his shoulders and smiled again. It was an
engaging, almost angelic smile. If this fellow was a rogue,
thought Cameron, then he had never seen a pleasanter-looking
rogue. He gave an impression of absolute cleanness—the cleanness that came from a close communion with Nature, with air,
sunshine and water. He was sleek as a young panther, with
glossy tanned flesh, and a neat head, as of that of the age of the

Greek athletic prize men. His blond, wavy hair had been bleached almost to silver by long exposure to the Mediterranean sun.

As the youth answered Cameron he showed a level line of white teeth.

"You must not think we are barbarians, m'sieur," he said, quietly. "We are——" and then, checking himself—"but my mother will explain."

"Your mother?"

"Donna Soudaikos is my mother," he said. "You see, m'sieur, I have come alone; I trust you. You could choke me."

The frankness of it made Cameron laugh.

"Thank you—but I can't return the compliment—and throttling young brigands is not my after-dinner pastime."

"Brigands, m'sieur!"

There was a protest in the lad's voice and eyes. Yes, actually he showed resentment! A little magnificent in his indignation, observed Cameron. In this sternness his place in the Parthenon frieze was even more indisputable.

"Brigandage seems your present occupation," said Cameron.

The lad did not answer for a moment. He was genuinely hurt, there could be no doubt of it.

"When you are ready, m'sieur," he said, with all the gravity of a court page, ignoring the insult.

Cameron got up from his berth, surveyed himself in the mirror, then turned to the youth.

"Since you're to be my gaoler, I may as well know your name?" he asked.

"Minio Mavrocordato Soudaikos—I am called Tino."

"Thanks—then, Tino, I am ready," said Cameron, and, for some reason, he could not forbear smiling at the youth, whose grave blue eyes flooded with sunshine in response.

He bowed, and Cameron followed him out, up the companion-way on to the deck. The yacht had left the lagoon,

and was well out of the Porto di Lido, whose lights flashed intermittently behind them. The swell of the Adriatic rocked the
vessel as she rode, one sail fully spread to the star-scattered night.
Cameron looked up to where the sail-tip glimmered ghostly
under a rising moon. Away on the starboard a line of lights
revealed land, with one conspicuous illuminated building. It
was the Lido Excelsior Hotel. Strange to think that friends of
his were taking coffee on the terrace overlooking this sea on
which he sailed a captive!

The youth led him along the deck towards a second companion-way. He seemed to have every confidence that Cameron
would follow. For a moment the idea of jumping overboard
and swimming landwards did enter his head, but the distance
to the Lido was a couple of miles, and the currents might prove
troublesome. Moreover, he was disinclined to inconvenience
himself, and his pugnacity was aroused. The Donna was not
to be let off so easily.

The youth descended the stairs, looked round to find Cameron
at his elbow, and then tapped on a door, before throwing it wide
open. He stood aside for Cameron to enter.

Surprise, not fear, transfixed the latter on the threshold.
There, amid all the refinements conceivable on board a private
yacht, in a salon that might have belonged to a Paris house, sat
two women, exquisitely gowned One of them rose from a
chair as he paused. Cameron recognised her as the Donna
Soudaikos. She came forward to greet him as though at a
reception in the Faubourg St. Germain.

"Major Cameron, this is a pleasure you do not perhaps
share?"

She smiled at him, superbly self-possessed. He stepped over
the threshold and bowed, but not with the reproof he had intended. The Donna turned to her companion, who stood up,
and Cameron for the moment completely forgot his situation
in the surprise of this meeting with someone so utterly outside
the nature of the adventure.

"This is my daughter, Nada,—Major Cameron," said the Donna. "You have already met my son."

The Donna pointed a fan she carried towards the youth who had quietly closed the door and stood within.

"I have. This is a family affair, Donna?" asked Cameron, satirically.

"Yes—won't you sit down, major? I have much to explain to you."

"It would seem so," he replied, acidly.

As he spoke his eyes met the girl's and the anger in them softened. Her beauty was of a kind so utterly opposite to her brother's that, for a moment, he was incredulous. But the resemblance to the Donna was infallible. Her colour was the same, but all her beauty had the virginal freshness absent from the mother's appearance. One was a hardened woman of the world. This girl might have newly come from some retreat of prayerful nuns.

He looked at her intently now. The black hair was firmly drawn back from a brow small and pure, with well-defined, arched eyebrows, as if an artist had drawn a charcoal curve across that ivory flesh. The nose preserved the traditional Greek line with the brow, but not assertively, and the beauty of the full red mouth softened its severity. It was a foreign face, foreign in that its contour and colouring were impressively individual, with that early maturity of the Latin which gives so much character to youth. Yet her years could not have been more than twenty.

In that first swift regard of her Cameron read something more appealing than mere beauty. Beauty was there, lustrous enough in those dark pupils, but under their glow he saw the unspoken appeal. Apprehension of this singular meeting had not effaced the implied trust in her swift survey of his face. Quickly she had glanced at him and then, with averted eyes, had resumed her seat.

Cameron sat down in a chair facing the Donna. The youth

remained standing at his side, but with no air of guarding him. Of the four persons in the salon he was assuredly the most at ease.

" My first words, Major Cameron," said the Donna, smiling, " must be those of apology. I asked you to dine with me, and you have had to dine alone."

" I have dined well," Cameron could not help saying. The situation was piquant.

" You are, of course, very indignant," continued the Donna. " You've every reason to be. I've decoyed you on to this boat and now hold you a prisoner here, a strange way of requiting your own kindness to me last night. But I am driven to desperate devices."

" Your desperation seems to have destroyed your senses, Donna," said Cameron. The deliberation of this woman annoyed him. " Whoever or whatever drives you does not concern me. I would like to know when you propose returning your guest to Venice? "

The Donna looked at her prisoner in silence for a few moments, and was undismayed by the hostility in his eyes.

" I cannot return you to Venice, major. We could call at Trieste in the morning, where you can be landed in time to catch the boat for Venice. You'll be quite free to go."

" Thank you," replied Cameron. " But you will have come to your senses a little late, Donna. I may not be quite so easy to dispose of."

The Donna shrugged her shoulders and fanned herself. A swift look passed between the girl and the boy.

" If I am free to go at Trieste, why have you taken such pains to trap me? " asked Cameron, irritated by the woman's composure.

" Major," she replied calmly, " let us not begin by quarrelling. I'm in desperate need of your help. You are in some measure to blame."

" I? " echoed Cameron.

"If you had not been so kind at that restaurant, and if you had not told me your name, I should never have resorted to this desperate trick to secure your aid."

"But what is it you want of me—money—a ransom?"

The moment he had spoken he regretted the insinuation. In his own heart he knew it was not that. There was a cry from the girl who had sat so still, and he saw the blood leave her lips. As for the lad, his eyes had a momentary gleam of anger, bright and swift. Then his face set rigidly.

"We are not brigands, m'sieur," he said, with dignity.

"Forgive me," answered Cameron, at once. His eyes sought the girl's, and her shy response touched him.

"There is nothing to forgive—you've every reason for suspicion, major," said Donna Soudaikos.

"Not suspicion, only anger, Donna," he corrected.

"Thank you—perhaps I may appease that, if you will listen," she said.

He nodded in assent.

"For six months, Major Cameron, I've been seeking for a brave man. It's been a difficult quest. There are many kinds of brave men, I find. There are men brave because they are reckless, men brave because they are desperate. There are adventurers who count no cost, but in whose characters I could have no confidence. I have interviewed many, and found none in whom I could trust. I know you are brave, your recent achievement has held the world in admiration. You are something more than a soldier of fortune. You are a gentleman of a race rightly esteemed for honour and courage in the four corners of the world. You'll know I am not saying this in mere flattery. I say it to explain my own desperate conduct towards you. It happens that chance or, as I hope it may prove, good fortune, brought me into contact with you last night. The *Gazzettino* had informed me of your presence in Venice, and when I met you I immediately determined upon my present plan."

" Couldn't you have told me your plan without kidnapping me? " interrupted Cameron.

" I could—but with little success. I doubt whether you would have assented, major."

" Do you think I shall now, by force? "

" No—not by force. I don't seek that. But you will realise there are many things a man will do, when certain obstacles are removed, that he would not consider on his own initiative. You would have said ' No ' to my request off hand. It would have seemed too troublesome, too fantastic."

" I shall probably say ' No ' now," said Cameron.

" That is as you decide," replied the Donna, smiling, " but if you can be persuaded to assent to my plan I shall at least have relieved you of the initial responsibility. You are now in a situation not of your seeking. I believe Englishmen to be somewhat quixotic. Once in a mess, they have a capacity for enjoyment until they are out of it."

Cameron laughed. The lady's psychology had at least the merit of candour.

" What do you want of me? " he asked.

Again there was a swift interchange of glances between mother, son and daughter. The boy looked anxious, as if uncertain of the wisdom of the Donna's act. But in the girls' face as she looked at Cameron there was nothing but implicit trust. Whatever they sought, this girl had no doubt of his capacity. Cameron had to steel himself against the flattery of this thought. He was no foolish young man to be hypnotised into any crazy adventure by a pair of lovely eyes.

" It's a long story, Major Cameron," began the Donna, " but I'll be as brief as possible. In telling you all I do I am placing absolute trust in your secrecy."

" Is that wise, Donna? " asked Cameron.

" I'll take the risk. Certain names for the present will be withheld. I am the only surviving child of an old Greek family. My mother was a Turk, my father a Greek, of Smyrna. I inherited much property after his death, most of it in Smyrna, all of which has been lost in my country's present unhappy state. Among my property, however, and, to us, the most valuable part of it, is an island off the Dalmatian coast. It has been in my family's possession for several hundred years, ever since an ancestor of mine, an admiral in the service of the Serene Republic, captured it from the Turks, following the Battle of Lepanto. The Venetian Senate, in gratitude, permitted him to retain it as a purely personal possession. It had, and has still, great intrinsic value, for it contains a rich lead mine. I am now solely dependent upon the revenues from this mine, and it is the only legacy I can leave my son and daughter. The island is about five miles long and one in breadth, very indented, with two small harbours, one to the east of the Castello in which I live, the other at the opposite end of the island, which is used for the shipment of the lead. There's a small village of about four hundred inhabitants, most of whom work in the mine."

"What is their nationality, Donna?" asked Cameron.

"I will come to that presently," replied the Donna; "it bears upon my present predicament. Until the Great War my situation was without difficulty. The island was my personal property and I possessed absolute rights in regard to it. Neither Italy, Serbia nor Greece had any control over it. It is one of those few surviving independencies like Monaco and San Miniato—a purely personal possession of its owner. But the Great War left me with tremendous anxieties. Under the vagaries of the Peace Treaty the Balkans and the Dalmatian coast have been converted into a Jacob's coat. There is a fine squabble proceeding over this patchwork, and there are all the explosive elements of a new war. My own island's situation is very precarious. I find myself wedged between Italy's new hold on the Dalmatian coast and the Czecho-Slovene State. On either side of my island lie the islands belonging to Yugo-Slavia, which casts an envious eye upon us, and is only restrained by Italy's jealous watchfulness."

" Are you under Italy's protection, Donna? " asked Cameron.

" No—and I am careful not to seek it. Italy so far has respected the traditions connected with my inheritance, but if she had any reason to occupy my territory I could never get her out again."

The Donna watched Cameron's face anxiously.

" You can understand that, major? " she asked, seeking assurance.

" Certainly, Donna. To Trieste, Pola and Zara, you fear they might add—I don't know the name of your retreat? " said Cameron, smiling.

The Donna turned and looked at her son.

" I think so, mother," said the youth, and as he spoke, the girl, who had hitherto sat with folded hands and lowered face, suddenly looked into Cameron's eyes and said :

" Its name is Sagusto—you'll not find it in any general map. We are two hours' sail from——"

The Donna checked her daughter with a swift look.

" We must not give the major any responsibility for our secret until we have his decision," she said, curtly. And turning to Cameron : " You will appreciate that? " she asked. " I want you to feel perfectly free in your decision. If you will not help us, then it's better that you should know as little as possible."

" But, mother ! " protested the girl. " If Major Cameron——"

The Donna made a commanding gesture for silence. The girl immediately obeyed.

" It isn't that I fear to trust you, major," explained the Donna; " it's because I wish to involve you as little as possible, until your decision is made."

Cameron thanked her. " But I am still unable to see my part in this business. What do you want of me? " he asked.

" I've come to that now. My island has no territorial status among all these grabbing Powers. The people on it are a mixture of Croats, Turks, Venetians, Saracens and Greeks— descended from the sorties and shipwrecks of centuries. Their speech is a Croatian *patois*. Some fifteen years ago I brought to the island a mine manager, a Greek, Condylis by name. Gradually he has increased his position until, of late, he has assumed the rights of a dictator. Five years ago I ordered him to leave. He ignored me, and since that time he's grown more and more insolent. It has come to such a position that this year he has seized the revenues of the mine and kept us prisoners in our own Castello. We've not been allowed to cross the bridge from the castle to the mainland. The people are in abject terror of this man, whose brutality has now reached the length of murder. Last month, fearing I might make some appeal somewhere for delivery from his violence, he built a blockhouse commanding the bridge over the ravine and forbade us to leave the castle. We were allowed only such meagre supplies as barely supported life. His intention soon became obvious : he was going to starve us out."

The Donna paused, and regarded Cameron in silence for a few seconds.

"Doubtless you are wondering if such things are possible in Europe to-day, Major Cameron. You may even wonder how much of my story is true, after my conduct towards you."

Cameron smiled a little grimly, and took a cigarette proffered by the youth.

"It certainly sounds like the Hundred and Second Story of the *Arabian Nights' Entertainment*," he said. "But, as I cannot conceive you would take all this trouble to kidnap me in order to tell me a fairy tale, I believe what you say. Why you should tell me all this I can only surmise; but surely, Donna, you don't expect me to take the rôle of bailiff and evict your troublesome tenant ? "

The Donna's eyes flashed, a little angrily, he thought.

"There is such a thing as justice, m'sieur—as the protection of a defenceless woman against a villainous thief ? "

The intensity of her appeal made it sound almost like an accusation against his manhood.

"I'm not exactly a soldier of fortune—a *condottiere*, Donna," he protested.

"You are a brave man, an English gentleman, Major Cameron —I'm appealing to you in my despair. You must see I cannot appeal except to an individual. I might apply to one of the Powers for help, which they might give, but I know sufficient of the ways of nations to realise that, once one of them took possession of my island, it would be to remain. You must see that?"

"I see it, Donna, well enough. What I don't appreciate is your choice of me, and this wild method of impressing it upon me."

"Then you will not help?" asked the Donna, desperately.

"I cannot—I'm expected in England immediately."

"That means you will not help me, Major Cameron," repeated the Donna. "You would not if you could?"

"I have not said that, Donna—although your request is such a strange one. I'm not a free agent. I have a position, a career and it might prove awkward if I became involved in some affair of violence that attracted political attention."

The Donna laughed bitterly.

"I didn't know brave men were so cautious," she said.

"Mother!" protested the lad, "you've no right to say that. Major Cameron declines to help. That is the end."

"It is the end of everything," added the girl.

The despair in her eyes stirred Cameron, but he checked an impulse to retract.

"We shall put in at Trieste and land you, Major Cameron," said the Donna. "I hope you will make no complaint to your Consul. In any case, it will be futile. We shall have gone. As for the future, nothing but bitter ruin confronts us. I have only my jewels. The whole of my fortune outside the mine has been expended in the purchase of this ship, and of arms."

"Arms?" queried Cameron.

"This is another confidence. At Venice we shipped all that might prove necessary to our attempt."

Cameron looked at the Donna in amazement. He saw in the determination of her mouth that she was making no wild assertion.

"You don't propose open warfare to regain your authority! Surely you——"

The Donna did not let him finish.

"I am confronted with an unscrupulous man who will not hesitate to shoot. He slew two of my servants in our escape from the island. My son and a trustworthy man eluded his guard and escaped from the island. I had some money in the bank at Trieste. Tino withdrew that, purchased this yacht, and under cover of darkness succeeded in evacuating myself, Nada, and the servants from the Castello. It will be occupied now by Condylis. He'll dispute every inch when we make a landing."

Cameron sat speechless with amazement.

"My dear Donna, you don't seriously propose attempting any such thing?" he cried.

"I shall attempt it, certainly! Tino and Nada are with me. Nothing but poverty confronts us otherwise. And, m'sieur," she added fiercely, "there is such a thing as justice and vengeance."

A strange scene that: the lighted, luxurious salon, this magnificent, fierce woman, at her side the girl, delicate, with a soft pervading beauty that touched Cameron to pity. And, standing now, erect, proud-lipped, the boy, a handsome young animal, a little scornful of him, thought Cameron, which aroused a sense of resentment. Dash it all, he was no deserter! He had not asked to be entangled in this fantastic affair.

They rose to their feet. There was a long silence, the pulse of the engine and the creaking of timbers audible as they stood.

"I will bid you good-night, Major Cameron," said the Donna, at last. "You may care to rest. My son will call you

B

at five. I have another confession to make. Your trunks are on board. They will go with you, of course?"

"My trunks—from the hotel! How did you get them?" stammered Cameron, in utter surprise.

"Had you consented, I wished to reduce the inconvenience so quick a decision would have brought. It was a simple matter. Your bill was paid at the hotel and your luggage fetched by a motor launch—you had met friends on a yachting cruise and had hurriedly decided to leave with them. The launch caught us at the Porto, where we dropped the pilot."

Cameron made no comment. The audacity of it left him dazed. This Donna Soudaikos, whoever she was, had the buccaneer blood in her veins. He began to feel a genuine if reluctant admiration for her.

"You seemed very certain that I should accept this mission?" said Cameron, at last.

The Donna opened her fan and closed it again with a snap.

"My son has been proved right. He said you could not be coerced," answered the Donna, coldly. "I still believe in the chivalry of Englishmen."

The girl at her side coloured slightly, as if the rebuke had been directed to her.

"We had hoped, Major Cameron, you might be persuaded—we are in a desperate condition," she said. "Won't you help us?"

Before Cameron could reply, the lad had moved towards the door.

"We must alter our course for Trieste," he explained, as the Donna looked at him.

The girl's eyes, dark, intense with pleading, watched Cameron's face. It was not her appeal, but something deeper in him that caused him to turn towards the youth.

"You needn't alter your course—I am with you."

Whatever reasons, whatever half-realised impulses crying for adventure surged within him at that moment—whether the call of the unknown, the thrill of action and the odds of a desperate chance—whatever they were, impelling so sudden a reversal of his attitude towards this crazy adventure, he had no time for self-analysis. The next action of the girl caught him in painful embarrassment. With a cry that came from the heart she had slipped to her knees, and seizing his hand in her own, pressed it to her lips. The passion in it perturbed him. It brought a swift realisation of all that was now centred upon his leadership. Stooping, he took her hands and half lifted her to her feet.

"Mademoiselle—please, please!" he said, quietly, stirred by her cry, by the sight of tears in her clouded eyes. Her frailty, the sweet dependence of her youth, were in such utter contrast to the Amazonian carriage of the Donna.

The lad had hurriedly come from the door. In an impulse of frank gratitude, his hand took Cameron's, now disengaged, all the light of youth in his splendid eyes, lit with excitement.

"M'sieur—that is like you! We shall win now. *Evviva!*" he cried, in the swift ardour of his seventeen summers. "Mother, you were right—you were right! We shall triumph! We shall triumph!"

Cameron had not the heart to check this exuberance. Nor would anything he could have said have done so. The lad was radiant, with a sudden happiness that had completely dismissed the grave, polite young gentleman who had made so taciturn a gaoler.

Donna Soudaikos had seated herself again. Cameron thought she had paled a little, and when she spoke to him there was a grave and tired expression in her face.

"I cannot thank you, major. We tried desperately to win your help, and our methods justify your indignation. I believe it is not these—I hope it is not—which have persuaded you?" she asked, and added, quickly, "Because I would not for a moment like any element of compulsion to influence you."

Cameron returned her frank regard of him.

"You know well, Donna, that compulsion could not effect

my decision. I have agreed, yet I don't know why. Perhaps it's the unknown, perhaps my own childish zest for excitement."

Donna Soudaikos smiled, and motioned Cameron to a chair. "You may tell us that. There is such a thing as chivalry, major—and I remember we have the same patron saint, St. George. Now we can tell you everything," she continued, "and submit our plans. Tino, lock the door and bring the maps."

III

Nearly two hours later Cameron, accompanied by the youth, regained the deck of the yacht. The night was moonlit and calm. Under full sail, trembling a little from the beat of her small engine, the white vessel bore southwards, a ghostly apparition cleaving the oily sea. The starlight of the cloudless heaven was shimmeringly reflected, sometimes breaking in a crescent of white fire where the ripple of water shattered the imaged stars. The warm air caressed the night like a lover. Beauty and calm engulfed them and made reality so remote that Cameron found himself wondering on what borderland they voyaged. Here he stood, embarked on a desperate enterprise, as unusual to the age to which he belonged as it seemed foreign to the tranquillity of this setting.

He glanced briefly at his companion. The boy's athletic head, with wind-tossed curls clouding the brow, and lips slightly parted in dreamy contemplation, was silhouetted against the light of the deckhouse. At a sound he turned sharply, and Cameron saw the sister appear, halt a moment in the bright companion-way and then come towards them. She joined her brother, silently, the breeze draping the filmy dress to her lithe, virginal body. They were a magnificent presentment of youth, opposed in pattern as in sex, she with her black hair, he with his gold. And Cameron realised then that it was for these rather than for the mother, capable and hard, that he had so suddenly consented. He was young enough to share their hopes, yet old enough to feel compassionate.

As if conscious of his thoughts, the girl turned to Cameron and regarded him without speaking. He heard a topsail shake out, and saw a star fall down the night into the oblivion of the eastern horizon. If his heart beat a little quicker, might not the sense of adventure be the cause? He, too, stood lapped by that silence of the summer night, happy in its tranquillity, stirred by the unknown to which they voyaged together.

CHAPTER V

THE next morning, at six o'clock, Cameron was awakened by the sudden cessation of the ship's engine. Dropping from his bunk, he went to the porthole and looked out. They were in a harbour, large but empty, except for great mooring buoys. Could this be somewhere near Sagusto? No, they were almost two days' distance, according to the youth. Hastily slipping an overcoat over his pyjamas, he went up on deck. There, beyond the quay, at the foot of a rising semicircle of hills, he saw the remains of a great amphitheatre, of Roman workmanship. In a moment, by that monument of Roman occupation, Cameron knew the name of the place. It was Pola, once the base of the Austrian navy in the Adriatic, now languishing under Italian annexation.

A footstep behind him caused him to turn. It was Tino, clad only in his pyjama trousers.

" Why are we here? " he asked the youth.

" For recruits, m'sieur."

" Recruits? "

" We are taking on ten more men; that will make us about twenty. It is too few, m'sieur, but we cannot carry more."

" Too few? But you don't seriously mean to make an armed attack on Sagusto? " asked Cameron, finding the whole scheme still more fantastic in the full light of morning. "And who are they? How've you got them?" he added.

Before the youth could answer, they were joined by Bandioli, the skipper from Ancona, who claimed an intimate knowledge of every island of Dalmatia.

"Good morning, signore. We are shipping the army!" he said cheerily. "Smart lads, too; I spent a week here getting them. Crack shots, every one!"

"Who are they—what nationality?" asked Cameron, watching the small boat that had put off from the yacht and was slowly crossing the green patch of water between them and the quay.

"Italians—young Italians, full of fire and youth, from Fiume," answered Bandioli.

"Some of D'Annunzio's legionaries?" asked Cameron.

"Ah, you remember them, eh! Splendid lads!" ejaculated the skipper. "We should never have left that place—still, we're there now; but those Yugo-Slavs want a little gunpowder under 'em to let 'em know we are."

Cameron made no reply. His opinion of the D'Annunzio tomfoolery would not be welcomed. This skipper seemed all too fond of gunpowder.

"I suppose these fellows know what they're coming for, or "—and here Cameron could not resist a smile as he addressed himself to the youth at his side—"have they been invited to dinner?"

The lad flushed.

"I hoped you had forgiven us that, m'sieur," he said, quietly.

Cameron placed a friendly hand on the boy's bronzed shoulder. "I have, Tino, I have—but I must have my joke. They do know, I suppose?"

"Certainly, m'sieur."

"That's just why they're coming. They are all single men, under thirty," said Bandioli, spitting contemptuously. "They'll fight for the love of it."

Cameron was about to say that it was what he most feared, but he checked himself. He would have a few words later with the Donna. Could she not realise that once she started this horde of wild youngsters shooting, there would be appalling bloodshed? With such a mixture of races on board, opposed to similar nondescripts on that island, discipline or restraint would be impossible.

They were watching the boat now. It did not go to the quay-side, but turned suddenly towards an erection built up in the middle of the harbour. It was a bathing-station, perhaps used by the sailors in the port. There was a railed promenade on the roof, and two flights of steps running down to the water from the cabins.

" That's my idea," said the skipper gleefully. " The port guard might want to know too much. There's no harm in those young men going for a bathe, and being casually picked up by a boat. And they've none of them more luggage than they can carry."

Cameron saw now that nearly a dozen men had suddenly come out of the cabins, which screened them from observation on the land side. As soon as the boat reached the steps they clambered down. Hardly a minute had passed before the boat had started on its way back. In the early light of dawn the harbour was quite deserted. From this manœuvre, and the haste with which the embarkation had been effected, Cameron realised the apprehension in Bandioli's mind.

" The authorities have no idea——" began Cameron, but as if anticipating his question, the skipper interrupted him.

" No. But once you buy arms the whole Intelligence Service begins spying. That's why we preferred to get our arms and our crew from different places. Once we are clear here we can't be stopped."

" You're going straight to Sagusto? " queried Cameron.

The Ancona skipper laughed.

" Well, not straight, signore. You can't go straight on this coast anywhere!" And then, in enjoyment of an after-thought, "Not in any sense, signore!"

Looking at the man, Cameron was sure he had reason to know. How had he found that scar running from the left temple to the chin? In his undersized alertness, with his quick black eyes, he gave the impression of a pugnacious terrier. He would be troubled by no fine points of honour.

The boat was drawing near now. Cameron and Tino went towards the gangway. The skipper left them to get the yacht under weigh. They were losing no time.

As the new arrivals came up on to the deck Cameron was relieved to find they were not a pack of low cut-throats. Indeed, three of them carried themselves with an air of breeding and command. They were all well under thirty, bronzed and lithe, but from their puzzled demeanour and the examining glances they threw about the yacht, it was clear they were not too certain of the mission on which they had embarked. They were conducted below by one of the Greeks, and while they were eating the coffee and rolls provided, Cameron got into conversation with them. He soon learned that they neither knew where nor for what purpose they were going.

"We are well paid—and the rest does not matter!" said one of the young men, shrugging his shoulders.

"But you do not look like a—like a mercenary," replied Cameron, to the young man. His face was honest and he had the manner of a gentleman.

The Italian laughed pleasantly.

"How does a mercenary look, signore? My father is a lawyer at Bologna. I fought on the Trentino, and, liking the adventure, joined D'Annunzio at Fiume. When you get used to this kind of life it is not easy to go back to the study of law."

"But what is the end of it all?" asked Cameron. He liked the frank air of this fellow.

"Ah, the end! Let us hope a bullet in the right place, when the end must come," he replied, shrugging his shoulders. Then, seeing dust on the black top boots he was wearing, he drew out a large silk handkerchief and stooped and wiped them carefully.

"Do you know where we are going?" asked Cameron.

The young fellow looked round, hesitated a moment, and then, moving away from his companions:

"You are English?" he said, ignoring the question. "What are you doing here?"

Before Cameron could answer, he gave a short laugh with a note of sadness in it.

"Perhaps none of us can return, signore—and yet we are not all bad."

The tragedy in this confession annulled the resentment Cameron felt at this inclusion of himself among the army of vagabonds.

"Yes, I know where we're going," the youth continued quietly, "although that old Ancona pirate thinks he's been so clever. They knew at Pola a week ago what we had been engaged for. Condylis has his spies there."

"Condylis—you know of Condylis?" asked Cameron, amazed. "And the island, surely you don't know——"

The young fellow's eyes looked confidently into his own.

"Sagusto—yes, I know we are going to Sagusto, although I don't know where it is."

Cameron looked round the cabin in which the men were eating and smoking.

"Come on to the deck—I want to talk to you," he said, and led the way, the young Italian following.

"Tell me," he asked, when they had gained the deck, "how did you learn all this? Despite what you have told me, I think you are honest."

The young fellow laughed, showing his white teeth. Not more than twenty-seven or eight, surmised Cameron, and a sad heart for all his bravado.

"Thank you, signore, and I believe you are—despite your presence here," he retorted. "I've come for money, and you

—I don't know what you've come for. That's not my affair. *Per Dio*—it's a strange business! You have met the Donna?"

"Yes. Do you know her?"

"No, I haven't seen her. But I hear she is *terribile*."

He pronounced the Italian word with such a rolling of the "r" that he conveyed to Cameron an impression she was capable of anything, and then, to support it: "She has killed one lover, and now wants to get rid of the second."

"Lover—you don't mean that Condylis——" began Cameron, in astonishment.

"She is tired of him, or he bullies her, or—— But then, signore, why does a woman change her lover?"

He laughed and lightly sang a bar of *La donna è mobile*. Suddenly, at the sound of footsteps, his whistling stopped, and, turning, his animation was suddenly checked by the sight of a young woman coming along the deck.

"*Per Dio*—then the voyage will not be——" he began.

Cameron snubbed his gay libertinism at once.

"This lady is the Donna's daughter," he said, severely, but as he spoke he found himself wondering how much respect this poor girl could command if one half of the Italian's gossip were true. She came straight towards them, and then, seeing the young man with Cameron, hesitated.

In an instant, with an assurance that supplied the key to the career of this young adventurer, the Italian had smartly advanced, clicked his heels and bowed.

"Permit me to present myself, Lieutenant Luigi, at your service, signorina," he said, agile and debonair.

The girl regarded him coolly, only a slight flush on her cheeks betraying her embarrassment. In that moment of self-possession Cameron found her still more beautiful, a mere child and yet with something, a poise, a command, that anyone save this arrogant young adventurer would have detected.

"Lieutenant Luigi—Luigi what?" she asked, her eyes meeting his calmly.

"Ah—just Luigi. I lost my other name with my character!" replied the young man, disconcerted and desperately asserting himself.

"Then, Lieutenant Luigi, while you find it, I will speak with Major Cameron," she said, dismissing him.

The young man bowed, and went, like a whipped dog.

"My mother would like to speak to you, major," she said, as soon as the fellow was out of hearing. "We have bad news."

"Bad? But how—from where?"

"From Pola—we've been watched, and our coming is known to Condylis. But my mother will tell you everything."

Cameron followed her down to the Donna's salon. As she greeted him on his entrance, her son Tino and Bandioli standing behind, Cameron was aware of something almost regal in her bearing. And yet that young adventurer from Fiume had said she was Condylis's mistress. It troubled him, not so much because of the complications that might arise if this were so, but more because of these two youngsters, Tino and Nada. How were they involved in such a relationship? He must find that out soon. He had not consented to this adventure as the agent of one partner in a broken liaison.

Motioning him to be seated, and after Tino had cautiously locked the door of the salon, the Donna looked at Bandioli, as if uncertain whether she should speak first. At a nod from him, she turned to Cameron. He met her gaze, suppressing a wretched suspicion that raced through his mind. Two lovers, had said that young man. Now Condylis was to be thrown out, and this Bandioli, perhaps, would—— No, he must not think that, not until he had better reasons than a young libertine's gossip.

"Major Cameron, something we have just heard, brought to us by one of these men from Pola, alters the whole aspect of our attempt," said the Donna. "It's probable that Condylis is aware of our coming."

" By what means, Donna? "

" We can only guess. One of these fellows says they've been watched before coming aboard. He has no doubt of it, they've been watched since the day Captain Bandioli engaged them. Who should do that, if not for some purpose? And who else but Condylis? "

" Have you any idea how Condylis has come to know of your plans? "

" None, major. It's likely he knows I shall attempt to regain my property. But throughout I've maintained the greatest secrecy."

" We've bought arms, and ammunition, and engaged men in different places for that reason," said Tino. " We could have done the whole thing at Trieste, or in Pola."

" I think that was discreet of you," answered Cameron. " But one thing's obvious. When you engage men of the type that will go on such adventures as these, you can't be sure of their characters. I've just been talking to one of them—he also knows our mission to Sagusto."

" The devil he does! " cried Bandoli; " then we land him! "

" No—that would be folly. He'd spread the facts wherever he went," said Cameron.

" Then what do you advise, major? " asked the Donna.

" Going straight on! "

" Thank you; I hoped that," answered the Donna, quickly. " It means you are aware what may happen? "

" Resistance from Condylis—yes, I am aware," said Cameron. The girl, who had remained silent and watchful, spoke.

" Mother—must we go on? " she asked. Yet there was no tone of fear in her voice.

" And why not? " asked the Donna, challengingly.

" For ourselves—it doesn't matter. But for Major Cameron —there may be trouble—have we any right to involve him? We did not foresee this position. Condylis may be strongly armed."

Cameron looked at the girl reassuringly.

"Thank you, mademoiselle. I made my decision, and I'm prepared for anything," he said. "If I have one fear it is not for myself, but for the Donna and yourself. Can't you remain somewhere until it is over?"

"At Zara or Sebenico—I have urged that," asserted Bandioli.

"Not for a moment!" cried the Donna, her white jewelled hand pressed flat on the table. "It is for my children here that you make your sacrifice—a mother is surely equal to anything others may suffer for them! Major Cameron, let me make one condition: I must be with you in all you do," she said, her eyes earnestly searching his face.

"And I," added Tino.

"And I," asserted the girl.

Bandioli cast a despairing look at Cameron.

"What do you propose, then, major?" he asked.

"That we try persuasion before force," answered Cameron.

"But that is useless," cried the Donna, at once. "You don't know Condylis. Nothing will persuade him to leave the island."

"Persuasion, with force behind it, Donna," said Cameron, "can sometimes be very effective. At least let us try. I wish to avoid bloodshed if possible."

"Are you going to talk to Condylis?" asked Bandioli, unable to disguise the scorn in his voice.

"Yes. The Donna tells me he has no right on the island, he is dismissed. I may make him see that further resistance is useless."

"But, major, you won't go on the island to talk to him," cried the daughter, exchanging a swift glance of alarm with the Donna. "He might kill you, or keep you a prisoner! You cannot know the kind of man you have to deal with."

"I don't think, mademoiselle——" began Cameron, but the sentence went unfinished. There was an imperative tapping on the door of the salon, and a shadow on the glazed panels showed someone there.

" See who it is, Tino. I said we were not to be disturbed? " said the Donna, turning to Bandioli.

The youth unlocked the door. A young Greek, who acted as steward, stood there with a large blue envelope in his hand.

" Donna," he cried, excitedly, " a launch raced us out of the port, and when she got abreast a man threw a bag on board. It had a stone in it, and this ! "

He held the envelope forward.

" Where's the launch now? " demanded Bandioli.

" Gone back, captain—it turned immediately, just as we cleared the harbour."

The Donna had taken the envelope and torn it open. Unfolding the sheet of paper within, she read slowly. Then, folding it up again :

" You can go, Meno," she said, quietly.

The Greek withdrew. Tino closed and locked the door, and not until he had done so did she speak.

" You see, it is not rumour, major," said the Donna, holding out the letter for Cameron. " Read it aloud, please."

Cameron took the letter and opened it; then, at a glance :

" But I cannot, Donna—it's in Greek."

The Donna gave a short laugh.

" I am forgetting," she said, taking back the letter. " Excuse me. Here is what it says :

I learn you are making an attempt to come back to Sagusto. You left more easily than you will come back. For every gun you buy I shall have two, and I warn you against any attempt to land. My men have instructions to shoot without hesitation. This applies to women as well as men. And, Donna, why Pola and Trieste? Rifles and cut-throats are cheaper at Ancona.

" That is all, major. It's characteristic. We've been watched."

" I'd like to get my hands on his throat," growled Bandioli.

" He seems to know Ancona ! " laughed Cameron, unable to

restrain a reference to the closing sentence. Tino and Nada joined in.

"It is a libel on the town, I assure you, major!" said Nada.

"You won't think of landing alone now?" cried Tino.

Cameron was silent a few moments.

"Yes, I shall land," he said, quietly. And then, seeing the alarm on their faces, "This letter in the first place seeks to intimidate the Donna by threats of violence. It is a bully's letter. It's quite improbable he is aware of any Englishman being on the yacht. I don't see how he can know that; my coming was so——" He hesitated tactfully, and seeing the grin on the youth's face—"I hardly knew of it myself! We've only made one call, at Pola here, and no one has gone from the ship. Do we call anywhere again?"

"Yes," answered Bandioli. "At Zara, to-morrow morning."

"Why?"

"For provisions—we thought it better to take as much as possible from our nearest base."

"How far is Zara from Sagusto?" asked Cameron.

"Twelve hours' sail," replied the Donna.

"Then it is better no one should land at Zara. I don't wish Condylis to learn I am here at all."

"We can fetch the provisions by the boat—Bandioli and myself," suggested Tino.

"Good—keep a good distance from the shore, if that is possible."

"It's quite possible, major. We can anchor in the roadstead, opposite the Riva," said Bandioli.

"And we shall want some paint, captain."

"Paint?" queried the Donna.

"White paint and black paint," said Cameron.

"We've got plenty. But why do you——" asked the captain.

"You'll learn, later. Can we approach Sagusto after dark?"

Bandioli looked at the Englishman intently. He did not like

this infringement of his command. He turned towards the Donna, and she, reading his thought, quickly said:

" Whatever the major suggests must be done, captain."

" *Va bene*, donna," he answered submissively. " Well, major, if we leave Zara about ten o'clock in the morning we could make Sagusto about nine."

" It will be dark then? "

" Not quite—dusk, and there's a half moon."

Cameron thought for a few moments. The company regarded him with a puzzled air. What was his plan?

" I shall want you to keep well away from Sagusto until it is quite dark—say ten o'clock. At eleven, after our preparations, you can go in to within boat distance. I shall land the next morning."

" You'll land! " echoed Tino. " Not alone? "

" We shall all land," said the Donna, decisively, crumpling the letter in her hand, in visible defiance.

" Pardon me, Donna—I shall go alone," said Cameron, firmly.

" But, major——"

" You must allow me to act," he said. " And now, I want three more things." He pointed to a long curtain draping one of the windows of the salon, and, ignoring their astonishment: " That curtain, a spare bed sheet, and a pair of scissors. For the present that is all. Later I shall seek your help, mademoiselle," he added, turning to Nada.

There was a silence, of amazement, of incredulity.

" Let the major have all he requires," said the Donna at last, in her deep voice. There was a note of tolerance in it, and Bandioli, after he had taken down the curtain, passed it to Cameron as if it were the cloak of a lunatic.

CHAPTER VI

CAMERON slept badly that night. His suppressed excitement may have been the subconscious cause, but uppermost in his mind was a continuous inquiry regarding the character of Donna Soudaikos. This powerfully-built woman, of such determination and daring as had characterised the kidnapping of himself and the planning of the audacious attack on the island, would at no time of her career have been troubled by scruples. She had all the appearance of a woman who, in her youthful past, had launched herself into many passionate affairs. That young libertine, Luigi, had somehow heard tales of her former associations. Cameron's difficulty was to fit these in with her devotion to Tino and Nada. Were they illegitimate, arousing in her that maternal passion often so strangely increased by the very irregularity of the union? Somehow Cameron could not bring himself to think Nada and Tino were the offspring of a liaison. The Donna was positive enough concerning her rights and those of her children. On the death of her husband she had continued her governorship of the island. Later the two children had been sent away to school—Nada to a convent in Venice, Tino first to Trieste and then to Lausanne, which accounted for his excellent French.

So much he had learned from the Donna. He now wondered whether the children had any memory of their father. He had died when they were young, while transacting business in Athens. It might be as well to ask them a few discreet questions.

But for what purpose? Supposing the whole story of the Donna was full of inaccuracies, in what way would it modify his conduct? That was the real question, and it troubled Cameron because it touched his conscience. Here he was, embarked on the craziest of crazy adventures, one that would make a story listened to with incredulity in any club smoke-room in London. His own advent had all the elements of melodrama, and his decision to continue the adventure had been quixotic in the extreme. Why, why, had he gone on with it when he might have been landed at Trieste and been well rid of the whole business?

Lying there in his bunk, with the creaking of a pitching ship in his ears, he regarded the white-enamelled ceiling above him, and transferred his gaze, through the porthole, unlocked now, to the blue, sun-smitten Adriatic Sea. It raced by, flowing into white crests, diamonded in the sunshine. Beyond, rose a dark, purple horizon, mountainous and barren, with half a dozen leagues of water between, jade green and belted with turquoise. For a moment he was puzzled, then startled by the appearance of land on the starboard bow. They were running south down the Adriatic, and all the land should lie on their port. What had happened? They were certainly continuing due south, as the flow of the water past his porthole showed. Suddenly the mystery was solved. He remembered studying the chart over-night. They were nearing the Italian town of Zara, on the mainland. Opposite lay a long island belonging to Yugo-Slavia; the roadstead, used sometimes by Italian warships, lay in between. This must be Zara, and its roadstead, to which they were drawing.

As Cameron rose from his bunk he heard the engine stop. The ship ran on her course for half a knot, then slowed down. As he dressed he heard the rattle of the lowered anchor. Then came a tap on his cabin door.

"Enter!" he called. He had just finished dressing, if the pulling on of a pair of white flannel trousers and a shirt deserved that term.

It was Bandioli, accompanied by Tino.

"Good morning, major—we're riding off Zara. The boat's going in now. I'm taking two men ashore who've never been there before—it's better, I think," he said.

"Much," assented Cameron. "And the ship's name on the bow and stern—they're covered?"

"Yes—I've had 'em painted over, as you wished."

"Good," said Cameron. "And on the boat you're taking also?"

"Yes," answered Bandioli.

"What do you want the black paint for, m'sieur?" asked Tino, surveying the strange array of cloth on the small table. What had the major been doing with that curtain?

"I shall want the black paint for painting in the ship's name again, as soon as we leave Zara—another name, of course," said Cameron, not satisfying the youth's curiosity concerning his handiwork overnight.

"What name, major?" asked Bandioli. He had not yet grasped the full import of this painting in and out.

"I think I shall call her," answered Cameron, stooping and lacing his buckskin shoes, "*The Three Castles.*"

"*The Three Castles!*" echoed both his companions.

"Yes—I think it's delightful, don't you?" he continued, genially. "It happens to be the name of my favourite brand of cigarettes—which all of you are so fond of accepting, and which, by the way, I regret to say are rapidly running out. When you are in Zara you might inquire whether you can get me——"

"But, major!" interrupted the astonished captain, now more firmly convinced of the insanity of all Englishmen, "you can't call this boat *The Three Castles*—it's an English name!"

Cameron laughed at the bewildered little fellow. For his part, Cameron was more than ever convinced of the transmigration of souls. This jumpy, blue-chinned creature had swung from a bough in his chimpanzee past.

"I can't see why we shouldn't call the ship anything we like, my dear Bandioli. She has no papers and her owner has no nationality. The one thing she must not continue to be is the *Lucciola* registered at Trieste. That would give us away to Condylis's agents if they are around. Do you see those pieces of cloth?"

Bandioli and young Soudaikos turned to the table with its oblong and triangular slips.

"The curtain I had from the salon has been mutilated beyond repair, as you see. But it happened to be red, which was the colour I wanted. Nada has contributed a bedsheet, and the ship's engineer, under protest, has had to give me his blue jacket, which I caught him wearing yesterday afternoon. With the aid of these, my scissors, and Mademoiselle Soudaikos's needle, we shall construct a Union Jack for this ship to fly to-morrow morning."

Cameron smiled in their astonished faces.

"I congratulate myself that I'm not an American. If I'd had to cut the Stars and Stripes," he said, addressing Tino, "your poor sister would have been crazy with stitching. You might be good enough to say I'm quite ready for her services when you go up on deck."

With an impulsive gesture the youth seized Cameron's arm.

"But, major—this is marvellous! It's a wonderful idea!" he cried, throwing back his hair with a toss of the head, his eyes glowing with excitement. "They won't know us when we get near—they won't dare to shoot!"

"The idea, as you have it, Tino," answered Cameron, disengaging his arm, and putting down the cloth, "is not quite correct, but it will do for the present. I daren't contemplate what may happen to me for unlawfully flying His Britannic Majesty's flag."

The lad laughed gaily.

"We'll go to gaol together, m'sieur!" he cried.

"If it's only a gaol we'll go to, I shall be much relieved," growled Bandioli. "I can't see Condylis being taken in so easily. When he finds out, he'll shoot, flag or no flag."

He turned to go, and halted in the cabin doorway.

"What's the name of those cigarettes?" he asked.

"Three Castles!" repeated Cameron.

Bandioli attempted the name, with the usual Continental difficulty with the English " th."

" Three—not tree ! " corrected Cameron. " Whatever will they think of a captain who can't pronounce the name of his own ship? "

" His own ship ! " cried Bandioli. " His own ship ! *Per Dio*—by the time we're through, nobody'll know whose ship it is ! "

" There may be no ship to bother about then," called Cameron, after the departing skipper. " And now, Tino, if mademoiselle will come——"

" M'sieur, I go at once. And, m'sieur," said the boy, earnestly, his eyes darkening with his serious mood, " I thank you with all my heart. My mother, my sister, myself, but for you, we——"

He could not finish, and turned away to hide his eyes.

" Foreign enough—emotional," thought Cameron.

" Pardon me, m'sieur—I go for Nada," he said, abruptly, and left the cabin.

Alone, Cameron ate the coffee and rolls that had been brought by Meno. He had sent for Nada, ostensibly to sew this Union Jack, but there was an ulterior motive. He was going to question her cautiously. The thought made him a little ashamed of himself. He was deliberately taking advantage of her innocence. He might have questioned Tino, but his instinct for character told him the boy would quickly become suspicious. With Nada he felt there was no such probability. Her faith in him was implicit. He could read that in the gaze of her dark eyes, in the half-wistful appeal that dwelt in them. He had been stirred by her on that night of his decision, when on the verge of refusing any participation in this adventure. Yes, let him confess it, but for her he would never have gone on with the thing. It was her innocence, her appeal, the thought that she was homeless and ruined, unless restored to her rightful heritage, that had drawn him into this enterprise. Her and the boy, of course, and the Donna, too.

No! let him be honest with himself. The boy and the Donna ranked in that appeal. But without Nada, without that utter trust thrown into her regard of him, the almost prayerful gratitude, as when she had come up on deck afterwards and stood in simple silence beside him under the starlight and the ghostly sail—without that vivid sense of her need of him, he had never gone into this thing, to end, God alone knew how.

Nada, the unknown. In his reverie he sat quite still, neglecting his breakfast. Was he in love with her? Had it come to that? Was that at the bottom of his enlistment in this strange enterprise? No, he told himself. She was a creature all men must notice, with her dark beauty, her beautiful lithe youth, all the softness of Southern places in her voice and eyes. No normal man could ignore her; but, then, everywhere around the shores of the Adriatic the potency of the woman brooded over human relationships, the woman as Madonna, the supreme fount of human devotion, of human self-sacrifice. Hence the ceaseless Madonna and Child of the churches, the shrines and galleries. The mother and child, symbol of human immortality amid human transience.

Yet it was not as a symbol he thought of this girl. In her presence he was conscious of no intensification of the sex impulse, neither for the gratification of the physical sense, nor for the fulfilment of that irrepressible instinct for the perpetuation of the race. There had of late, with the passing of his first youth and the acquired sense that this world was something more than an entertainment, been born in him the desire for close human relationship, intimacies, children. They were fleeting desires, but persistently recurring. Yet, for want of some definite person, they had achieved no fixation. At twenty-eight, with the friends of his boyhood marrying, he was growing conscious of a solitariness. There was his mother, beloved beyond all measure of thought, but one day that irreparable tie must be broken. And then?

No, it was not Nada that had created these thoughts; they were always there, she stirred them anew. She stood for the fragility, the beauty and potency of her sex, and his life in the strange lonely places of the world kept him fresh in his appreciation of all the emotional subtleties that stirred in the presence of the woman. Away there in England, Northern, colder, with the repression consequent upon such latitudes, he felt this appeal, but never so strongly. Here, she was the vessel, the receptive earth, the imprisoned instinct of generation, bursting with the springtide of life, ardent and prolific.

A quick tap on the cabin door shattered his reverie. Good heavens! whatever had he been thinking? That was Nada, and an inward sense of shame at the liberty his thought had taken with her found him unready to face her. His answer not being forthcoming, she tapped again, and this time he bade her enter, rising as she came in.

"You want me, major?" she asked, and whether his self-consciousness betrayed him, he never knew, but the smile on her face quickly vanished, and she regarded him with solemn eyes.

"Thank you—Tino has told you," he said, awkwardly. Then, turning towards the porthole, "Do you know Zara?"

"Oh yes—I've often been there. Won't you see it?"

He continued to stare out over the blue water to the great hills, trembling now as the haze rose in the absorbing air. For the moment he felt he could not trust himself to confront her. Even her voice had a disturbing effect upon him. It was preposterous! Surely in the midst of the task he had undertaken there was not going to be the harassing question of personal relationships? He gave a short laugh at the absurdity of the thought.

"Why do you laugh, m'sieur?" asked the girl, and this time he was obliged, from politeness, to turn and face her. In the white light of morning streaming into his cabin he saw her eyes more clearly than he had ever seen them. They were dark brown, ringed, and their unusual beauty thrilled him. The lashes were so long and heavy that they seemed to create a blue shadow under them. The eyebrows went up in a perfect black curve, defined as if an artist had drawn them in charcoal.

"I laugh at a thought you could not follow, mademoiselle," he answered, at last, "and it is of no importance, anyhow."

She watched him and smiled, with a steady, slow regard that perturbed him. He had seen women in the churches of Italy looking like that, before the altar of some saint of whom they sought succour. He was no saint, and the last thing he could tolerate would be adoration; moreover, it made him profoundly uncomfortable.

He would have been still more uncomfortable had he known the thought behind that quiet regard of his face. So this was what an Englishman was like! Hitherto they had belonged to the legends, to the half-caricatures of the press, the impersonal representations that had filtered through the careful sequestration of her convent life. Later, she had seen Englishmen in her walks in Venice. There had once been a naval lieutenant, very handsome and kind, who had shown her over his battleship, anchored in the San Marco basin, but as he could speak little French and less Italian, their conversation had been confined to "Oui" and "Vraiment?" and, in moments of apparent emotional distress, to "Oh, God!" which, however had never seemed in the nature of a prayer.

Then, too, she had never clearly settled the difference between these English and the Americans. When, by desperate devices, she had communicated her difficulty to the young officer, he had again exclaimed, "Oh, God!" She had never forgotten him, fair, blue-eyed, the rose and white mantling his cheeks— nor the pressure of his hand as he had helped her down to the gondola.

This Englishman was of the same type, square-faced and thin-lipped. He had that direct, alert look of the athlete, and, in the simple open-necked shirt he wore, he had a boyish air, despite the lines at the corners of his eyes, the legacy of desert days She liked him, liked the square thickness of his wrists, the way he held his pipe, clumped in his big hand. She liked his boyish laugh and his sudden gravity, the straight brown hair, swept back glossily from a good broad brow. She liked the freckles on his neck, just where the hair turned sandy, the upturned curve of his wide nostrils, giving him a quizzical air. There was about his appearance, as in his manner, a cleanness, as if he had been shaped by the winds of heaven rather than mortal mould.

And in those odd moments of grimness, as when his indignation had been turned upon her mother, or his manner towards Bandioli had suddenly subdued that resentful nature, there was an impression of strength, undemonstrative, but nevertheless sure, in whose reliability she felt the same security as the Donna. Her mother's instinct, seldom fallible, had found in this Englishman the best agent for her purpose.

All this passed through her mind as he talked to her, explaining the pattern he wanted her to keep in sewing the pieces.

"I'm afraid I'm giving you a lot of work, mademoiselle," he said, after the pattern of the thing had been explained. "It's an intricate thing, like the British Empire."

She gathered up the strips, and looked down at her hands a moment before she rose to leave the cabin.

"M'sieur, you call Tino, 'Tino.' Why must I remain 'Mademoiselle'? You make me feel so old and grave!"

She laughed, with a silvery ripple of her voice, the singing voice of the South, and it gave her a sense of pleasure to see the question had embarrassed him. Actually, for all his experience, he was a shy man!

"I'm sorry if that displeases you," he said, at length. "What would you have me call you?"

"Oh, just Nada—we are Tino and Nada," she answered, simply.

He looked at her then, her eagerness emphasising the girlish air she had, so strongly contrasting with her serious moments, when, to him, she had the aspect of a matured woman.

" You are very young, and perhaps ' mademoiselle ' is a little elderly. If I may call you Nada——"

" I'm just twenty-two," she volunteered, "and Tino's seventeen."

" That gives you authority over Tino, then," laughed Cameron.

" I adore him ! " she said, passionately.

" Tell me," he began, approaching his purpose, "does he take after his father, or the Donna? I, too, am fond of your brother—he's a likeable lad."

" My father? I don't know. You see, we never knew our father, we were such children when he died. I was five and Tino was just born."

" And the Donna never married again? "

" Married again? " repeated the girl. " Oh no, mother has never married again. Perhaps it had been better. Condylis wouldn't have dared to act as he has."

There was no hesitation in her answer, he observed, and no sign of suspicion in her face. He would try further.

" Since when has Condylis been so dictatorial—do you know? "

" Always, I believe—as long as I've been here."

" At Sagusto? "

" Yes. You see, I only came back three years ago, when I left the convent at Venice. Before that, I came to Sagusto once a year, for two months, to be with mother."

" And Tino—how long has he been home? "

" About a year—since he left Lausanne."

" I know so little about this Condylis," said Cameron, feeling he had better change the subject.

Tino had only just been born when the father died. Neither of them remembered the father. These facts did not necessarily support the suspicions aroused by that gossiping Italian. Also, they did not dispel them. The children had been sent away from the island until recent years. Was there a purpose?

"Oh, Condylis!" cried Nada, shrugging her shoulders. "He is a villain!"

"That's positive enough," laughed Cameron.

"You cannot imagine how he treated my mother! As if— as if——" she paused, in difficulty for a word, and also reluctant to find it.

"As if?" repeated Cameron.

"As if he possessed mother!" affirmed Nada.

Her exact meaning was not clear to him. He could not believe she intended a confession in its worse sense.

"Possessed?—you mean he ruled her?" he asked.

"He terrified her at times! Mother isn't a woman easily cowed, as you can see, major. But I couldn't help noticing how Condylis seemed to hold her at times. She would never allow me to discuss it. She was so much in his hands, she said, for controlling the mine and the islanders. He would come up to the Castello and force himself upon us for days together."

"With the Donna's consent?"

Nada shrugged her slender shoulders, and looked at Cameron.

"Not her willing consent, I'm sure. He pretends to be fond of Tino, always wants him with him."

"And Tino—how does he feel about this!"

"Major, he hates him! hates him!" cried Nada, suddenly stirred. "Do you know what I fear? One day Tino will kill him. I can see it in Tino's eyes. Oh, how he hates him! It's for mother's sake more than his own; he worships mother."

"Does Condylis know this, Nada?"

"He must—although Tino hides it. Tino is a wise boy, he's been learning all he could at the mines. One day, I know it, he'll turn on Condylis—and then——" She broke off, her face in anguish at some thought of that hour.

"I see," said Cameron, sympathetically; "you fear there will be trouble, a fight——"

"Murder!" corrected Nada, quietly. "One will kill the other."

"We'll hope not. If we succeed we'll avoid that," assured Cameron.

"Avoid!" echoed the girl, surprise sounding in her voice. She turned burning eyes on his face. "You must kill him, he must never be able to return! We should never be safe. He must be killed!"

Cameron stared at her. This fierceness, this sudden flaring of a barbaric spirit in the girl whose manner had been so quiet, so dependent, suddenly gave Cameron a new sense of the material he was handling. This was the Southern spirit, inflammable. Generations of clannish warfare, waged with barbaric ruthlessness, stood behind the nature of this charming young Greek. It was a shock to Cameron, but he was wiser for it. It explained the readiness to fly to arms which, on the Donna's part, had seemed a little hysterical. They intended shooting. If they did not kill Condylis, Condylis would kill them.

Cameron stood stilent. This was his first deep realisation of the enterprise he was committed to. Up till now it had had an element of the unreal. He had believed in the existence of the island, in some kind of injustice done to this woman and her children. They were entitled to their heritage. For the rest, the nondescript crew, the arms and ammunition—all that had seemed but the melodramatic apparatus with which these Southern races loved to surround themselves.

"Nada," he said, at last, "you can't think I'm going to deliberately commit bloodshed? If Condylis won't listen to reason, of course, then——"

"Condylis will listen to no one!" affirmed Nada. "My mother will never know happiness so long as he lives."

"If we drive him from the island——"

"He will return," said the girl, quickly; "he'll impose himself on my mother, he'll——" She broke off, and with a sudden passionate appeal to Cameron: "Oh, he must never be able to return—he must be beyond that possibility! He must be killed! Do you understand that?" she cried.

"I'm afraid I do not," answered Cameron, slowly. "Our views of the value of human life are perhaps not the same."

"I shall kill him myself," said the girl, quietly. "When we get him I shall kill him myself," she repeated, in slow determination.

"Nada, my dear girl, you mustn't talk like that!" cried Cameron. "We shall find a way out."

"Mother must be released from this intolerable tyranny. Oh, it is terrible, terrible!" cried the girl, and suddenly, covering her face with her hands, she collapsed in the chair, her young body shaken with sobs.

Cameron stooped over her, incapable as all men in the presence of tears. He let her cry, partly because he felt it would relieve her, partly because he could do nothing else. And as he looked at her, a suspicion grew in his mind, more sure, more substantial than when that glib Luigi had first awakened it. This girl had not told him all, could not tell him all without overwhelming herself in shame. Cameron would have liked to have faced the hideous thing at once, to have asked her outright what were, or had been, the actual relations between Condylis and the Donna. But now he felt he could not. He reproached himself for forcing this scene upon the poor girl sobbing in the chair.

"Nada! Nada!" he said, kindly. "You know I'm your friend. You can trust me to do all that's possible. I'll see it through, whatever the end."

If she heeded him or understood, he knew not, for suddenly, gathering up the materials he had given her, she rose and left the cabin without a word, her pale young face averted to avoid his eyes.

CHAPTER VII

I

CAMERON's view of Zara was confined to what he could see through his glasses. The side of the little town facing the roadstead was modern and well-planned. The long quayside, or Riva, was broad, planted with palms and plane trees, and extended for about a mile, running from the fort towards the old wall and gateway of the town at the extreme end. Along this Riva a number of modern hotels had sprung up. In the past it had been a favourite resort of the Austrians. Now the Italians were seeking to develop it and to prove to the Bosnian and Czech population that a new prosperity had come with them. It still bore the evidence of old Venetian occupation. Here had waged, around its citadel, those fierce, bloody assaults of Turk and Venetian depicted so luridly in the great paintings in the salons of the Doge's Palace at Venice.

Cameron could see along that Riva, with its gay flower-beds, an almost exotic luxuriance of flower and foliage. The water lapping the quayside was of the bluest of the famed Adriatic *azzurro*. He looked at the place with an interest apart from its historical wealth as a Roman, Turkish, or Venetian stronghold of those old days when nation after nation contended for the mastery of the Adriatic. It gave him an indication of the nature of the island to which they were bound. Sagusto had probably been the one-time stronghold of a corsair, perhaps had, in turn, been governed by Roman, Saracen, Greek, and Venetian. The Castello, in which the Donna dwelt, dated back, so she had told him, to the thirteenth century. The harbour was much older, with clear signs of Roman construction.

As Cameron looked at the distant Zara, to which Bandioli had departed for provisions, he began to realise one other fact. These places, these nests of men accustomed to desperate strife in the long centuries when brigandage, piracy, and casual warfare had been the chief occupation of the people inhabiting them, were natural strongholds. A little fortification had made them almost impregnable.

It was likely that Sagusto was such a place. The presence of a castello indicated a history of assault and defence. What manner of defence could not Condylis make, had he the mind? With this poor little auxiliary yacht, a couple of machine-guns, and some two dozen rifles, they could achieve nothing against an old castello strategically placed, with all the strength of mediæval masonry. More and more, as they journeyed, the insanity of this enterprise grew upon him. Even now he would counsel turning back were it not that his pledged honour was involved. And the others had all the spirit, the desire for the thing. That recent scene with Nada, the sudden revelation of her fierce wish for the death of Condylis, indicated the feeling underlying the calm of the Donna, of Tino even, and Bandioli. The last, he saw clearly, was merely an adventurer, but the love of strife was there, however much he might care to ensure his personal safety.

Bandioli was back by eleven o'clock, his boat loaded with provisions bought in Zara. They proceeded at once out of the roadstead, purposely running north in case any observation of them was being made from the shore.

"I deliberately spoke of our running north," said Bandioli. "They think we've come up from Corfu. I'll keep this course for an hour. We'll put her about then, and keep well away from the coast. We should make Sagusto about nine."

"You know it?" asked Cameron.

"No—but I've an idea where it is. I've heard of it. Signor Tino has the bearings, he'll pilot us in. There's a perfect maze of islands to run through. I once had a fishing fleet at Ancona; I know the coastline pretty well, but not Sagusto. We never called there."

Bandioli grimaced, and spat overboard.

"Why not?" asked Cameron. "Out of the way?"

"That—and inhospitable. Visitors were not encouraged, I heard."

"In what way?"

"Well—how do you find out you're not wanted? I never heard of anyone who touched Sagusto say they'd had a warm welcome."

Bandioli laughed grimly, and walked off towards the deck-house. Cameron went below. He wanted to have a long talk with the Donna. The campaign, down to the smallest detail, must be settled before they came in sight of Sagusto.

II

That evening, as they voyaged south, a storm leapt upon them, in the manner of the Adriatic. After dinner Cameron went up on deck. He watched the dim coastline, now dark and almost lost in the deepening night. There had been a crimson sunset, of wonderful stormy hues, the water almost luminous, its calm surface kaleidoscopic with patches of green, mauve, lemon, and purple. Suddenly the sun was gone below the horizon. It was then about seven o'clock. In an hour they would be approaching Sagusto, the unknown. Until now there had been no deviation from their southern course, but, as he watched, the ship bore south-south-east, and gradually, on the port horizon, a long low line of black hills was just discernible. Half an hour later they seemed to be entering a channel running along a mountainous island on whose northern cape a solitary light intermittently flashed.

Presently Tino came on deck and approached him.

"Where are we?" asked Cameron.

"That is Scyrea—where the lighthouse is. We are entering the channel now," he answered.

"You know our course?"

"A little—but I'm not sure of navigating it. I'm feeling my way."

"Then how did you take off the Donna from the island?"

asked Cameron, quickly. A moment later, when the boy had answered, he regretted his quick suspicion.

"We went south, to Sebenico—I know that course, our lead boats go regularly," explained the youth. "Here's Nada with your flag."

They turned, and saw her coming along the deck, the Union Jack in her hands. She shook it out for Cameron to inspect. He felt satisfied; only an expert eye could detect the faults. He gave it to Tino.

"Ask Captain Bandioli to fly that at once. You have handed out the rifles and ammunition?"

Tino nodded, he also tapped his hip, where he carried a revolver holster. "We are ready for anything—even Nada here!"

Cameron looked at Nada, not understanding her brother's reference, and then it was that he saw she too wore a revolver belt.

"But you mustn't be mixed up in this," said Cameron, quickly—"not even if it comes to trouble. You and the Donna must keep below."

The girl gave him a quick, defiant look.

"I shall be where the others are!" she replied, her dark eyes shining with suppressed excitement. "And I want to be the first to shoot."

This spirit permeating the ship alarmed Cameron. They were spoiling for an encounter, and if it came to it, he would regard their cause as lost. What chance had a mere handful of nondescripts against an armed population, with all the advantages of land defences? Moreover, he was determined to avoid bloodshed. That young fire-eater, Luigi, had urged storming the island, and, to Cameron's dismay, the Donna had even considered the possibility of success.

Now, as he looked at the girl, he recognised something utterly foreign in her nature. There was a ruthlessness in her, contrasting with her soft beauty.

c

" Until I say otherwise, the Donna and yourself must remain below as soon as we reach the island," he said, quietly.

" Remain below? " she asked, derisively. " Do you think——"

The protest died on her lips under Cameron's cold glance.

" I am now in command, mademoiselle," he said, curtly.

" *Mademoiselle!* There, I've upset you! I'll do anything if you won't call me that! " she laughed, throwing back her dark curls.

" Then obey me! "

" I will," she said, quickly, but there was a twinkle in her eyes as she added: " But mother won't! "

The ship slowed on her course. Over the stern now floated the Union Jack. She had become *The Three Castles*, as her name, painted on bow and stern, proclaimed, the private yacht of a wealthy Englishman cruising for pleasure in the Adriatic.

Tino returned to them. " In half an hour we shall see Sagusto," he said.

" Then summon all the men below," commanded Cameron; " there must be nobody on deck except the hands when we approach. We must not risk observation, even at night."

Tino departed to carry out the order, but Nada did not move. Some unspoken thought held her, and she watched Cameron's face, inscrutable in its expression, as he gazed ahead through the rapidly falling darkness. They had again changed their course, and a succession of shadowy headlands rode by. There were no lights and no signs of life on any of these small islands between whose black shores they ran. Cameron watched, the girl silent at his side.

He had been writing all the afternoon. There was no foreseeing the end of this business, and he had written a long letter to his mother, and another to his solicitors. They were to be posted only in the event of his death. It had seemed absurd, of course, but he was beginning to realise that he had embarked on a grim adventure. In Abyssinia he had been in constant peril, and yet never had he had the sense of danger. Here it was otherwise. This boat voyaging through the quiet sea, between the dark, unknown islands, holding within its timbers some twenty young men, armed and careless of life, awoke in him a consciousness of peril he had never before experienced. Perhaps it was increased by the presence of these two women, particularly of the Donna, a virago certainly, brooding over her wrongs and stirred by the lust of revenge.

He glanced covertly at Nada, at his side. The night breeze lifted the stray wisps of her black hair. She was staring landward, as if searching that dim horizon for some sign. In her eagerness, with half-parted lips and bright eyes, she was exotically beautiful, the vital spirit in her quickened by the approach of the unknown. Suddenly a cry escaped her.

" There ! "

Cameron looked, following the line of her white outstretched hand.

" The light—do you see it? That's the harbour light ! "

" Sagusto? " asked Cameron.

" Yes—the headland's there—with the Castello on it. Look ! can you make out the shape? "

Cameron peered into the night, but could not see the land. Something was there, but it may have been cloud or sea.

" There are no lights in the Castello," said Nada. " I wonder if anyone's there."

As she spoke the ship's engines slowed down, then stopped altogether. Their momentum carried them in silence through the black water. After a short time the yacht rested idly on the water. Cameron heard the anchor paid out. This was their resting-place for the night. They had reached the mysterious Sagusto at last.

He looked long at the dark mass on the horizon, and slowly it grew more definite in his sight One end was low, running down to the sea's level, along whose shore he could see some lights, yellow and steady, through the darkness. They marked the village and the small quay, where the boats for Sebenico were loaded. From this flat plain, perhaps a mile in length, the land gradually rose, until the plateau was reached. At the northern extremity of this, so Tino had told him, there was a precipitous declivity, dropping some eight hundred feet to the bed of a small stream, which ran through the gorge separating the mainland from a solitary headland. The latter rose to a thousand feet, on whose utmost crest was perched the mediæval fortress which, for three hundred years, had been the ancestral stronghold of the Soudaikos family.

Across this gorge, to effect a quick and easy access to the northern end of the island, a strong bridge had been built. Tino had enthusiastically described this piece of Turkish masonry. Some former Governor had built it, of solid Istrian stone. It spanned the gorge, which fell sheer to the bed of the stream six hundred feet below, without any support save that given by the skilful cambering and the massive keystone of the great arch. The architect of this daring achievement had utilised two projecting ledges of rock on either side of the precipice, down to which a narrow approach had been cut. The east tower of the Castello commanded an extensive vista of the gorge and the bridge. The only other means of approach to this natural stronghold was by a deviously winding track, descending to and ascending from the level of the stream. The head of the gorge was impassable to all except experienced mountaineers.

"Then the place's impregnable," had said Cameron, at the close of Tino's description, aided by a plan and some photographs.

"Quite—the bridge can be covered from the east tower. There are only two other approaches—the track round the bed of the stream, and the direct ascent from the northern shore, which is impracticable."

"Why?"

"It's only a narrow staircase cut into the rock's face, overhanging the sea. It's an hour's climb. We came down that way when we left the island. It may have been used by the corsairs who once held the place, before the track and the bridge had been made."

Cameron had sat silent a few minutes, and, turning to the Donna, had said:

"It seems to me that if Condylis has taken possession of the Castello it is quite useless to attempt to drive him out?"

"Quite," she replied. "But I don't think he'll be there. You see, it's right away from the mines and the village. He has a house down in the village."

"Then we need not bother about the Castello?"

"No—it is the quay that matters—that is vital to us, and to him."

Cameron had pondered over this. The necessity of landing by the quay, in full view of Condylis and the villagers, made the task formidable. Condylis was certain to have guarded this approach with the utmost caution. That letter at Pola had revealed his readiness to repulse any attempt to land by force. To Cameron now, as he stood on deck, peering through the darkness at the low tongue of land where the lights glimmered, the need for diplomacy rather than force was incontestable. He began to realise how desperate were the chances of the Donna.

In his own mind he had already evolved a plan of campaign, in which he hoped not a shot would be fired. He had not revealed it, and would not, until the ultimate moment, for, apart from the Donna, Tino, and Nada, he trusted no one on board. Men who could be bought for such an enterprise as this could be captured by the highest bidder. They were mercenaries with no interest save their own, and no honour to sacrifice. He had not told the Donna this; perhaps in her shrewd mind she already knew, for he observed that, outside her family, her only confidants had been Bandioli and himself.

Cameron looked at his watch. It was nearly ten o'clock, the time he had fixed for a conference below. He went down the hatchway, halted a few minutes near the men's quarters to satisfy himself they were obeying the instructions to keep as quiet as possible, and then tapped on the door of the Donna's salon.

Tino quickly opened it, and Cameron found the Donna, her daughter, and Bandioli awaiting him, their impatient curiosity regarding his scheme showing in the alert faces they turned upon him. Only Bandioli seemed quite at ease, with little evidence of strain. Obviously his life was one long adventure, and he accepted everything with which Fate crossed his path. His round face and beady eyes smiled at Cameron, the wrinkles and the great scar making him look more likely for the rôle of the villain than that of hero.

As for the Donna, as always, she was regally superb. In these last few days, when she hazarded her whole future on this throw of the dice, she had never revealed a weak moment. Cameron's task had been to curb her daring, and to point out that diplomacy won more kingdoms than gunpowder. In one respect she was a true child of her Balkan *milieu* : she was more ready to shoot than argue.

" Well, major, what's to be the move? " asked Bandioli, first, as soon as Cameron had seated himself. " I have all the men ready for a landing."

" Will you make it before daybreak? Tino and myself will go in the first boat—we know the harbour," said the Donna. " We can land here, at the end of the sea wall "—she put a jewelled finger upon the plan before her, drawn by Tino for Cameron's guidance. " If there's resistance then, we can take cover."

Cameron looked quietly at the tense faces around the table. The boy was slightly flushed, the girl pale and highly strung. Only the Donna and Bandioli seemed to approach this problem as a matter of business.

" Donna, that isn't my plan. There will be only one person land—myself," said Cameron.

" Yourself? " echoed the Donna and Bandioli together.

" Listen. You've seen the precautions we've taken to make

this ship a private one, owned by an Englishman, obviously cruising in the Adriatic? Well, there's a purpose in it. What use is it attempting to force a landing if, as he has warned you, Condylis is prepared for it?"

" That's probably bluff—as you said yourself," interrupted Bandioli.

" Probably it is," repeated Cameron. " But there's no reason to try violence until other methods have failed."

" What are they?" asked the Donna, slightly incredulous.

" To-morrow morning, at nine o'clock, I shall be rowed ashore—by two Italians for preference. We've no English crew—it may seem natural enough for me to have taken on some Italian hands. I shall step on to the quay the most obvious English tourist, out to see the sights of Sagusto. I shall naturally be most interested in the native life and work, which includes the lead mines and the old Castello."

" He'll not let you see anything," growled Bandioli.

" That may be. But I've two eyes, and at least I can get the lie of the land. Also I want to talk to Condylis."

" But, major, he may suspect. In which case——" began the Donna.

" That is the risk I must run. But I don't think he will."

" He's expecting an attack," said the youth.

" By a boat coming from the north—and anything but an English boat, flying an English flag. Don't you see," continued Cameron, " that my very impudence is my best defence?"

It was Nada who now spoke, leaning forward, her hands clasped on the table.

" Major Cameron—it's a great risk. Must you do it this way?" she asked. " To go alone like this—anything might happen!"

" It would be dangerous to go any other way, my dear young lady," replied Cameron, smiling. " With yourself, for instance, or the Donna, much as would be my pleasure. Once we are seen together, our connection is known. That is why

I have given such sharp orders that in daylight you are all to keep below as long as we are anchored here."

They were silent for a few moments, revolving his plan in their minds. Obviously, they had little faith in it. Its utter simplicity gave it an air of impossibility.

"If you land, and see Condylis, what then, m'sieur?" asked Tino, breaking the silence.

"The moment you mention my name he will guess everything," said the Donna. "I can't see what you can gain, major."

Cameron smiled assuringly.

"Donna, I wouldn't propose this step if I hadn't the next in mind," he answered, quietly.

"Which is?" demanded Bandioli, patronisingly.

"One I shan't reveal just yet," replied Cameron, blandly.

The Donna drummed with her fingers on the plan.

"I should have thought an attempt to seize the Castello had been the first thing. If we can get that, many of the villagers would come to join us—they only want a lead," she said.

"Tino is certain that is impossible," answered Cameron. "There is only the rock staircase from the shore—unless we landed here"—he pointed on the map—"and fought our way up to the plateau."

"It's not impossible, m'sieur—but it is very difficult," said Tino. "We are nearly two miles by road from the Castello. Also, if it's defended, we could never get across the bridge—it's covered from the east tower."

"That's why I propose the staircase," persisted Donna Soudaikos. "They'd not expect an attack from that way—it's too risky. We could take the ship round by night and land under cover of darkness."

"It sounds too desperate," answered Cameron.

"We are attempting a desperate thing, major," said the Donna. "We don't mind any risk that's shared. But I can't see your going alone into the hands of Condylis."

"There's little risk, believe me," persisted Cameron. "In any case, I insist on taking it. Since you've given me this command, I must take the responsibility."

By the tone in his voice they knew he could not be dissuaded.

"I must consent, then," answered the Donna.

"Thank you," said Cameron, and, turning to Bandioli:

"At nine, captain, I shall be rowed ashore. The men must be unarmed. If you can display a little washing drying on deck, so much the better."

"Washing?" asked the perplexed captain. His glance travelled from face to face, in confirmation of his suspicion of Cameron's sanity.

"Anything which tends to give those on shore the impression that we're living a normal, unconcerned life supports my rôle as a casual visitor. There mustn't be a gun seen. Until I return, no one but the deck hands must show a head."

"When will you return, m'sieur?" asked Tino.

"I shall signal from the quay for a boat to take me off. Please keep a look-out, therefore. I may want it in an hour, or in two or three."

"Or not at all," jested Bandioli, grimly.

"Or not at all—if Condylis offers a boat," retorted Cameron. "I hope I have made everything clear?"

"Quite, major—I'm very sorry to consent to it," said the Donna. "I shall never take my eyes from the porthole."

"Then I must hurry my return!" laughed Cameron. And turning towards the pale, anxious face of Nada, he was glad to see that his retort provoked an answering smile, for she had been looking at him throughout this council as though he were a doomed man. The anxiety of both the Donna and her daughter revealed something more than a mere selfish desire to use him. As for Tino, the lad followed him about for the rest of the evening, seeking in a hundred little services to give voice to his dumb devotion.

CHAPTER VIII

I

In the full light of morning Cameron was able to make a general survey of the island through his glasses. It had been very faithfully described by Tino. At the southern end, where the cliffs gradually broke down to the sea, lay the small village. He could just discern the flat-roofed houses, pink and white, some of them with the familiar green shutters that kept out the glare of noon. They rose in terraces from the quay, whose single wall, of Istrian stone, ran out into the placid blue sea. Here and there the water fretted the arid rocks on which the quay had been built. Beyond, the boats themselves hidden, he saw the tops of lateen sails, furled. They might be the boats that took lead to Sebenico.

Around the village rose the uplands, the slopes well covered with groves of olives. It was a rich soil, as the luxuriant growth of palms and lemon trees proved. Higher, the land had been scored with vine terraces that rose up the valley towards the feet of the encircling mountains on the north-east. The morning mist still veiled those heights whereon, so Tino had reported, was a great plateau running north to the gorge.

He sought that break in the range now, and a momentary clearing of the mist, rolling upwards under the absorbing sun, suddenly left the precipice revealed. From the schooner it was impossible to see the depth of that sudden break in the great wall of the mountains. It was so abrupt that it appeared as if the pinnacle, crowned by the sturdy Castello, were an island, broken away from the mainland by some cataclysmic force of Nature. Perhaps, indeed, it had been so, for as Cameron looked, he could scarcely believe that a mere stream could have wrought such a fissure in that rocky mountain.

As a defensive position the Castello was ideal. No wonder those old corsairs, and the successive conquerors of this historic sea, had made it a stronghold. Sheered up by colossal buttresses, and built to the very edge of those precipitous rocks, at whose feet, one thousand feet below, the blue sea seethed like filmy lace, it was impregnable. The massive walls were now golden with age, and the old fort nursed its secrets. There were few windows opening seawards, and, such as they were, so deeply set in the masonry that they seemed blind eyes. Above the crenellated ramparts the morning sun glinted on the bronzed tiles of some internal buildings. The extreme end finished in a massive bastion, carrying a flag-mast. There was no flag on it.

Sweeping his glasses southwards again, Cameron searched for sight of the mines, but failed to find them. He had been told they lay behind the village, at a distance of about half a mile. Possibly they were behind that barrier of foothills cutting the sky.

Seen in the morning sunlight, with its green uplands, its luxuriantly wooded valley, the arid, rose-hued rocks, and the great purple wall of the encircling mountains, it was a beautiful spot. Well might a man settle here and dream his days away in idyllic bliss. In these almond and olive groves, amid the vines or the meadows of asphodel, there was something of an Arcadian setting. So remote that history was dumb concerning it, human life had ceaselessly flourished here. There had been scenes of bloodshed, doubtless, of siege and assault, of wild terror and rapine. That old Castello bore witness to changing fortunes, but even so, life had had its Elysian moments. The cultivation of the vines, of the lemon, of aniseed and tobacco, had occupied the easy labours of a peasant population. The conquerors had troubled themselves little with the soil, plunging into the richer bowels of the mountain, where the lead mines offered wealth.

It was in these mines that man's infamy, his insatiable cruelty, had been shown to his fellows. Hundreds of miserable captives, naked, flogged, starved, had perished in that dark underworld. It had taken the life of the strong barbarian, bowed under the Roman lash, of the proud Venetian captured in some foray against the Turk, or, in turn, of the arrogant Turk himself. Tino, who had related this, had also related another horror, of that time following the Battle of Lepanto, when two hundred prisoners, unwanted by a water-logged galleon returning from victory, had been walled up in a disused arm of the mine. That wall and its horrors beyond had never been unsealed.

But this morning it was all a scene of sunlit luxuriance, of sub-tropical plants and flowers, of a peaceful cluster of white and pink dwellings, with a semi-Venetian bell-tower rising aloft, the blue sky shining through its open belfry. Around the small harbour, and upon the rugged coastline the morning sea-mist wavered like steam. As it lifted from the lower slopes of the hills, Cameron could see, amid the vineyards and lemon and olive groves, the tiny whitewashed dwellings of the peasant cultivators.

Such was the Donna's demesne, fair enough in all truth, and one for which rightly she might take arms against a usurper. It was the nature of this usurper Cameron was now about to investigate. So far, he had heard only the Donna's story. It sounded true enough, and all he could learn, from Nada and Tino, corroborated her story in the main. But there was a mystery in her relations with Condylis. He had been some eighteen years on the island, and this break in their relations after so long a period required explanation. Nominally, as her employee, Condylis had no claim; actually, he had, by some means, established himself as the dictator of the island. And for some reason he had driven the Donna out of her possession. It might be an act of tyrannical theft, or it might——

"How do you like Sagusto, m'sieur?" asked an eager voice at his side. It was Tino, his brown skin gleaming with water. He squeezed the brine out of his hair, fresh from his morning swim.

"It looks attractive, Tino—I hope it may prove so," said Cameron, and then, glancing at the youth's lithe figure, "I hope you've not been showing yourself to the enemy?"

" Oh no, m'sieur ! I swam on the other side of the ship."

A pool gathered at his feet as he stood rubbing the water from his limbs. Cameron stooped and played with Kim, the lad's Dalmatian hound, that rarely left its master.

" M'sieur ! "

" Yes ? " answered Cameron. There was the note of request in the youth's voice.

" If I disguised myself couldn't I come with you—as one of the boatmen ? "

There was an eager appeal in his voice, but Cameron turned a deaf ear to it.

" No one can come with me, Tino. It might spoil everything. Besides, you would be sure to be spotted."

" But you run such a risk, m'sieur ! What if he makes you a prisoner ? "

" I must run that risk. It's the very danger that makes it safe. At the worst, if he suspects who I am, I don't think he'll detain me. The one thing he wants is to keep us off the island. He wouldn't know what to do with me, if he got me. And there's another point. I'm a British subject—but I don't want to rely on that. I've no right to start dragging the British Empire into rescuing every mad fellow who mixes himself up in an island feud."

Disappointment was in the lad's face. He had set his heart on going with Cameron. And suddenly he gave voice to all that was in his mind.

" M'sieur, you do all this for us—you risk your life; and we treated you—oh, abominably ! Do you know what I would like to do ? "

He asked the question with such passionate earnestness that Cameron saw the boy was labouring under the stress of great emotion.

" M'sieur, I would like to die for you ! "

His voice rang as with the protestation of some holy vow, his eyes aflame, his young body tense with determination. Cameron checked the laugh that half rose to his lips, arrested by the genuine depth of this emotion. It was no melodramatic impulse, but the vow of a young squire to follow his knight. He regarded Cameron as a crusader, and his whole being was at the service of his master, for life or death. As Cameron looked at that face, purified by its hero-worship and self-negation, he loved the boy. He had always loved youth, its clean lines, its clear head, its quick impulse. The youngsters under his command, those English youths, hiding their emotions and patterned to their accepted creed, were to him the flower of the earth. Tino was not of this race, but the unifying spirit was there. It caught at Cameron's heart, in all its simple nobility.

Perhaps no hint of this escaped him, only a little added warmth in his tone there may have been, as he rested his hand on the boy's slim shoulder.

" Thank you, Tino. I shan't forget that. Meanwhile, there's one thing I want you to do."

" M'sieur ? "

" To live, both for myself and your mother. You've much to do, and, after this is through, you've a man's work. This island will need you."

And then, to change the subject, as one embarrassed by any sign of emotion : " Get dressed now, we'll breakfast together," he said.

II

Punctually at nine the boat was waiting at the foot of the accommodation-ladder, which had been lowered for Cameron's departure. He did not know that by Tino's orders another boat waited, on the other side of the ship, containing six men, all armed, under the command of Lieutenant Luigi. They had strict orders to shelter there. If any treachery showed itself towards Cameron, then Tino would lose no time in sending help. All this was unknown to Cameron.

After greeting the Donna and Nada, who kept to their salon as requested, Cameron went to the companion-way. Like Tino, the girl was very jumpy, and he'd have sworn there were tears in her eyes as he left her. The Donna, as became her bearing throughout, showed no sign of her thoughts. The next few hours meant much to her, but nothing of this penetrated the mask of her bold face.

Tino said good-bye to him at the foot of the stairs, after looking at him in open astonishment. He had not seen the major so carefully groomed before. Clad in flannel trousers, with yachting cap and blue reefer coat, he looked every inch the English " milord," wealthy, as became the owner of a private yacht. One thing in particular astonished Tino.

" A camera—you take a camera ? " he gasped.

" Certainly—that's the badge of the tourist. How else should I go to look at Sagusto? " exclaimed Cameron. " Did you expect me to carry a gun ? "

" You've a revolver ? " asked Tino.

" Nothing offensive or defensive—I can arouse no suspicion, naked or clothed."

He laughed at the youth's puzzled face, smacked him playfully on the back, and calling " Au revoir ! " ran up on deck. A few moments later he was seated in the boat, which immediately pulled off from the ship.

Yet, for all his light manner, affected to give the rôle he wished those on board to maintain, there was deep anxiety in his heart. None knew better the hazard in this throw of the dice. If Condylis suspected nothing, then he was a step nearer his scheme. But Condylis might be suspicious, in which case he would need all his wits. Despite his reference to British nationality, in order to assure the anxious Tino, Cameron knew well enough that a desperate man, standing on his own territory, acquired by force, would be prepared to protect it by force. He would shoot on the slightest provocation. But the plan Cameron had in mind made it well worth this risk. If it succeeded it would bring a swift and bloodless triumph to the Donna's cause.

As the boat drew nearer to the quay there were signs of life in the harbour. He caught the gleam of wet brown bodies, where half a dozen boys dived and splashed about a mooring buoy. Still nearer, he was aware of several figures standing at the end of the jetty, watching his approach. As the boat touched the wall of the quay, before it was possible for Cameron to put a foot on the iron ladder running up it, a man, as thorough-looking a ruffian as one could imagine, yelled something to the men in the boat. Neither they nor Cameron understood. Whatever it was he said, in some unknown tongue, his object was unmistakable. He leaned over, a formidable iron bar in his hands, gesticulating ferociously. He did not intend that they should land there, and kept pointing, amid a torrent of words, towards the inner corner of the harbour.

Cameron told his men to row across to the place indicated. It now occurred to him that an unforeseen obstacle to his purpose might have to be confronted. These islanders spoke some form of Czech, a *patois* in any case, and communication was going to prove difficult. He began to wonder whether Condylis spoke any other language save his native Greek and this *patois*. If not it would prove extremely awkward to carry out his scheme.

At the corner of the inner harbour a flight of stone steps ran up from the water level. And here Cameron observed what had been hidden from him by the high quay. A man, with a rifle slung across his shoulder, sauntered up and down, his beat ending at the jetty's extremity. There was something placed there, shrouded under a tarpaulin, that Cameron's eye readily recognised. It was a machine-gun.

It would have been idle to deny that he experienced a shock at the sight of this. It was very visible evidence of the reality of affairs. This island was prepared for an attack, and it was grimly prepared. Condylis's letter to the Donna at Pola had been, then, no empty threat.

As soon as the sentinel with the rifle saw the intention of the boat to effect a landing for its distinguished-looking occupant, he ran quickly towards the steps, unslinging his rifle and pointing it recklessly at Cameron, who had begun to mount them. Deliberately ignoring the man and his loud exclamations, Cameron turned and dismissed his boat, watching it depart with studied unconcern. As the gesticulating man rushed up to him, the muzzle of the rifle shifting its direction with every word he spoke, a crowd began to gather, of half-clad boys and fishermen, who gazed in speechless awe at the faultlessly dressed stranger.

The words of the excited guard were wholly unintelligible to Cameron, but a man in the crowd who spoke Italian offered himself as interpreter. Between the accent of this fellow and Cameron's limited knowledge of the language, they made little headway. Eventually he made it understood that he wished to visit the island, and was met with "*Non possibile*" in endless reiteration.

Undeterred, Cameron moved towards the village. At first the guard sought to obstruct him, and put out a detaining arm. With a show of outraged dignity, Cameron cast off the fellow's hand, and resolutely stepped forward, breaking through the ring of loafers who had encircled him. The guard hesitated a moment, and then realised this move was to his own advantage. In the village he would have support. This was no ordinary invader. He looked a "milord," one with authority. Falling behind, he kept close to the heels of Cameron, his rifle held nervously at the full cock, so that at any moment he might have shot someone in the crowd that danced along beside the foreigner.

From the small open square fronting the harbour, and containing half a dozen poverty-stricken shops, a narrow street, cobbled and dirty, led out between two rows of overhanging balconied houses, up the hillside. It was obviously the main road through the village. If he went up this he would get nearer the centre of things. The church, whose tower he had seen from the ship, must be somewhere up this street. He marched on, showing no hesitation, and the guard made no effort to check him.

His progress had aroused the whole village. Dark-faced women, with blue eyes and the flat nose and broad nostrils of the Slav, came to the shop doors, or leaned down over the iron balconies of the houses. The types were indescribably mixed. In the course of that quarter of a mile Cameron saw Greeks, Italians, Slovenes, and many indefinable half-breeds, the Hellenic, the Jewish and the Slav nose marking the racial source. Upon all their faces was the impress of poverty and fear. They were what he would describe as rat-faced, bred and reared in semi-starvation, and the prey to panic. The utter misery of their condition depressed him. Here was all the ferocity which, given opportunity, would reveal incalculable cruelty. They were serfs, born of generations of serfs, and instinctively Cameron felt that Sagusto was, and always had been, for all its beauty, a place of tyranny.

A few hundred yards up the street they encountered the village priest. By his long black cloak and the conical cloth hat he wore, Cameron judged him to be a Father of the Greek Ortho-dox Church. He was a man of medium height, with a long black beard flowing over his chest. Unlike his flock, he looked well-nourished, but the eyes under the iron-rimmed spectacles were myopic.

He hesitated as Cameron approached, folding his hands placidly over the end of his beard, and looked at the stranger, expressing neither curiosity nor fear. Cameron saluted him, to which he responded with a dignified bow. To the first words, addressed to him in English, he shook his head, slowly repeating " No—no—no—too leetle Eenglesh. *Parley-vous francais*, m'sieur? "

Immensely relieved, Cameron immediately spoke French.

" I have just landed from my yacht," he said, " and would like to visit the sights of the island. This is Sagusto, isn't it? "

The priest extended his hand, and Cameron, wishing to give every tribute to his position, removed his cap, and, raising the hand of the priest, kissed it. The old fellow was obviously pleased by this tribute. It increased his merit in the eyes of the villagers, a fact Cameron well knew.

"This is Sagusto. But there are no sights, m'sieur—except those of our poverty," he replied.

"You have a church here?" queried Cameron.

"Yes—there is little to see. I have a missal of——"

Here the guard, feeling himself ignored, angrily pushed himself between Cameron and the priest, saying something to the latter that was explosively rude and meant for all the onlookers. Cameron immediately took hold of the fellow by the shoulders and swung him round, out of place, cowing him with a look of strong disapproval. The priest observed all this, his expression never changing, but he said in a quiet voice:

"You see, m'sieur, I am accorded no dignity. You are a stranger here, and you are most unwelcome. We have fallen upon evil days, and our island is suffering terribly. You will be wise to go no further, lest harm befall you."

"Harm—what harm? I only wish to look around," said Cameron. "What is the matter, Pappa?"

"It is dangerous for me to talk. Pray let me escort you back. This fellow is suspicious. You will do well to return, I beg of you."

The priest was earnest in his request. Cameron saw his eyes anxiously watching him.

"I'm sorry, but I never give way to fear. The English can be stupid, Pappa."

"Ah, you are English!" sighed the priest, as if it explained everything. "If you must stay, then it were better you saw the Governor—Colonel Condylis."

"Colonel Condylis?"

So the fellow was a colonel and had styled himself Governor!

"Without his permission you may not visit the island. If you wish, I will conduct you to his house. But I can't promise you a reception, m'sieur. I have no authority with him," he said, and added, sadly, "Indeed, m'sieur, I am quite ignored."

There was such pathetic resignation in the priest's voice that Cameron knew at once here was no ally of the Condylis régime. That might prove useful. He would do all he could to ingratiate himself.

" I really wish to see your church, Pappa, and, if I may, to photograph it. Perhaps, as you suggest, I had better call on the Governor first. Please conduct me. I suppose this fellow here will take me, in any case? "

He asked the question jestingly. Without looking at the fellow, the priest led the way, and, as he walked at Cameron's side, spoke guardedly, as though he feared being overheard.

" These are troubled days for us," he said. " We are living without liberty. All our hopes died when the poor Donna was driven out."

" The Donna? " queried Cameron, with feigned ignorance.

" Donna Soudaikos, m'sieur. She was a noble lady, the owner of this island. Ever since the death of her husband she fought against the encroachment of her agent, Colonel——"

He broke off, apprehensive of the listening guard.

" The Donna you speak of," questioned Cameron, " where is she? If this is her property, surely——"

" The poor lady was driven out, m'sieur. Where, we know not. She fought nobly—for herself, her children, the islanders. This man is evil, he was evil towards her, but she scorned him, she——" He paused, fearful that he might be overheard.

" More I must not say, m'sieur. I can do little for my flock, and the evildoers have the ear of authority. Our hope is that the Donna will return one day, with help. Until then we suffer."

He fell into silence then, and replied to Cameron's questions with monosyllables. It was obvious he did not wish to talk, fearing he had already said too much.

They had come out of the street now, into a small square that had pretence to dignity. Perhaps in the old days it had been seignorial. In the centre of the square there was an old well-head, carved in marble, and probably one of those Venetian *pozzi* that invariably marked the terrain of the Serene Republic. In confirmation of this, Cameron caught sight of a stone column supporting the winged Lion and Book of San Marco.

So the Venetian lords had reigned here! It accounted for the faded dignity of this treeless square, well paved and surrounded by houses whose windows were decorated with Gothic–Byzantine pillars and architraves. The house to which the priest was now leading him, with a porticoed façade, approached by a flight of steps, had probably once been the headquarters of the Capitano del Popolo—the chief administrator.

On the steps the priest halted. He would go no further. "The guard will ask for Colonel Condylis. I wish you pleasure in your visit to Sagusto," he said, with much dignity.

Before Cameron could answer he had bowed and gone down the steps, the small gathering opening silently for him. A fellow at Cameron's elbow was speaking. He was armed like the guard, but more respectably dressed. Obviously he desired Cameron to follow him, making himself understood in Italian. They went through a heavy wooden door, studded with iron. It clanged behind them, shutting out the crowd.

The scene confronting Cameron made him catch his breath in the quick surprise of its beauty. The door gave access to one side of a covered gallery that completely surrounded a small courtyard. The gallery had two storeys, the roof of the ground one being arched and painted with the arms of the successive Captains of the People.

The upper storey, open to the courtyard as the lower, had a double colonnade of Carrara marble, each pair of pillars being set upon the apex of the arches in the lower storey. The centre of the courtyard itself was paved, and contained a small garden, in which the great fan-leaves of a banana tree rose above beds of crimson azaleas and the exotic blooms of the hibiscus. A green-plumaged parrot fluttered from branch to branch, screeching through its vermilion beak at a little marmoset that gibbered insolently from the upper colonnade. An outside staircase, wide and ornamented with carved escutcheons supported by griffons, connected the courtyard with the upper gallery.

Cameron was kept waiting for some time on the ground floor, the guard never leaving his side. Presently, through a door at the end of the colonnade, the second guard appeared, summoning Cameron to approach. He went forward, traversed a short corridor, and was shown into a room at the end. The door closed behind him. He was alone.

Again he had a pleasant surprise in the prospect opened before him. This was the back of the house, which was evidently set on the crest of the hill up which the long street had run. Through an open French window, giving access to a small balcony, he looked down on the other side, over orchards, maize plantations, and small houses buried deep in vine pergolas that lifted a green network to the morning sun. Somewhere he could hear the creak of a cart and the familiar cackle of hens. Whatever Condylis might or might not be, he had established himself in very pleasant quarters. The rich landscape fell to what must be the east side of the island, and between a fold in the near foothills Cameron thought he discerned a glint of the sea. But the haze of the morning was still over the scene.

It was then, looking closer, attracted by a noise immediately below him, that Cameron noticed the high-walled courtyard. The ground on this side of the house must have been much lower than on the front, for he was surprised to observe that the balcony which he now approached was on the second storey.

Two horses clattered their hoofs restlessly in this cobbled yard below him. They were saddled for riding, their bridles tethered to a post in the centre of the court. It was this post, and what he saw on it, that sent the blood rushing back to his heart. There were two padlocked bars of iron on either side, each with a pair of loops whose use was unmistakable. These were hand manacles, and the whole apparatus could serve one purpose only. It was a flogging-post!

For a few moments Cameron stared at it, and then laughed involuntarily at his own foolishness. It was a relic of those bad old times when bloodshed and torture had been part of the day's work. Elsewhere, these fiendish implements of mediæval modes had been swept away. Here, no one had taken the trouble to remove them.

It was while his eyes were still upon the post that a voice broke the stillness. It came from underneath the balcony, an angry voice, pouring forth a tirade wholly foreign to Cameron's ears. The voice belonged to a man, a heavy throaty voice, and against it rose another. It was a pure treble, protesting, pleading—a woman's? The next moment there was a scream of pain, and out into Cameron's line of sight ran a boy.

He was not more than fifteen, sturdy, with bronzed shoulders and strong neck. His head was covered with close black curls, and his body was bent so that Cameron could not see the face, but judged the age from the lad's figure. He wore nothing but a pair of ragged green shorts, tied round his waist with a red sash. A peasant, obviously, mahogany-coloured with exposure to the burning sun. But the depth of that tan on the strong young shoulders could not hide the angry red weal that lay across them—the mark of a lash.

So that explained the scream of pain!

Cameron saw the boy turn, half-enraged and defiant, saw another figure emerge, that of a heavily-built man, horsewhip in hand. He was pyjama-clad, and slithered forward in a pair of Bosnian slippers. Again the lash descended, circling the shoulders of the cringing lad, accompanied by a torrent of abuse.

For a moment, astounded by that sickening scene, Cameron was irresolute. Then he stepped towards the balcony. He would make himself seen. It would perhaps check this bully. But before he could emerge, the man turned, exhibiting a dark, coarse-featured face, and was gone, leaving the lad crying, his face buried in his arms as he leaned against the saddle of one of the horses. A few moments later he seemed to recover himself, crossed the yard, and disappeared through a doorway into what appeared to be part of the stables. He soon reappeared, carrying a box containing brushes, and proceeded to brush down one of the horses.

He was a stable-boy, then, concluded Cameron, watching him from the cover of the room, indignant as he saw those two red weals across the lad's brown back. Acting on impulse, he took from his pocket a half-empty packet of cigarettes, and taking aim, threw it at the lad. It fell short, but he saw it as he stooped to change his brushes.

For a moment the boy stood like one paralysed, staring at this small packet that had dropped from the sky. Then he went forward, picked it up, and was still more astonished by its contents. Straightening himself he searched the wall of the house with a puzzled face. Suddenly, seeing Cameron, standing there on the balcony, smiling, the mystery was cleared. Immediately the tear-smudged face brightened into the sunniest of smiles, teeth and eyes gleaming in glad recognition of the gift. The next moment he made a gracious little bow that would have done credit to any court page. Cameron placed a finger on his lips to signify silence, and withdrew. A look told him the boy understood. He had pocketed the cigarettes quickly and resumed his work.

Cameron now examined the room into which he had been ushered. It was plain enough, except for the ceiling, that retained a faded memory of past glories, whereon mouldering nymphs reclined, while blotched cherubs emptied cornucopias into their ample laps. The furniture was scanty and simple : a couple of oak chairs, a faded couch, and an old oak table. On the last was an ash-tray containing some stumped-out cigarettes and some magazines. The familiar cover of one of these made Cameron look closer. He was surprised to find that it was an American periodical, nearly a year old. Then someone in the house probably knew English. The condition of the room suggested that it was used as a waiting-room.

Cameron sat down. Outside, from the meadow and the hill, came the bleak rasping of the cicadas in the growing heat of the day. Time passed and still no one came. The boy had led off the horses he had brushed down. Then, after a long wait, there were sounds of footsteps. The door abruptly opened and the same young guard entered, still carrying his rifle slung over his shoulder.

"Colonel Condylis wants to know what your business is, also what's your name," he said, but not without a certain politeness in his tone, despite the request.

"Cameron's my name—Mr. Cameron. I've no business at all. My yacht, *The Three Castles*, put in here last night, and I thought I would like to see the island. I understand it's private property?" asked Cameron.

"Yes," replied the guard. "If you'll wait I'll tell the Colonel."

He was already impatient with waiting, but before he could make any answer the man had withdrawn again. Cameron sat down to wait developments. A few minutes later the door opened. But this time it was not the young guard. A man stood in the open doorway, a bushy, thick-necked fellow, dark-featured, and with a head of black hair that was slightly curly. He was clad in pink-and-white striped pyjamas, open at his red neck. Instantly Cameron recognised him as the man he had seen thrashing the boy.

Springing to his feet, he stood without speaking, while the other man returned his scrutiny, his cunning eyes missing no detail.

"Good morning!" he said curtly, advancing, a half-smoked cigar twirled between his fingers. He spoke English, and Cameron thought he detected an American intonation. "I'm Colonel Condylis—you want to see me?" he asked.

"Please. I hear you speak English," began Cameron.

"I was two years in Texas—mining—but I'm forgetting it. Won't you sit down?"

Surprised by this invitation coming from so rough a character, Cameron sat down, wondering how he should begin his excuse for this intrusion. But Condylis did not wait for him. He seated himself on the edge of the table, which creaked under his bulk, took a draw at his cigar, blew out the smoke, and said:

"I'm told you want to see Sagusto. Well, there's nothing to see. It's private and——"

"I'm sorry if I'm trespassing," said Cameron.

"You are. But you needn't be sorry. What brought you here? We're supposed to be off the map."

There was no suspicion in the question; it might have been as casual as it sounded.

"Yes—I should think you are! I saw it was marked 'Sagusto,' and wondered if there was anything worth seeing. I'm just cruising—coming up from Corfu on my way to Venice. These Adriatic islands are often interesting, with their Venetian and Saracen remains. I see this place was once held by Venice?"

Condylis drew again at his cigar. From under his dark bushy eyebrows he had made a close scrutiny of his visitor. Obviously an Englishman, this, with too much money and time on his hands.

"Yes, it was Venetian—you've seen the piazza on your way here? And the Castello——"

"The Castello?" echoed Cameron, deliberately. "Oh, is that the Castello at the end of the island, which I saw from the yacht? Is it worth visiting?"

Condylis felt angry with himself for mentioning the Castello. The sooner this fellow cleared off the better.

"No, it isn't worth seeing, and it's difficult to get at. Besides, it's closed now. We don't use it," he said.

There was an awkward silence.

"I suppose you don't mind my taking a few photographs?" asked Cameron.

Condylis glanced at the camera he held.

"No,—if you see anything worth while."

"I thought perhaps the church," suggested Cameron.

"I've never been in it," said Condylis, with a surly smile. He scratched his hairy chest. In his youth he had possibly been a handsome fellow. Now he had got slack and coarse. "What's your tonnage?" he asked abruptly.

"Six hundred."

"When are you going?"

The directness of the question found Cameron unprepared. He laughed and looked at Condylis.

"Well—very soon if there's nothing to detain me," he said. "Would you care to come on board? I could——"

"I'm busy, thanks," interrupted the Greek.

"I could give you a drink," continued Cameron.

He saw the sudden interest awakened in the man.

"Say—how much liquor have you got on board?" asked Condylis, leaning forward. "This damned place's dry as a bone, except for wine—and poor stuff that."

"Liquor? You mean——"

"I mean whisky. It's a year since I saw the colour of it."

"Oh, whisky!" laughed Cameron. "Why, of course, if that's what you like."

"I'll buy it," said Condylis, bluntly.

"No, you won't," contradicted Cameron. "Come and lunch with me on board."

"I can't—I'm at the mines this morning," he answered.

"Mines?"

"Lead mines here—that's what I'm doing in this hole."

"It seems a beautiful spot," said Cameron.

"Beautiful—oh, if you want poetry-stuff, it's here all right," cried Condylis, contemptuously. "Say, I don't want to miss that drink. If you'll let me buy some, I'll——"

"Can't you come and dine to-night? You can sample my store," said Cameron, lying gamely, now he had begun. So far as he knew, *The Three Castles*, or the *Lucciola*, or whatever she really was, or had been, had never smelt whisky. But this bait was too attractive to be lost.

"Well, that's hospitable of you," said Condylis, lurching off the table. "See here!—you stay to lunch with me after your sight-seeing, and I'll come to dinner to-night. Sorry my hospitality isn't very enticing. By the way, when are you going?"

There was something fidgety in the manner in which Condylis repeated his question. He alternated between a desire to be hospitable and a churlish resentment against this invasion.

"We'll weigh anchor early to-morrow—I'm making for Zara from here," answered Cameron. He noticed now that Condylis limped slightly, carrying his great bulk on his left leg.

"Lunch's at twelve," said the Greek. "You can have a look round the village until then. But don't go up to the north end—it isn't safe."

"Not safe?"

"No—that's why some of my fellows are armed. There's been trouble with the miners here—the scum!" said Condylis, fiercely. "But I'll send a guard with you."

This was precisely what Cameron did not wish. So far his luck had been marvellous. He was on the island, he had found Condylis, and had apparently broken down his suspicion. If only he could be free between now and the lunch, he could make valuable use of his time. He wanted to take the lie of the land. It would have been useful also to have got hold of that scared priest and learned exactly what the local position was since the Donna's flight.

But he fully realised the impossibility of making any suggestion that he should go unguarded. It would immediately arouse Condylis's suspicion. So, thanking him, he left the house, the second guard being attached to him this time. It was now nearly eleven. Lunch was at twelve. He had an hour in which to move about. At first he thought he would attempt to give his guard the slip, but decided this would be unwise. It would certainly be reported to Condylis, and nothing must be done to awaken suspicion. His invitation to lunch presented a problem. When he did not return, those on board *The Three*

Castles would be certain to feel anxious. Should he take this opportunity of going to the ship, and return immediately after he had informed them? No, he decided—that, too, might prove unwise, as also the sending of a messenger. Any kind of communication with the ship would be sure to be observed and reported. It were better that he kept away.

It was then, as he retraced his steps down the street, still followed by a few curious urchins, that a turning, revealing a mountain spur on the right, gave him an idea. He remembered having seen this boldly defined foothill rising beyond the tower of the church. It cut sharp against the bright sky, and anyone walking on its ridge would be silhouetted against the light. Those on board the ship were keeping a sharp lookout through their glasses, and it was certain, if he mounted to that ridge, he would be seen.

After much trouble he made his wish understood by the guard, also indicating that the gaping children must be got rid of. A few lavishly administered knocks on the head did this, and they turned up by the church into a lane that ran between the high walls of the gardens. Cameron vainly hoped that he might encounter the priest in this vicinity. He went into the church, and his hopes rose when he noticed that the guard, from some instinct of reverence, remained with his rifle at the door. But the gloomy little place was empty. After a brief glance at a highly-coloured plaster effigy of St. George, and at the tawdry altar, Cameron came out. They resumed the path leading towards the hills. Twenty minutes' hard walking brought them to the crest, along which Cameron displayed himself, for the benefit of those on board. They would know now he had not been killed or imprisoned.

Apart from the motive that had brought Cameron to this crest, he felt amply repaid by the magnificence of the vista before him. Below lay the squat buildings of the village, with its surrounding orchards, its olive groves and vine terraces. The palm, the lemon, the orange and the citron trees testified to the softness of this climate, to the luxuriance of this island lying on the bosom of the blue Adriatic. He could see the harbour, its still water like a mirror, the sea beyond, wrinkled by the light breezes, stretching in ever-changing zones of green, azure, and purple towards the faintness of the hyaline horizon. Their own yacht lay like a paper boat on that coloured sea.

Then, turning north, he looked up to the reddish rocks beyond the upland plateau. A road wound up to those heights, like a white ribbon cutting the grey-green, its upper part sharply zigzagged as it approached the steeper edge. Perhaps that road led ultimately to the Castello, hidden from sight by the great shoulder of the mountain. An eagle hovered over a sun-smitten crag, its shadow sweeping the face of the cliff.

Southwards the land fell towards the sea—pasture land this, dotted with small homesteads. But what was wholly new to Cameron was the eastern prospect. He now saw what lay behind this ridge. In a valley hollowing out towards the sea he discerned a cluster of outbuildings built against the bluff of a cliff. Around these ran truck lines that entered dark openings in the very face of this rocky amphitheatre. They were undoubtedly the lead mines, the source of the Donna's wealth, and the spoil of Condylis.

Impressing the whole panorama firmly on his memory, without betraying himself to his silent guardian, he turned and made the descent to the village.

CHAPTER IX

CAMERON was again shown into the small waiting-room overlooking the stable yard, and as he looked out of the window he saw Condylis ride in, accompanied by a young fellow with a revolver in his belt. Evidently it was unsafe to ride about Sagusto unarmed. There was something more than the fear of an attack from outside—there was a danger within the island itself. That could come from only one source, the people themselves.

It conformed entirely with the unspoken thought growing in Cameron's mind. When he had first seen the island, black under the clear starlit sky, the sight had filled him with a sense, not only of the mysterious errand on which he was bound, but also of the aura of malevolence, of repressed evil that lay upon the place like a thunderous cloud. This morning, again, despite the colour, the sunshine, the exotic beauty of the place, he had the feeling that human nature had gone awry in this Eden. The scared, starved looks of the natives, the sense of repressed emotion, the half-said warnings, the furtive glances, and, above all, the unrelievable gloom of that priest—all contributed to this atmosphere of quiescent evil.

The wild thrashing of the boy, the sinister survival of that post, the necessity of going about armed, and the half-fear that lurked in Condylis's manner, seemed to have their basis in some survival of barbarism. As Cameron watched Condylis dismount he noticed that, despite his bulk, he had retained his agility. He leapt down from the saddle, casting the reins over the horse's neck, and strode off, clumping over the cobbles in heavy, spurred riding-boots. His companion called to someone, and Cameron saw the stable-lad come out from one of the doors. He took the reins of the horses, and, from the smile answering some remark of the young man's, he saw that these had a pleasanter relationship than that exhibited by Condylis. There was no fear on the lad's face now. He laughed back at the man's remark and made a light answer.

A swift opening of the door behind him, and Cameron turned to find a negro standing in the doorway. By this time he was prepared for any kind of sight, but a negro, and such a negro, caused him to stare with amazement. He was a young black, slightly built, and faultlessly attired in a waiter's evening suit. The bow and white shirt, contrasting vividly with the black face and crisp curly hair, were immaculate, as also was the cut of the coat. The only departure from custom was the wearing of a bright green apron round his waist, that gave a bizarre touch to the fellow's appearance. He looked like some bird of rare plumage that had fluttered out of an African jungle. His smile was expansive and ingratiating.

"Will you come this way, sah?" he said, in the softest English.

The voice, the accent, the manner, brought back a memory of a lunch Cameron had once attended at the Century Club in New York, when, as a youth, he had there met his first negro servant. Those fellows had worn coloured waistcoats, he remembered. This negro, with his green apron, was even more startling.

"You are an American?" asked Cameron, as he followed the man.

"Yes, sah, from New Orleans."

"However did you get here?"

"I was the Colonel's servant at Fort Worth, sah," he answered, softly.

He stood aside, to usher Cameron through double doors into what, at a glance, he saw must have been a salon in more splendid days. A massive gilt mirror covered the end wall, and a great marble fireplace, elaborately carved with floral festoons, was opposite. The long side of the room had six windows overlooking a garden, with sub-tropical trees, and gorgeous flowerbeds that blazed under the noontide sun. Brown awnings drawn over each window reduced this glare and gave a softness to the light in the room.

As he entered, Condylis, who had stood near the mirror, came forward. Cameron saw he was not alone. For some reason, he had never expected the presence of a woman in this house, and yet, the moment he was presented to the opulently dressed lady seated on the crimson couch, he realised, what he should have known from the first—that Condylis belonged to that class of man who could exist nowhere without a woman at his side.

"Donna Emilia Granados Gonzalos," said Condylis, grandiloquently, and the Donna, regal on that couch, lived up to the euphony of her name. She gave a swift flicker of her plumed fan of orange-hued ostrich feathers, smiled with glowing eyes in a dead white face and showed perfect teeth between scarlet lips. Her shining black hair was tightly drawn back from her pale brow and carried a great jade comb set with emeralds. The hand she extended, with an artistry that would have graced a Bernhardt, was highly manicured and of flawless beauty. Cameron saw it rest in his own like a work of purest ivory. He raised it to his lips and caught the Donna's eyes peering at him from under their long painted lashes, all the coquetry of Andalusian beauty in their measured regard of him.

" I hear you are English, señor? " she asked, motioning him to be seated at her side. " It is pleasant to greet visitors to Sagusto—we are recluses. The Colonel doesn't mind, but I long for the fleshpots! After Mexico and Bucharest——"

" Mexico—you know Mexico? "

" I was born there, señor. Do you know it? " she asked.

Condylis brought up the young man who had ridden with him.

" Mr. Cameron—Lieutenant Mahassein, my secretary," he said.

The young fellow clicked his heels together and bowed. Cameron began to wonder what nationality he could be. Swarthy, he had a thin, alert face, grey eyes revealing much intelligence, and a jaunty air. He enjoyed life, was prepared to accept it as a gay adventure. Cameron saw this in the ease with which he had greeted him, in his subsequent half-playful chattering with the Donna, who used him as a foil to her elaborate coquetry.

They sat down at a table bright with flowers and choice glassware. There was an air of luxury about the service of this meal, well-cooked and varied. By some means Condylis had commanded most of the luxuries of the rich man's table. It seemed a singular commentary on the nature of mankind that,

D

situated in such a paradise, with every apparent refinement, Condylis should crave whisky to round off his existence. If Cameron's plan worked, whisky would prove this fellow's undoing, as it had many another's, though in a far different sense.

Cameron had not long to wait before he could place this dapper little secretary. He was an Armenian, driven out of Trebizond by a massacre. There seemed to be no capital in Europe in which he had not resided. Like his master, he wore brown doeskin riding-breeches and top-boots. Condylis, however, wore a jacket of dark grey cloth that had a military cut. On the shoulders at some time there had been epaulettes.

"You are in the Greek army, colonel?" asked Cameron, as they reached dessert. The negro footman had waited upon them throughout.

"I was," answered Condylis. "I retired some years ago—before the Balkan Wars claimed my carcase."

"Have you been in Sagusto long?"

Cameron wondered if he would shy at the question, but, intent on the peeling of a fig, Condylis gave no sign.

"About eighteen years—since I inherited this place."

It was Cameron's turn to control himself.

"Oh—it is a private island entirely?" he asked.

"Entirely," replied Condylis, looking at him. Then, his eyes meeting those of Donna Emilia, a swift look of understanding passed between them.

"It would be a very pleasant place, Señor Cameron, if it were not for the people," said Donna Emilia.

"So would the world—the human race spoils it!" laughed Mahassein.

"That's not true!" replied the Donna. "I should find it an impossible place without men in it."

She looked archly at Cameron. She could not be a day younger than fifty, and her size gave her a matronly figure, utterly at variance with the absurd childishness of her face and manner. She turned to Condylis, and with her white jewelled hand stroked his cheek.

"Shouldn't I?" she cooed.

He gave her bare arm a pinch and winked his heavy-lidded eyes.

"Ah, you see the Donna's not been here long enough to get tired of us," said Mahassein.

Cameron glanced round the table. A Spanish-Mexican, a Greek, an Armenian, and Englishman, sitting round a well-furnished table, after an excellent lunch in a house at Sagusto. This did not appear the setting for a fantastic drama. The expedition of *The Three Castles* became a little unreal. Was it possible that even now he was plotting to kidnap his host? And that host a bully and a thief, who had driven a defenceless woman out of her property?"

The Donna graciously excused herself. She was going to have her siesta. In turn each of them received a look of adoration. She sighed, laughed lightly, and, fan spread out against her magenta skirt, jewelled hand and white wrist gracefully displayed in the act, swept majestically from the room. A heavy, overpowering creature, reeking with romance and attar of roses.

The men moved on to the loggia overlooking the garden, and the negro brought cigars and coffee. Closer observation increased Cameron's respect for his adversary. This man was no fool. His courage was probably commensurate with his cunning. There was great determination in that swarthy chin and the thick firm lips, thoroughly sensual and brutal. Side by side with his assistant the contrast was so striking that, at first, Cameron wondered what rôle Mahassein could play. The Armenian was the quicker-witted of the two. He reminded Cameron of a lizard at the side of a cobra. Nothing escaped his quick, bird-like glance. He had pestered Cameron with questions, all of which, so far, he had successfully parried.

"Is your crew English?" he asked, lightly, drawing at the cigarette delicately held in thin fingers.

" Not all—I've some Italians, taken on at Ancona."

" Ancona ! "

The alertness of the tone told Cameron at once that he had blundered.

" Then they must have told you about Sagusto? " asked Mahassein, turning his eyes enquiringly upon Cameron.

" No—you see, I never talk to them. Do they know this place? " he said. He was aware of Condylis watching him covertly from the corner of his eyes, while he pretended to be engrossed in scratching the head of a wolfhound that had come to him.

" Ancona is one of our nearest calling places," replied Condylis. " They know this place, of course, by repute. But they don't come here. There's nothing to come for. We're right off the track. That's why you surprised us. It's not easy to find."

" I didn't find it, colonel," laughed Cameron, " I just blundered into it, pottering around these islands."

" It's a dangerous coastline—and there's currents," said Mahassein, casually. " You've a good pilot? "

Again Cameron was conscious of an attempt to trap him. This little Armenian might not suspect anything, but his questions were difficult to answer. He observed, too, that Condylis let him do all the talking, and contented himself with listening. A sound attracted his attention after Mahassein had talked a while. Condylis's head had fallen forward and his stertorous breathing was shaken now and then by a snore.

" That's his daily nap," said Mahassein, casting a glance at the collapsed figure in the wicker chair. " He'll wake up in ten minutes. I never can doze in the day, can you? P'r'aps you'd like a stroll in the garden?—there's a fine view at the end."

Cameron assented, and they rose, walking to the end of the loggia, where a flight of steps ran down to the garden. Condylis was evidently an enthusiastic collector of cacti. In one section he had a great variety of these convoluted, evil-looking plants.

"They're sinister, I grant you—look at that, just like a bunch of snakes. The Medusa's Head, I call it. But that's characteristic of this place," said Mahassein.

"Characteristic?" asked Cameron, not understanding.

The little Armenian raised his hands towards the sky, grimacing with his face.

"This looks a paradise, doesn't it?" he exclaimed, satirically. "Well, get out of it as quickly as you can!"

Cameron stared at the fellow. There was a ring of sincerity in his voice that broke through his suspicion.

"Why?"

"I can't say more, m'sieur—but get out of it."

"Do you suggest I'm in danger? Surely Colonel Condylis——"

"We have troubles here—things you cannot understand," went on Mahassein. "One day, sooner or later—but, m'sieur, why worry you with it! Isn't this view magnificent?"

They had emerged from an orange pergola on to the end of a terrace on the slope of the hillside. The village lay below, pink and red-roofed. A deep shadow fell on the eastern side of the mountain. Afar lay the dark blue sea, with the harbour, the jetty, and beyond, their white ship, motionless on that unbroken surface.

The Armenian gazed at it pensively. In these last few minutes his mood had changed entirely. All the tiresome monkeyishness had gone out of him. There was something pathetic in this sudden listlessness.

"You don't want a hand, I suppose?" he asked, half-heartedly.

"A hand?" echoed Cameron, mystified. "Do you mean on board?" And then, just as he asked the question, he saw through the whole manœuvre. This strange half-expressed fear and dislike of Sagusto was part of a ruse to gain confidence.

"No—I've a full crew," said Cameron firmly.

"I'd be glad to get out of here," sighed Mahassein.

Cameron made no answer. They stood for a few minutes looking at the panorama, neither speaking. This fellow's desire to get on board, following those questions about the pilot, revealed his train of thought too well. Condylis had accepted his call at Sagusto as a casual event. This Mahassein had suspicions. If he communicated them to Condylis, anything might happen. They were all of them very jumpy. It would be wiser, thought Cameron, to do something that would allay Mahassein's curiosity. He made a bold move.

"I've asked Colonel Condylis to dine with me on board to-night. If it would give you any pleasure, I should be delighted if you joined us," he said.

Mahassein shook his head and smiled affably.

"Thank you, m'sieur. I cannot, much as I'd like. One of us must remain," he answered.

Cameron checked a desire to ask why.

"We'd better go back," suggested Mahassein, "the Colonel will be awake now. I could set a watch by his doze."

But when they regained the loggia Condylis was nowhere to be seen. At once Cameron felt uneasy. He was walking in a lion's den, and at any moment it might pounce. Why had Condylis gone, against all habit, according to this Armenian? They were not kept wondering. From an upper floor came voices, voices in angry debate. One was Condylis's, the other— there was no mistaking it, for it shrilled like a parrot's. It belonged to Donna Emilia Granados Gonzalos. Its pitch pierced the noonday quiet like a country sawmill. It used words as a deluge, which the lower voice of the man vainly sought to stem. What language they belonged to Cameron could not tell, but they were the words of a woman enraged to the pitch of hysteria.

The Armenian looked at Cameron with a wry face.

"Pardon, m'sieur," he said, gravely. But his eyes belied him. "We have birds of exotic plumage in the island, and, as you know, the more gorgeous their attire the worse their voices."

Cameron laughed. The man and the woman in the room

above were declaiming, without regard of each other's words. Suddenly there was a crash of splintering glass, and a piercing scream. Had he killed the woman? But one glance at Mahassein reassured him, for he was calmly lighting another cigarette.

"*Mon Dieu!* That's the last mirror in the house. The Donna has a passion for mirrors. We'd ruin a glass factory. It is all over now. She always finishes by smashing a mirror. Let us go in, m'sieur."

What was Mahassein—a knave, or a light-hearted adventurer? Cameron asked himself this question. If a knave, he would prove far more formidable an antagonist than Condylis. He was deft and quick-witted. As with most of his race, he had a virgin mind that absorbed facts like a sponge. These fellows were hopeless as executive officers, they would argue away an empire, but at intrigue they were adepts. Cameron had encountered them in his Asia Minor days. His contempt was mingled with caution.

Mahassein conducted him through the dining-room back into the waiting-room where he had left his hat. At first he feared that he was not going to see Condylis again, but the latter joined them in the gallery.

"I will send my boat at six-thirty, colonel, if that will suit you?" asked Cameron.

"Thank you—I'll be at the quay. At six-thirty, then. Au revoir, m'sieur."

He held out his heavily-ringed hand, which Cameron shook. His manner had changed: he was not so at ease as during the luncheon. What had transpired in that scene between himself and the Donna Emilia? Jealousy was the motive, surmised Cameron, for throughout the meal the lady had flirted outrageously. He had responded. It was his policy always to make allies in the camp of the enemy, and he had subtly flattered the Donna, by the obvious pleasure he had taken in her conversation, and by all those little signs and attentions that she received as the tribute of a conquest.

Mahassein must have seen this, and his thoughts ran parallel to those of Cameron. He conducted their guest as far as the village street, the armed guard once more taking charge of the stranger, but less ostentatiously this time.

"Donna Emilia has enjoyed your visit," said Mahassein, mischievously, "but it seems to have left discord behind."

Cameron was not a little surprised at the Armenian's frankness, but the fellow was certainly a chatterer.

"You mean—perhaps I was too attentive?"

"No—I don't think that's the trouble. The Donna doesn't like being left this evening."

Cameron wondered whether this was a hint to extend the invitation. That he could not do. It was essential that Condylis came alone. Two Donnas on board, with such contrasted interests, would make his plan impossible. He ignored the hint.

"How long has Donna Gonzalos been visiting Sagusto?" he asked.

"A month," replied Mahassein. "But I think she's ceased being a visitor, she intends becoming a fixture."

There was, apparently, no limit to the fellow's garrulity. Cameron grew bolder in his questions.

"But if Colonel Condylis wished to get rid of her?" he asked.

Mahassein laughed, and struck his riding-boot with the stock he carried.

"Men are strange animals, m'sieur. I've never seen the woman who could manage Condylis until this one came. He's afraid of her. It's extraordinary."

"There were other women?"

"Mon dieu, yes—a procession, and when Donna Soudaikos made a protest he drove her out."

"Donna Soudaikos?" echoed Cameron, as if he had heard the name for the first time.

"Yes—she owns the island actually. She lived up at the Castello, and had nothing to do with him towards the end."

" She is living—at the Castello? "

" Oh no.   It's locked up.   She vanished one night—starved out, actually.   Condylis is dictator here."

" And you're his second in command? "   Cameron could not refrain from saying.

Mahassein took the remark as expected.   The fellow was a weathercock, turning himself to whatever wind blew.

" One must live, m'sieur—but I have my views."

He halted, and took a glove off his hand, preparatory to saying farewell.   A coxcomb, this fellow, with his absurd little black moustache, heavily waxed, his pomaded hair and highly manicured hands.

" I will leave you here, m'sieur," he said, " the guard will take you to the quay."

" Will you tell me one more thing?   You've been very kind and have told me much that's interesting.   Why must one walk about here with an armed guard—is there any danger? "

The Armenian shifted uneasily and then he looked Cameron full in the face, as if hoping he would be satisfied by the answer in his eyes.   They said plainly, " There is danger.   I don't like this place.   I'm scared, for all my bravado."

" M'sieur, I have told you much, in confidence——"

" You need have no fear," said Cameron.

" There's danger—at any moment it may come.   Anything might happen."

" Where is it coming from—the inhabitants? "

" Yes, m'sieur—those mines.   *Mon Dieu!*   It's terrible."

" How? "

The Armenian looked at Cameron, but he said nothing in explanation.

" Condylis fears an outbreak? " pressed Cameron.

" Not only that—there may be something else."

The Armenian looked round.   The guard was standing a little way off.   He lowered his voice so that there was no possibility of being overheard.

" He's not got rid of the Donna—Donna Soudaikos," he whispered.

Cameron purposely assumed a mystified air. He was not sure yet how far this weasel-faced creature was luring him on to confidences.

" But you said Donna Soudaikos had been driven out? "

" Exactly, m'sieur—and she may return, despite Condylis."

" Ah! " exclaimed Cameron. " By force? So that explains your precautions here—and on the quay? "

" The quay? "

" Yes—I know a machine-gun when I see one, despite the tarpaulin. Well, perhaps the sooner I leave this island of yours the better for my comfort. We shall sail to-morrow."

" I wish I were coming with you," said Mahassein, presently. Then, casting a swift glance at the guard. " I must go—au revoir, m'sieur. Have you a boat? "

" I shall signal for one, thanks."

" And, m'sieur! "

" Yes? "

" I've spoken in confidence."

" Absolute—don't worry," said Cameron, assuringly.

The little fellow bowed, stuck out his chest and strode off. Cameron watched him go, wondering how much, in the hour of need, he could be bought for. The trouble with these fellows was that their vanity often struck attitudes towards bribery. They would refuse gold for the mere pride of exhibiting a quixotic honesty.

The boat was not long in answering his signal from the quay. Five minutes later he was ascending the accommodation-ladder of *The Three Castles*. The deck was deserted, as he had instructed but at the foot of the companion-way Tino and Bandioli awaited him anxiously.

" What's happened? " asked Tino, breathlessly. " We saw you on the ridge, but wondered where you'd gone afterwards."

" I've been lunching with Condylis," said Cameron.

"Lunching with Condylis!" echoed the youth, in utter astonishment. Bandioli gave a great laugh.

"Is the Donna in her salon?" asked Cameron.

Tino nodded in assent. "Do you want her?"

"Yes—let's go along. "We've much to do," he said, and led the way to the salon, Bandioli and Tino following.

CHAPTER X

FOR the first time, Cameron observed traces of nervous tension in the demeanour of the Donna. Hitherto there had been a statuesque poise in her manner. It had attracted his attention from that momentous evening in the restaurant at Venice, when her superb air had won his sympathy and drawn him to her rescue. She had carried her serenity through the subsequent scenes on board, never flinching for one moment from the most daring commitments. In the spirit in which she had kidnapped him she had carried on her whole plan. The daughter was perhaps more high-spirited, but she had moods of despair and anxiety. Tino treated the enterprise as youth treats everything that is spiced with uncertainty and adventure. Compared with Nada and Tino, the Donna was a sphinx. She had entrusted her cause to Cameron from that moment when he had made his decision to come to her aid, and every suggestion from him had met with her immediate support.

With the approach to Sagusto a change had come over her. She had not openly opposed his excursion on shore, but she had not liked it. Now, as Cameron entered the salon, her pallor had increased even in a face always white, with its deep, flashing eyes. She stood, the moment he entered, a little breathless with anxiety, and came forward holding out her hands, which he took.

"You are safe! It has been terrible waiting here," she cried. "Nada and I have imagined everything!"

Cameron laughed cheerily and looked round the salon. Nada had put aside some sewing, and came to him, her cheeks flushed with pleasure, her eyes shining in the delight of his presence.

"Major, you must never go like that again," she said imploringly. "We can't endure the suspense, even if you can. It's been terrible, terrible!"

"But how foolish of you all! Really, there was no danger," he said.

"You saw him—he received you?" asked the Donna, excitedly.

"Yes, I saw him. He's not pleasant, but certainly not dangerous. Sit down, please; you shall hear everything."

He glanced round the small company. There were Tino, Nada, the Donna, and Bandioli, who stood by the door.

"We are quite safe from interruption?" asked Cameron.

"Quite," answered Tino. "Shall I lock the door?"

"Please—and now won't you sit down—closer? I wish to talk as quietly as possible."

Briefly he narrated his adventure. One thing only he withheld—the information supplied by Mahassein. He even omitted all mention of him. He had been pledged to confidence, and that apart, there was also no purpose in naming this potential ally. He would not raise false hopes. He made no mention of Condylis's coming until the end.

"You've asked him to dinner—on board!" cried the Donna, incredulously.

"He won't come!" declared Bandioli, not attempting to hide his contempt of Cameron's simplicity.

"Why not?—if he suspects no one?" asked Tino.

Suddenly Nada clapped her hands together ecstatically, in anticipation.

"It's magnificent!—he comes on board, we seize him, and then?"

She asked the question, excitement in her eyes, but as Cameron looked at her the deep voice of the Donna made answer:

"We shoot him!" she declared, exultation in the tone.

Cameron swung round to her, in utter amazement.

"Shoot him?—in cold blood!" he exclaimed.

The Donna's dark eyes, fierce with a light he had never seen before, unflinchingly held his own.

"You have a strange idea of my character, Donna, if you think I'll lure Condylis here to be murdered," he said, coldly.

These momentary revelations of the mentality he was associated with profoundly shocked him. The sanctity of life never entered the minds of these people. That girl with her revolver, the boy aching for conflict, the desperadoes gathered in at Pola, the Donna's unemotional intention to shoot Condylis, all this showed how sundered by race and clime was his own nature from that of these people. It was useless to express indignation. They simply regarded human life as of no consequence if it stood in the path of their progress. Sickened, for the moment Cameron felt like abandoning the whole thing. He had no regard for Condylis. The fellow would act exactly as the Donna—given the opportunity, and at the best he was a libertine, a bully and a thief. But even so, it was not in Cameron's unwritten yet inexorable code to lure a man to cold butchery.

He conveyed this as best he could to the Donna, knowing well she could not comprehend his attitude. That the girl, too, shared this fierceness filled him with sorrowful despair. There was in her such beauty, such gentleness, that he could not understand a nature capable of these extremes of kindness and cruelty.

"Then why get Condylis here at all?" asked Bandioli, when Cameron had made clear his objections to any violence. "Is it to be merely a social call?"

Cameron ignored the question.

"Please listen to me, Donna—you must leave this matter entirely in my hands. Condylis will come by boat from the quay——"

"His own?" asked Tino.

"No, Lieutenant Luigi will fetch him, but in mufti. There must be nothing to arouse suspicion. On arrival he will be shown down into my cabin. It's my intention, Donna," he said, smiling at her, "to borrow your excellent idea."

"My idea, major?" repeated the Donna. "What do you mean?"

"You'll remember I, too, was invited to dinner—and was shown into that cabin!"

They all laughed, the Donna loudest of all.

"*Per Dio!* So that's the game!" cried Bandioli. "And when we've got him, what then, major?"

"He'll be detained, until we have made a landing in force. It's my opinion that without Condylis the opposition will be negligible. He's the driving power on the island, and unless I'm mistaken, he rules by fear."

"There's no question of that," said the Donna. "The people are with me!"

"Except the miners," interjected Tino, looking at his mother.

"Why the miners?" she demanded, a little fiercely.

The lad shrugged his shoulders, intimating that the Donna knew well enough.

"We've never paid them properly—they can't love any of us," he said, looking towards his sister, as if seeking support in this opinion.

"You are a boy—you know nothing about it!" retorted the Donna, fiercely. "Major Cameron, I don't follow your plan. Even if we land successfully—what are we doing with Condylis?"

"I will ask you to leave that to me," replied Cameron.

"We've got to do something with the fellow—he won't sit still enjoying your hospitality!" said Bandioli, failing entirely to approve of these kid-gloved methods. Now a bullet— from anywhere—got rid of such a problem as the disposal of Condylis.

Cameron regarded them a little impatiently. After all, these people, with their primitive hates, were children in everything, except the appalling intensity of their passions.

"When you are safely in possession of Sagusto I must return at once to Venice. My only means will be by this yacht, which I hope, Donna, you'll place at my disposal."

"Most certainly, if you wish."

"Thank you. With me, to Trieste, will go Condylis, where he will receive his liberty. That will have given you time to consolidate your position. I don't anticipate any trouble from him at Trieste. He's not likely to lodge a complaint with the authorities, and you assure me they have no jurisdiction over Sagusto."

"But he'll return!" cried Nada.

"You can make that impossible," answered Cameron. "And I don't think he'll attempt, once you are in possession."

"You won't stay on the island—for a time?" asked the girl, anxiously.

He saw that his proposals pleased none of them. Bandioli looked contemptuous, the Donna was inscrutable, Tino and Nada were obviously alarmed. A glance passed quickly between Bandioli and the Donna. They did not know he had seen it, but Cameron required no second thought to read its meaning. The death of Condylis was sealed in that look; they meant murder. Cameron suppressed a sense of nausea. More than ever he regretted his quixotic decision to countenance this crazy adventure. Between his code and theirs yawned an impassable gulf.

In the question addressed to him by Nada there had been something more than anxiety. In these few days she had not hesitated to show the feeling he had aroused in her. Her unguarded demonstrations added to his anxiety. He was not in love with this wild, beautiful creature who looked at him with the deep eyes of entire devotion, much as Tino himself looked, but with the added intensity of her aroused sex. How far the Donna was aware of it he knew not. She seemed too engrossed in her enterprise to observe anything else. For Cameron, the necessity of escape from the *milieu* was intensified by the personal question. He would see it through, in fulfilment of his promise, but at the first moment he would leave—for England and sanity.

" You won't leave us—not at once? " cried Nada, when she saw he evaded her first question. " There may be trouble on the island. Condylis has his lieutenants."

" Your men will be able to control that," answered Cameron. " I'll be responsible for the safe custody of Condylis. But let me proceed. We've no time to lose. When Condylis is locked up, Tino, Lieutenant Luigi, myself, and the men will make a landing. It will be dusk then. We won't attempt the harbour. It's guarded, and I don't want the village arousing. They must wake up to find us in possession. I noticed this morning a small cove to the south of the harbour. It's used by some fishermen, I believe."

" I know it," said Tino. " There's a path runs up to the meadow behind—it leads back to the village."

" Is there anyone near the cove? "

" A cottage, m'sieur—one of the fishermen lives there."

" We must risk that, and prevent him giving the alarm. Our next move must be to surround Condylis's house—his second in command, Mahassein, is there."

" Mahassein—I've never heard of him," said the Donna.

" An Armenian—about twenty-three or four."

" I don't know him—he must be a newcomer."

" Very well. If we get him we'll be able to stop any counter-attack. Without Condylis and his assistant, they will be like sheep."

" There's the guard at the harbour ! " said Bandioli.

" I've thought of that. When the village is in our control, we can approach the harbour. If we're opposed we must fight. I don't think the guard consists of more than four men. All they can do is to retreat—with the sea behind them. There's a machine-gun on the jetty, but there's the night and the element of surprise in our favour.   Have I made everything clear?"

"And what are we to do?" asked the Donna, speaking for Nada and herself.

"Wait, Donna.   You can leave the ship when we are masters of Sagusto."

"We're to do nothing?" cried Nada, rebelliously, the love of battle shining in her eyes.

Cameron had perforce to smile.

"Nothing, Nada," he replied.

"You'll want me to stay on the ship?" asked Bandioli.

"Yes—I give Condylis into your safe care."

None of them failed to notice the emphasis on the word "safe."

"Now will you fetch Lieutenant Luigi?—we'll hold a council of war.   There must be no hitch in our programme," said Cameron.

For the next hour they were engrossed in details of the landing.

CHAPTER XI

At five o'clock Condylis rode in from the mines.   Throwing the reins across his horse's neck, he marched across the yard and entered the house by a small door under the balcony where Cameron had stood that morning.   He was back early because he had to change before going on board the Englishman's yacht. This was one of those occasions when he wore uniform.   Once a colonel, always a colonel, held Condylis, even though an ungrateful Government withdrew your commission and asked you to leave its country.   That was twenty years ago, and by now the Government had undoubtedly forgotten his irregularities in that little Balkan affair.   When a man had fought for his country he had fought for it, whatever view it took of his subsequent conduct. He had been a colonel truly. He would remain a colonel. Moreover, the uniform suited him. For a man who governed an island a uniform was necessary. Also, the Donna Gonzalos liked him in it.

He looked at her now as he stood in front of his long mirror, unbroken because so far it had proved invulnerable to her attacks. She lay on the bed, a great hulk, shapeless, behind the mosquito net. The book she had been reading had fallen on to the floor. One hand, one of those hands she was so justifiably proud of, hung down, the fingers laden with rings. It was Condylis's hope she would not wake up before he had gone. In his present condition of nerves he dreaded these scenes. He had never been afraid of a woman in his life, but she had a voice that went through him when she raised it, which was often.

She was an unreasonable creature. That sceen this afternoon had risen because he had not procured her an invitation to dine on *The Three Castles*. He knew well enough why she wished to go. Cameron had flattered her with his attention. It was obvious the señor had desired her company also, but Condylis was jealous, he had determined to go alone and deprive her of the pleasure.

It was in vain he had denied this. There had been high words, and finally, as often, a handbrush had cracked a mirror. Now, exhausted by her display of passion, she lay asleep, unaware of his presence. Condylis, regarding her, began to wonder how he should get her back to the mainland from which, in a weak moment, he had brought her on a visit to Sagusto. But she showed no intention of returning. Sagusto suited her, she declared, and nothing short of forcible deportation would shift her.

Satisfied with his appearance, having waxed his moustache and sprayed some of the Donna's scent over himself, he softly stepped from the room. He feared she might even yet insist on going with him, so eager was her desire to encounter that charming young Englishman again. And they wanted no women about this evening. Already the pleasurable anticipation of that whisky filled Condylis with well-being. It was quite a year since he had tasted any, and it had been of wretched quality, obtained from an inn at Sebenico. He had never met an Englishman who carried a bad whisky. Cameron was not the man to let down his nation's reputation.

Punctually at half-past six, an imposing figure in his tight jacket, tight riding-breeches, and glossy top-boots, he stood on the quay, where already he found the boat from *The Three Castles*. The guard saluted him, a few loungers gaped at their resplendent dictator. His breast blazed with decorations, and, by the aid of corsets and determination, he had pulled in his girth, so that his figure was not too preposterous in a uniform which clung to him like a rubber suit. His cap, worn at a dare-devil angle, and his much-waxed moustache, gave him the desired fierceness, to which he added a glitter and a clink with a quite unnecessary sword and still more unnecessary silver spurs.

But the sun sparkled on him, and his heart at that moment had a boyish zest for the rôle he had carved out for himself on this island. For his career, could it have been reported, had been a remarkable one. It was unfortunate that certain minor incidents necessitated a discreet silence. He had been rich, he had been poor. At seventeen he had run a revolution in Bolivia, at eighteen an oil well in Texas, at twenty-one he had married a Mexican heiress, and at twenty-two had had to flee for his life from non-approving relatives. He had left Europe in the filthy hold of a guano-manure boat, he returned to it in the "millionaire suite" of an Atlantic leviathan, staying sufficient time in London to float a Panama diamond mine company, which had sunk the moment his enthusiasm and the first subscriptions had been withdrawn. Paris held him for three months, and a fluffy little creature, all silks and simpers, extracted more diamonds from him in those three months than were ever found in his Panama mine.

It was characteristic of the contradictions that are inherent in humanity that throughout all his vicissitudes, including a period as colonel in the Greek Army and as convict in an Italian colony he had never failed to send his old mother in Greece a monthly remittance. When she died, her last sight lingering on the ruins of Mycenæ, seen through the windows in her hut, leaving nothing but a flock of mangy goats and a much-kissed photograph of her son, he wept for a week. He placed around his neck the little iron chain carrying an oxidised Greek Cross that had been worn by his mother. When a certain lady in Bucharest, finding it on him, had laughed, he promptly struck her in the face and departed forthwith, hurrying from her house of accommodation into a church, to exorcise the desecration that had touched this relic. For although at any time of the day or night he was ready to shoot a man or blaspheme against his God, he was prompt to defend the adoration of his mother.

His splendid appearance on the quay filled one young gentleman with envy and some annoyance. To render proper honour to the embarkation of Colonel Condylis, Cameron had placed Lieutenant Luigi in charge of the boat party. He, too, had wished to wear uniform, that uniform he had carried so proudly when D'Annunzio had defied Europe, and advertised himself. He would have worn his hat at an even more rakish angle than the Colonel, and the cut of his breeches, nicely outlining a muscular though lean thigh, was even more adventurous. In the lustre of his top-boots, that constant preoccupation of Luigi's life, he could have outshone this popinjay. But Cameron had robbed him of his splendour and had insisted on mufti.

For no reason at all, or perhaps just because of this overpowering reason, Luigi took an immediate dislike to his passenger.

But nothing of this appeared in his behaviour. Running to the top of the jetty steps, he was the pattern of courtesy.

" Colonel Condylis? " he asked.

Condylis nodded curtly, wondering why, to give a proper flourish to this embarkation, he had not brought Mahassein in uniform, as his aide-de-camp. He descended the steps, holding up his sword in a lavender-gloved hand. He left behind him as he went down a heavily perfumed air, and the young Italian behind breathed it contemptuously, keeping his dark eyes concentrated on that red apoplectic neck, so constricted in its collar that it bulged like an overblown tyre.

The boat pushed off, Condylis sitting in the stern and Luigi at his side. Again, he could not forgive the lavender gloves. He also had a pair in his kit, but he had never thought of wearing them. Whatever annoyance rose in his heart, however, was fully appeased by contemplation of the service he was rendering the unsuspecting fellow. For Lieutenant Luigi had been entrusted with the secret, and there was a moment coming when his revenge would be adequate.

Slowly, the four men steadily rowing, the boat drew near to *The Three Castles*. The moment that it ran alongside the accommodation-ladder, Major Cameron appeared to welcome his guest. Cameron, now that he was committed to this desperate expedient, had dismissed all hesitancy, and treated his task with zest. Not a little of its appeal was to his sense of humour.

A very desperate enterprise lay behind this kidnapping of the Colonel, but there was an element of fantasy in the fact that he, the kidnapped, should be now repeating, in the same ship, the very act that had aroused his indignation.

"Ah, colonel, this is a pleasure," exclaimed Cameron. "Allow me to present my skipper, Captain Bandioli."

The two men shook hands, measuring each other with a look. Cameron, comparing, scarcely knew which appeared the bigger adventurer. He met Lieutenant Luigi's laughing eyes, and reproved him with a glance. The fellow was visibly exulting over the destined victim.

"Now, colonel, before we join the ladies, let's have a drink in my den," suggested Cameron, slipping his arm through the Colonel's. What a mixture of blackguard and popinjay, he thought, seeing and smelling this swaggering bullock of a man.

"The ladies? Ah—ladies on board—how delightful!" cried Condylis.

They crossed the deck. Not a man was to be seen in the late afternoon. Around them the water lay like a mirror, with Sagusto reddening in the dropping sun. Two houses on the mountain slope flashed like burnished shields. They descended the companion-way, Cameron leading, Condylis next, with Bandioli and Luigi covering the rear as far as the cabin door. The two men entered. In a glance Condylis saw that it was probably his host's stateroom, small but comfortable, with some Italian papers and books lying about.

"Ah! I've not seen a newspaper for a fortnight," exclaimed Condylis, picking up a copy of the *Corriere*, after he had accepted his host's invitation to sit down. "You know, the worst of Sagusto is——"

The sentence was checked by a peremptory knocking on the closed door. Cameron, expectant, opened it.

It had been exactly timed.

"Could you speak to the captain a moment, sir; he doesn't ——" said a voice outside in the corridor.

Cameron turned to Condylis, now scanning the headlines of the newspaper.

"Will you excuse me a moment?" he asked. "I'm so sorry, but——"

"Certainly, certainly, Mr. Cameron," replied Condylis.

The door closed. Cameron was outside. Bandioli and the young Italian were waiting there. The captain quietly turned the key. Their man was fast. It had been a mere repetition of that evening when Cameron himself had been made a prisoner.

In response to the captain's nod, one of his crew, for he would trust no one else, stood sentry by the door. They knew presently there would be cries of rage and noises from within. But it would be useless.

As they came up on to the deck again, Bandioli mopped his

brow.   Without a word they all went forward to the Donna's quarters.

" Well? " she asked, as they entered, Tino and Nada on either side of her.   Their anxiety showed in the nervous manner in which they had leapt to their feet.

" We have him ! " replied Bandioli, exultantly.

But in Cameron's face there was no sign of triumph.   It was grim, and he remained silent.   The girl was the first to notice his reserved manner.

" There's something the matter ! " she exclaimed, impulsively.

" The matter ! " echoed the Donna.   " What's the matter? "

She looked at Bandioli, at Luigi, at Cameron.   They none of them spoke.   She caught at Cameron's arm and held her face close to his.

" You've got him—there's nothing gone wrong? " she demanded, desperately anxious.

Cameron laughed, more at himself than at her anxiety.

" Oh no, Donna—there's nothing wrong.   We've got him in my cabin—but I don't feel elated."

" Why not, m'sieur? " asked Tino.   " Everything's gone all right, hasn't it? "

Cameron looked the boy straight in the face.

" I'm wondering what I shall do next for you," he said, but in such a manner that the lad knew Cameron was addressing his question to the whole company.   " I don't feel it's been very clever or creditable.   I hate tricking people, and this poor beggar's had no kind of a chance in the game.   He's been cooped up there like a hen."

" It was your plan ! " retorted the Donna, acidly.   " You dislike violence."

" Yes, it's my plan, Donna," said Cameron, a little sadly.

Somehow all the romance had gone out of the thing.   If the fellow could have made a fight of it, he would not have felt thus. That he was a blackguard Cameron had no doubt, but one was not excused in one's conduct even towards a blackguard.

Perhaps the slight tone of self-reproach in Cameron's voice was heard by the girl, for she immediately came over to his side, placing her small hand through his arm.

"Major Cameron—whatever the end of this, you have acted splendidly towards us. We can never forget it. And you are incapable of anything dishonourable. We all know that!" she exclaimed, looking earnestly into his face.

"But for you I'd have put a bullet through the fellow," declared Bandioli. "It may be necessary yet," he added, grimly.

Cameron turned impatiently to the Donna.

"Let's sit down—there is no time to be lost. One mistake and our hopes will be shattered. Here's the order of the landing. Lieutenant Luigi knows exactly what he must do."

They seated themselves at the table. It was obvious Cameron had omitted no detail. He was to go in the first boat, Luigi in the second, each with five armed men. The first landing would be made at nine o'clock. The boats would then return and land the remaining men. Cameron read out their names.

"They must be provided with rations, captain," said Cameron, addressing Bandioli. "We must be prepared for all eventualities. Please have both boats ready on the port side. After the landing, the boats must wait within hailing distance on the shore. If we succeed in reaching Condylis's house, and taking possession of it, we shall next move towards the harbour—you must keep a look-out in readiness for our signal there. My aim is to get possession of that machine-gun on the jetty. If we can do that, I don't fear much resistance."

"And Condylis—what are we going to do with him?" asked the Donna.

"He's to be left under strict guard in the cabin," answered Cameron. "What we do with him depends upon the course of events in Sagusto. I've only one anxiety—these men of ours."

"I can answer for them, major," said Lieutenant Luigi. "They're a lot of wild boys, but they've pluck."

" It's their wildness I fear—there must be no shooting unless it becomes an absolute necessity—they understand that? "

" Perfectly, major," affirmed the young Italian.

Cameron glanced at his watch.

" It's now seven o'clock. We must all have a good meal at once. At eight-thirty we'll muster the men on the deck. I shall want to inspect them. Tino, get the map I marked with you this morning."

The youth rose, unlocked a drawer in a cabinet and drew out the map of Sagusto. Nothing was left to chance. Bandioli, observing, began to revise his opinion of this Englishman. Under his indifferent air there was an alert intelligence at work. Now, as he listened, Cameron elaborating each point, he came to think the Donna was not so crazy, after all. He had not forgiven her for not entrusting to him the sole command of this expedition. His resentment of this divided authority sprang from something more than vanity, however. Cameron was in this business merely for the love of adventure and some queer strain of chivalry. He, Bandioli, never confused business with sentiment. He was here because he was to be well paid. The price of that payment, in the event of success, might be more than the Donna intended.

In the presence of Cameron he saw someone who might frustrate his intentions. Listening now, he realised that, with Cameron beside the Donna, his price would have to be considerably modified. The position left vacant by the ejected Condylis might now have a candidate other than himself. He had watched with growing dissatisfaction the cordiality existing between the Donna and Cameron, between Tino and Nada——

Bandioli was watching the girl now, and in her absorbed interest, as Cameron outlined his plan of campaign, in the unguarded admiration of her face, he found the confirmation of something he had begun to suspect. This girl was madly in love with the fellow. She hung upon his words as of those of a demi-god. Actually, the fellow was quite unaware of the feelings he had aroused. But a time might come when this Nada might not be content with an unexpressed passion for Cameron. In such a development Bandioli saw a further weakening of his authority, of his indispensability.

Listening, he sat acutely observing the group around the table, and when the conference ended, after some three-quarters of an hour, he realised that the course of events had relegated him to the position for which he had been engaged, namely that of captain of the ship. There had been moments when he had seen himself as the new master of Sagusto, the sole instrument of the Donna's will. Cameron's coming, and his undoubted efficiency, had put him in a strictly subordinate place. It was not unreasonable of him, he reflected, to wish this fellow no success, even while he wished the Donna no harm.

As for that young woman, Nada, at a certain moment it might prove advantageous to enlighten the Donna as to the exact nature of her daughter's feeling for Cameron. For he had always seen in the Donna a temperament that brooked no division of authority. Being a man of quick decisions, he made one now.

As Bandioli left the salon at the end of the conference, Cameron spoke to him.

" Let's have a look at our prisoner—I suppose by now he's no doubt what's happened," he said.

" You're going in to him? " asked Tino, amazed.

" Oh dear, no," replied Cameron, " but we can hear if he's subsided."

" Hunger will do a lot," laughed Bandioli.

" I had thought of that—as did the Donna," answered Cameron, a ghost of a smile hovering over his face.

" I? " she queried, puzzled over his remark.

" Condylis will have found by now the covered tray of food, and a polite note regretting his forcible detention. I have passed on your forethought for myself, Donna," explained Cameron.

CHAPTER XII

HALF an hour later, having visited the guard outside Cameron's cabin, they dined together, the Donna, Nada and Tino, Bandioli, Luigi and Cameron. They were a silent party throughout most of the dinner, for by this approaching venture the fate of their enterprise might be sealed. Condylis, after a noisy protest, shouted through the door, had subsided into quiet.

Cameron refused to satisfy Bandioli regarding his intentions in dealing with their prisoner. Actually he had decided, the moment their position on the island was secure, to lose no time in having the ship under weigh for Trieste. He would deposit the fellow there, and if he exhibited no gratitude for not having come to a violent end, then Cameron would let him make what noise he could.

For himself, he was looking forward to that hour when he had finished with this mad adventure, and could board the Paris-bound Orient express at Trieste. Having restored Sagusto to the Donna, it would become her business to retain it. Beyond that he would not go. With Tino and her hired retainers, it should not prove an impossible task. Moreover, from all that he had learned that morning, the islanders themselves were ready for a change. One thing had been certain, to which the priest and the scared populace had borne witness : Condylis was feared, not loved.

So that when, in the course of the dinner, to which none of them did justice because of the suppressed excitement, the Donna asked Cameron what he proposed doing with Condylis, he replied, " That depends on the course of events, Donna." His instinct told him she would not readily consent to the fellow's liberation at Trieste. Nada, too, had not hesitated to reveal her own view. She preferred Condylis dead. It was possible in the next twenty-four hours he would be defending Condylis from this ruthless spirit of revenge. It was a turn of events entirely in keeping with the whole expedition.

Cameron looked at the Donna, as she presided at the head of the table. Within an hour her attempt might have ended in failure, in the death of some of her retainers, including himself, or it might have restored her to the wealth that Condylis had wrested from her. Yet of this, of anxiety, or any kind of excitement, she revealed no trace. She ate and talked, magnificently serene, her dark eyes observing everything, her voice deep and placid amid their broken, nervous utterances.

Even Bandioli showed something of the strain, leaving much of his food untouched. Luigi and Tino were flushed with excitement, Nada looked at Cameron from time to time, a slow smile of encouragement passing over her face whenever he met her eyes. The Donna excepted, it was an uneasy meal. While they ate, the last rays of the sunset glowed crimson through the portholes, the dusk deepened over the incarnadined water. Then Meno, the Czech steward, switched on the lights.

" Have you a match, major? " asked the Donna, opening her cigarette case as the coffee was brought in. The dinner had been an excellent one, had they been of a mind to appreciate it.

Cameron struck a match, but at that moment, as he leaned forward, there was a sharp unmistakable sound. They all heard it, sitting alert, wordless as they looked at each other. It was the report of a rifle.

" *Per Dio !* One of those fellows——" began Luigi, angrily rising to his feet. But the sentence went unfinished, for again, twice in swift succession, came the sound of firing.

They all jumped to their feet, in confused speculation, and simultaneously the door was flung open, to reveal Meno, breathless and wildly gesticulating.

" What does he say? " demanded Cameron, not understanding a word of the fellow's utterance.

" Condylis ! *Mon Dieu !* Condylis has escaped ! " cried Tino, hoarsely.

CHAPTER XIII

THERE was a moment of absolute silence following the shock of this news. Then Cameron spoke.

"Escaped!" he echoed. Without another word, pushing the still-gesticulating steward aside, he left the room. With a bound he went up the companion-way, followed by Tino, Luigi, and Bandioli.

They ran along the deck towards the men leaning over the gunwale. One of these, rifle to shoulder was shooting across the water, now leaden in the dusk. They turned at the approach of Cameron.

"He's there, signore—swimming there!" cried one of them, pointing excitedly.

Again the rifle cracked. They all strained their sight in the endeavour to find something in that dusk, more baffling than darkness.

"Stop shooting—it's useless," said Cameron. "Where's the guard?"

"There, signore—with him!" exclaimed one of the men, pointing shorewards. "We heard a splash and looked overboard; there were two men swimming—they must have dived, signore."

Bandioli broke out in a torrent of oaths.

"Stop that!" cried Cameron, curtly. "They're not to blame. Let's go down and see."

But Tino had already gone, and met them at the stairway.

"*Mon Dieu!* It's treachery! The door's been opened for him. Look!"

He held up a sword and a boot.

"Condylis must have known—he's half undressed, his boots and uniform are there!" added Tino.

Cameron looked at the sword in the lad's hand, then at the glossy top-boot, so envied of Luigi.

" Then the guard must have——"

He did not end the sentence, and walked on. Bandioli, still cursing, followed.

Tino was right. Condylis's finery was strewn about the cabin. He had discarded sword, spurs, top-boots, breeches and jacket. The most significant fact, however, was that the door showed no sign of having been forced. It must have been opened from the outside, by an accomplice in the escape.

" Ah—here they are ! " cried Luigi, excitedly.

He had been peering down along the passage outside the cabin door. " Look ! " he exclaimed, holding up a pair of heavy nailed boots. " These belong to the guard ! "

" Who is he? " demanded Cameron.

" Kosrev, the Russian—he relieved Yanin, who's in the landing-party," answered Bandioli.

The three men stood in the cabin, none of them speaking. There was something more disturbing than the loss of Condylis, the collapse of their plans.   There was the realisation of treachery in their midst.

" Where did Kosrev come on board? " asked Cameron.

" With us—at Pola," answered Luigi.   " It's a pity the guard was relieved."

" You said you wanted Yanin in your boat," said Bandioli, angrily turning on the young lieutenant.

" I didn't ask for Kosrev to relieve him," retorted Luigi. " We knew nothing about Kosrev——"

" We know nothing about you," sneered Bandioli, and a heated quarrel in Italian, which Cameron could not follow, sprang up.

" That's enough ! " he called, sharply. He was trying to solve a problem that had suddenly presented itself. If Condylis had an accomplice on board, then the fellow had not been able to warn him before boarding the ship. It was obvious that Condylis would never have come had he had the slightest suspicion of the trap prepared. His accomplice, by some means, had communicated with Condylis after he had been locked up in the cabin. There was also the probability of bribery. Kosrev had perhaps been bought. The mistake had been made in changing Yanin, whose loyalty was above suspicion. But Cameron refrained from saying this. Their tempers were already sufficiently tried, without the beginning of fresh re-criminations.

"What are we going to do?" asked Tino, looking at Cameron despairingly. "If we attempt to land now——"

"That is impossible—the whole island will be aroused in half an hour," interrupted Cameron. "We must talk with the Donna. This alters everything."

They found the Donna white-faced but outwardly calm. She had already learned the facts. Cameron had been prepared for blame, or despair. Instead he found her alert and anxious for revised plans.

"We must land at once," she urged. "Every hour they will be more prepared."

Cameron looked at her steadily.

"You know what this means?" he asked.

"Yes—those who don't wish to come can stay behind!"

He ignored her taunt, her fighting spirit compelled his admiration.

"You should know me better than that," he said, quietly. "But there is nothing to gain by mere folly. If we lose our men, what then?"

"The major is right, Donna," intervened Bandioli, mopping his brow. "But if you insist on a landing, there's only one place."

"Where?" asked Tino.

"As far from the village as possible—if we can get there before Condylis can send a warning round," answered Bandioli. "Why not try the Castello?—it would make a base, if a landing must be made."

"It must—at once," said the Donna, emphatically. She turned to Cameron. "You realise the necessity of that?"

"If you mean fighting—yes," he said, and by the flame in her eyes he saw she would not draw back. There was something heroic in her obstinacy, for all its folly.

They seated themselves round the table, clearing aside the used dinner-things to spread out the map. There was no time to lose.

The Donna, Bandioli, and Tino favoured a landing at a cove at the foot of the headland crowned by the Castello. It was at the extreme north end of the island, and Condylis could not possibly reach it overland before the afternoon of the morrow. If the Castello was not occupied, it would serve as a base for future operations on the island. Bandioli proposed they should sail for the headland at once, make a landing just before dawn, and let a scouting party advance to the Castello by the stairway cut in the face of the cliff. If the Castello was defended they could retreat back to the yacht.

It was a desperate plan, but their case was desperate. Cameron accepted it. He saw the Donna was determined to make the attempt. Nada, too, made light of the danger. She joined her mother in one stipulation. They would make a landing with the men, and share their fortune, good or bad.

At ten o'clock *The Three Castles* weighed anchor, and in the wan light of a clouded moon, passed softly as a wraith northwards up the coast to the headland.

CHAPTER XIV

So what he had most feared was now to become a fact. It was in vain that Cameron sought a way out of this *impasse*. His careful scheme, so successful in its preliminaries, had been shattered by treachery in their midst. He and the Donna had reviewed every possible circumstance and person that might yield a clue to their betrayer. Cameron found it hard to believe that Condylis, by the mere offer of money, had corrupted a strange guard standing outside his cabin. Moreover, he seemed to have gauged the exact moment when he would be safe from detection—while the party was at dinner in the salon. Kosrev had, of course, helped him in this. Had the Russian, from the moment of coming on board at Pola, been Condylis's agent? If he were, it was obvious he had not been able to communicate with Condylis and prevent him coming on board.

All the way along the coast, as he paced the deck, the problem was uppermost in Cameron's mind. They were committed to a landing now, with force of arms, and no one could foresee the issue of the next forty-eight hours. Their one hope was to entrench themselves in the Castello, and then use it as a base for an approach to the lower end of the island.

The deck was almost deserted. All the men were below, making their preparations for the landing. If the Castello was vacant they would occupy it at once, before Condylis had time to get there. Near the deckhouse the sound of footsteps made Cameron alert, but he smiled when he saw who had set him listening. It was Nada, an almost unrecognisable Nada. She was clad in breeches and shirt, her dark hair covered in a green scarf, worn turban fashion. A revolver holster hung on her right hip. Altogether she looked quite a dangerous character, and Cameron told her so.

" I hope I'll live up to my appearance ! " she said   " Do you know, I'm almost glad this has happened ! "

" Why ? "

" I didn't like the idea of Condylis slipping out of it so easily," she answered.

" I suppose you think I'm very squeamish about taking life ? " asked Cameron. " I certainly find it difficult to realise that a nice civilised young lady like yourself is capable of such fierceness."

E

" Then you do think I'm civilised? " she laughed.

In the darkness he could just see the sparkle of her teeth and eyes. She was entrancing in this dress, and rather like the principal boy in a pantomime, he reflected. Now he came to think of it, these people regarded the whole affair as something in the nature of a pantomime. Was he, after all, taking everything too seriously, including Nada?

" I think you are the most extraordinary mixture I have ever encountered," he answered.

" Thank you ! "

" Thank you ? " he echoed.

" I should hate to be thought commonplace. I know you don't believe I can shoot, or that I like shooting. Well, you're going to see. I'll make you take me seriously before long ! " she declared.

" By shooting me ? " laughed Cameron, provokingly. But the moment he had spoken a change came over her. The bravado, the boyishness vanished. He saw her mouth tremble and the dark eyes grow troubled with the reproach that came into them. Then, as suddenly, she turned on him, flashing with a quick anger that made her still more beautiful.

" You laugh at me—always you laugh at me ! There are moments when you make me hate you, when you treat me like a child ! " she cried. " How can you be so unkind? "

" My dear Nada ! " protested Cameron, in utter surprise, " whatever makes you talk like this?—I have never laughed at you. On the contrary, I—but you don't mean it," he said, abruptly.

He would have looked away, hiding the discomfort she had aroused, but the next moment he felt her hands clenching his arms, her face thrust so close to his that he was aware of the perfume she carried, of the slender rope of emeralds encircling her olive throat, where it was exposed by the open shirt collar.

" You are unkind—you laugh at me—I can bear anything but that ! " she said. Then, with a quick glance towards the bridge, as if she feared someone up there might overhear her, she changed her manner.

"You suspect someone—who?" she asked, in a low voice.

Cameron did not reply for a few moments, unprepared to answer such a question.

"What makes you think that?" he queried.

"I see it in your face—you are suspicious of someone—on board here. I'm right?"

He gave an uneasy laugh. He had uttered no word throughout their conference, but this girl must have watched him closely.

"Shall I tell you who it is?" she asked, drawing closer to him.

He gazed into her intense young face, and slowly shook his head.

"I've no certainty—and it's wrong to act on surmise," he answered.

"But you believe in instinct?"

He shifted uneasily. Her questioning embarrassed him. He did suspect someone, but there was no evidence.

"I'll tell you who it is," she whispered, persistent. "It's Bandioli!"

"Bandioli?" he repeated. She had divined rightly, and he found it impossible to contradict her. He felt that his suspicion had been based on pure aversion, an unreasonable aversion felt from the first moment he had seen him.

"Why do you suspect Bandioli?" he asked.

"Why? Because—oh, I feel he has betrayed us!" she answered.

"That is no reason at all."

"It's better than reason," she asserted, "it's instinct. I have never trusted him. Why do you?"

She glanced swiftly round. In the darkness of the night they were aware of every sound, of the water racing by, of the engine beating, of the voices indistinctly coming from below, and of the regular footstep of the officer of the watch on the small bridge.

Cameron waited in silence. Her manner, her words, had given a dramatic tension to the night. He felt this forward urge of the boat as due to something more than an engine's propulsion. They were being drawn as by a destiny awaiting them. He knew perfectly well that the feeling arose from the presence of Nada. She had a quality of dramatising everything. Even her silences were pregnant with suggestion. She spoke little, her movements were almost unnoticeable, her attitudes often statuesque, but always there was in her and about her a dramatic quality.

Knowing this, Cameron was reluctant to confirm her suspicion. True, it accorded with his own, but she had no more reason or evidence than he had on which to base it. For her, instinct was an all-sufficient guide; for himself, he always mistrusted it.

They stood there, under the shadow of the mast, at whose tip a lantern rode through a network of stars. Beyond them, half imagined, lay the island. They were each busy with their thoughts, and to Cameron came the certainty that this girl was more concerned with his safety than with her own. Throughout she had questioned his right to jeopardise himself on their behalf. Her warning sprang from no self-fear. She was utterly fearless, to the point of rashness.

Her voice broke the silence again. She smiled at him, confidently.

" You needn't answer me," she whispered. " Good-night ! "

To his surprise she was gone, as swiftly, as quietly, as she had come. Mysterious, elusive creature ! Suddenly almost ferociously bold, and then so reticent, so withdrawn. He realised that he understood her less than anyone on board.

A few minutes later he went below and was busy until midnight, superintending the preparations. Then he went to his cabin for a short sleep. At four o'clock, on the verge of dawn, they were to attempt the landing.

CHAPTER XV

CAMERON was awakened by a tapping on his cabin door. He was awake instantly, and found Meno at the side of his bunk with hot coffee. It was half-past three, and there was no glimmer of day to be seen yet through the open porthole. Hastily dressing, he went up on deck. The air was cold, the sky still starlit, but in the east the first discoloration of dawn already extinguished the stars. All around him there was a movement of men quietly collecting their things in final preparation. The ship was stationary, and on that scene of dark tranquillity it rested softly as a shadow. A glimmer of light, and it seemed as if all the world about them might vanish.

Gradually, in his accustomed sight, Cameron became aware, on the starboard side, of a great headland rising into the darkness. Afar came the long, dull noise of waves breaking on shingle. Straining through the dark, he found the faint summit of a vast rock, where the Castello must be situated.

" All's ready—the boats are launched," said a voice behind him. He turned to see Bandioli, who had been on deck all night.

" Good," replied Cameron. " How long before daybreak? "

Bandioli glanced at the sky.

" Not more than half an hour—you'll just get to shore in time."

They were joined then by Luigi and Tino, both armed. Cameron greeted them.

" The men—are you all ready? " he asked the lieutenant.

" Quite, m'sieur. Shall I give the order to embark? "

" Yes, you know the order. I'll take the second boat. Let's have a look at your fellows."

He followed Luigi, who had lined them up on the aft deck. Each man was armed and carried rations. All told, excluding the Donna and Nada, there were twenty-three. They were as fussy and alert as hounds at a meet.

"Good," said Cameron, well pleased with all he saw. "Get them down into the boats. What about their water-flasks?"

"All full, m'sieur," answered Luigi. "We're prepared for anything."

"Is the Donna ready?" asked Cameron, turning to Tino, whom he had appointed his aide-de-camp.

"They're waiting in the salon, m'sieur."

"I'd rather they didn't come!"

"I know, m'sieur, but they insist. My mother's determined to land with you," said Tino. "You can't argue with her," he added, wearily, and stooped to pat his dog Kim, who seemed to know something was afoot.

Cameron laughed and slapped the boy on the shoulder.

"Anyhow, I've put them in the third boat, to be out of the way. I'll make Luigi responsible for them."

He made his way below deck to the salon, where he found the Donna and Nada, muffled up in leather greatcoats. They were just finishing their coffee and rolls as he entered.

"Good-morning, major. Coffee?" cried the Donna, as lightly as if she were setting out by car for a day's excursion.

Amazing woman! He stared at her a moment. It was the first time he had seen her clothed for a journey. Yet the scarlet on her lips and the rouge on her face were applied as heavily as when he had first noticed her in the restaurant at Venice, five—or was it fifty?—nights ago.

"You haven't changed your mind, then?" he asked.

"No!" she replied, decisively. "I shall die on Sagusto."

"Die! I hope it won't mean that—or I shouldn't let you go with us," laughed Cameron.

She looked at him with that direct, forceful glance of hers, no answering laughter in her own eyes.

"I mean I shall not leave Sagusto once I have landed there," said the Donna, in her quiet, low voice. "Nada and I have sworn that—not if we have to face Condylis alone!"

Cameron shrugged his shoulders. There were moments when these people were impossibly melodramatic—veritable children.

"You need not anticipate that, Donna—I'll see it through."

"I wasn't doubting you, major," she replied, quickly. "I was only voicing an instinct. You're ready for us?"

"Yes," answered Cameron, standing by the door.

Without another word or glance, the two women rose, passed up on to the deck, and took their positions in the third boat. Precisely at four each boat, manned by men from the crew, pushed off from the ship. The last person they saw was Bandioli, standing at the top of the accommodation-ladder, searching the headland through his binoculars.

It was a mysterious embarkation, silent, in the chill of that summer dawn, not yet heralded but soon to break over them. The water, as they rowed, glimmered slightly phosphorescent where the oars dipped and rose. Gradually the headland hove into sight, immense, black, and inscrutable. There was a silence around, intensified by the long murmur of the sea fretting the shingle. It was as though they drew near to the island of Death, and Cameron recalled a swift memory of a picture in his room, some German print that had thrilled him as a boy.

In compliance with strict orders, no one spoke, the men sitting hunched up, their rifles upright between their knees. Tino piloted the first boat, Cameron followed in the second. After some ten minutes they approached the shore. In the darkness it looked an impossible task, but every inch of this coast was known to the lad. Suddenly he swung the boat hard over to starboard, apparently running it straight on to an evil-edged rock, barely submerged, but another quick deviation revealed his course. They went in through a narrow opening between two masses of fallen cliff. The water beyond was calm as a pool. The boat ran with a long sigh up the shingly beach. They were in a little semi-circular cove, apparently inaccessible save through this sea-channel, and walled in by the immense overhanging cliff.

Tino was the first to land, followed by Cameron and the men. The boat with Luigi came last, holding the Donna and Nada. Under this cliff the darkness was profound, but looking seawards they saw the first light of dawn breaking grey over the still water. Rapidly the sea changed, absorbing the shifting colours of the east. From their position they could not see the rising sun, but suddenly something caused Luigi to exclaim.

"Look!" he cried, pointing upwards, and there, as if caught in a pool of fire, the crimson ray of dawn struck a high crag, the sentinel of the advancing day.

They unloaded their kit. The boats pushed off, successfully navigated the narrow channel, and were lost to sight on their return journey to the ship. The party on the beach was as silent as possible, and Cameron had them placed well within the cover of the overhanging rock, to avoid any detection from above.

It was lighter now. Around them the morning mists swirled, lifting here and there like a curtain, to reveal patches of green-blue sea, of crimson-hued rock and headland, then veiling them again in white shrouds. Already that chill before the dawn had gone, the air was warmer, there was a sense of stirring life about them. A few perturbed gulls swept in and out of the rocks with fretful cries.

"I hope those birds won't give us away," said Cameron, anxiously.

"They can't be seen from the Castello; we're hidden by the cliff," answered Nada. She had discarded a great cloak that had enveloped her like a conspirator, and now stood in her breeches and top-boots, barely distinguishable from the men about her. Cameron noticed that she had also armed herself with a rifle, in addition to her revolver.

Their plan of campaign had omitted no detail. Tino and Cameron were to ascend first, leaving the party on the shore, until they had reconnoitred the position. If the Castello was unguarded, then they would all advance immediately, take possession of the place, and signal to Bandioli, who would proceed to land supplies.

At a quarter past four the light was sufficient to enable Tino and Cameron to start the ascent of the two thousand steps, cut zigzag fashion across the precipitous face of the mountain. They hoped to return within one hour. Luigi, meanwhile, was to have everything ready for the advance of the whole party should the way prove safe.

With little formality they took their leave of the Donna and Nada. None of them made any reference to the risk he might be running. Tino and the Donna were confident the Castello was not garrisoned. Cameron, for his part, was prepared to find a guard there.

Slowly they rose above the little cove, and a turn took them out of sight of their party. It was rough going. The steps had been hacked out of the rock, friable in places, so that often the track was barely marked.

It had fallen into disuse for almost a century, and only Tino had used it on odd occasions when he had gone down to the cove for a bathe. There was one part, half-way up, said Tino, where the cliff face was so precipitous that the path had been laid over a platform built on iron stanchions driven into the face of the rock.

After twenty minutes' work they paused for a rest. Cameron had now an opportunity of observing the view. They were already some three hundred feet above the sea. It lay below them, a marvellous spectacle of kaleidoscopic colours. The sun, now risen, had burnished the face of the water, but the sea-mist, swirling in strange convolutions in the air currents stirred by the new warmth enfolding this world, had absorbed all the colours of the dawn. Turquoise and emerald belts of water gleamed like mountain valleys between diaphanous clouds of mist, shadowed with the purple of dawn and stained with the rose of day.

" Shall we get along? " said Tino, at last, after he had finished breaking some biscuits for his beloved Dalmatian. " We're not half-way yet. We'll lose sight of the ship now, we work round to the east."

They rose, refreshed, and for another twenty minutes made good progress. But the way was treacherous in places, where the weather had worn away the friable rock, sometimes quite obliterating the hewn track.

" Do you think we'll get our party safely along this, Tino? " asked Cameron, anxiously, after a few yards of extremely difficult footwork rounding a bluff of the rock. They paused again to wipe the sweat from their faces. The chill of dawn had completely gone, and the great mass up which they toiled was full in the morning sun. Below, the sea had cleared, and sparkled in the radiance of the new day, a diamond floor to the world.

" We must ! " called back Tino. " It's the only way, except round by the east harbour."

" There is another way, then? "

" Yes—but almost impossible. Our boats would be certain to be seen—there are several cottages overlooking the old harbour, which was used by the Castello, before the one at Sagusto was built for the ore-boats. Besides, it's a five-mile journey to the Castello that way. You have to descend to the bed of the Yana and up again, unless you use the bridge. Condylis would be there, long before us, and we'd be hopelessly trapped. You see, m'sieur——"

He stopped suddenly in his explanation, and Cameron saw the youth halt. He was staring at his dog, which had been running ahead. It had now come back and stood full in its master's path, looking up into his face. Then, in a moment, Tino turned and put a finger to his lips. The dog had given a warning of some kind. Was there anyone beyond the bend?

With quickened hearts they waited and listened. Not a sound broke the stillness of the morning. Five hundred feet below them the sea fretted itself into a white surge about the base of the rugged shore, but no sound of its labour came to their ears. It was then, after an alert pause, that Tino observed something singular about Kim's attitude. He did not turn, with pricked ears, in the direction whence the enemy might be stationed. He stood stolidly in front of his master, looking towards him with a quizzical, perplexed expression on his intelligent face.

" What is it—what is it, Kim? " whispered Tino, but the dog only wagged his tail slowly, not moving otherwise. The youth turned and looked at Cameron, unslinging his rifle.

" If there's someone—I'll go on," he said. " I hope Kim's not betrayed us."

" He'd have barked," suggested Cameron, likewise unslinging his rifle.

" No, I've taught him not to. Let me go ahead—I know the bends; you can follow closely, m'sieur."

Cameron let the youth go on. He was on familiar ground. For a couple of minutes he crept close, when suddenly the tense silence was broken by a cry from Tino. He had halted and waited for Cameron to come up, dismay in his eyes.

" Look," he cried, pointing to the face of the cliff, revealed by a sudden turn in their track.

Cameron looked as directed, and could see nothing at first to cause his alarm. But in a few moments of closer observation he saw what had filled Tino with such sudden dismay and had turned back the dog. Where the track had been there was nothing, for some twenty feet, except a few gaunt iron stanchions projecting from the bare face of the rock. They rose, spoke-like, above them, a few loose boards hanging to some of the iron rods, but for quite twenty feet there was nothing at all joining the broken path where they stood and the splintered end of the stairway running up beyond them.

" It's been blown up? " asked Cameron, the first to speak after the dismay created by this sight.

" Perhaps—or perhaps not. Look ! " replied Tino, pointing

downwards to a mass of debris littering the steep slope below them.

"There may have been a mud-and-rock avalanche, caused by the rains. It would carry away the platform."

He lapsed into silence again and stood sadly contemplating the ruined track. It meant the death of their hopes and a return with the bad news to the expectant party below.

"There's no other way?" asked Cameron, realising, as he spoke, how futile was the question.

"None, m'sieur," answered the lad, slowly.

"Then we face the inevitable—that's all!" said Cameron, affecting a cheerfulness he could not feel.

"You mean—fighting our way in?"

"Yes."

The youth looked at him earnestly for a moment.

"You wanted to avoid that—at any cost?" he asked, quietly.

"I wanted to avoid it—except as a last extremity," corrected Cameron, "because of the Donna and Nada."

"My mother has no fear—neither has Nada."

"I wish they had," replied Cameron, earnestly.

The lad looked down at the dog a moment and then raised his face, turning his serious eyes on the Englishman.

"You can't understand us—I know that, m'sieur. But this island is in our blood, and we'll have no life away from it—it will be our home or our grave," he added. Then, with a swift change of mood: "We must go back— there's one possibility yet."

"Which is?"

"We can try the east harbour. Perhaps we could force a landing before Condylis reaches it. We can go at once in the boats."

"How far is it?"

"Three miles, m'sieur."

"Good,—we'll try."

They turned and retraced their steps. By his wrist watch Cameron found they had been away three-quarters of an hour.

In half an hour they could regain the cove. It would then be nearly six o'clock. They might go to the east harbour and attempt the landing by seven. Every minute was now vital. It was certain that Condylis would lose no time in blocking every way to them.

They worked downwards as rapidly as safety would permit, no word passing between them. Once more they came to the bluff, negotiated it, and faced the north-west again, and the sea where the yacht rode——

" *Mon Dieu !* "

The words were half-screamed by the lad, and in the same second Cameron saw what Tino saw. There, far below them, leaving a white semi-circular wake on the blue expanse of sunlit water, was *The Three Castles*, a mile out to sea, and steaming south, full speed ahead !

In that moment of utter consternation they both knew the meaning of this thing they saw. The lad turned to Cameron, speechless, his eyes staring, his face working under the emotion that shook his young body. And then, his passion half-strangling the sob that broke in his throat, he poured forth his wrath upon the traitor, with a frenzy bordering on hysteria. Finally, exhausted by this outburst, he sank to the ground, his head buried between his knees, his body shaken by a storm of tears that had in it all the abandon of a child.

Cameron stood by, silent. It was un-English, this demonstration, but he could not help pitying this high-spirited boy. He had been sustained by such hopes and had borne the strain with a quietude that made him a Spartan figure.

After a time, when the lad had subsided into a despairing silence, his head still bowed in his hands, nervous fingers interlocked in his hair, Cameron touched him on the shoulder, but did not speak.

The boy looked up, and it was a schoolboy's face that gazed a little sullenly into Cameron's. Then, after a pause :

" You think me contemptible, m'sieur ? " he asked, pathetically, all the tragedy of youth's complete, though momentary, despair in his eyes.

"No—but I do think we're wasting very valuable time, old son," said Cameron, kindly. "And for all your whimpering I'm glad you're with me in a very tight corner."

Without another word the lad rose to his feet and strode fiercely on. Ten minutes had passed, and they were nearing the cove, before he spoke one word. Then, his face flushed with a thought that brought back hope again, he turned to his companion.

"We'll do it yet, m'sieur," he exclaimed, exultantly.

"Do what?"

"Get to the Castello by this track. I'll swim to the harbour, land round by the jetty, cross the gorge and go up the other side to the Castello. From there I can get to the upper half of this track."

"But it's broken away!"

"Yes—we can replace it—the stanchions are there. I can lower a ladder or rope from above, we can make it fast at both ends, and the men can scale up!"

In his optimism he paid no heed to Cameron's doubts. He saw deliverance again, and youth triumphant swept away all shadows of despair. A three-mile swim, a dash for safety, the crossing of a gorge, the climb to the Castello, the possibility of its being occupied, the difficulty of repairing that gap in the track—these Herculean trials to be endured gave Cameron little hope of success. But the lad had no doubt in his own mind.

"Swim three miles!" he exclaimed, in reply to a question of Cameron's. "But, m'sieur, you have never seen me swim!"

His expression was so pained at this doubt cast upon his powers, that Cameron had to laugh, forgiving him his boastfulness. He found himself wondering, amid many grave questions, how often this impetuous child had been spanked, and whether any castigation or repressive system, so thoroughly applied according to stern English traditions, could have wrought any change upon his mercurial temperament.

But with the approach to the cove and the party awaiting their return, graver thoughts supervened. They were the bringers of heavy news.

CHAPTER XVI

IN all the moments during which he had observed the Donna there was none that revealed her to Cameron as this, when her fortune seemed at its lowest ebb. She realised from their faces, before either of them had spoken, that their task, for some reason, had failed. But her expression did not change, and Nada, at her side as ever, seemed to take from the Donna her imperturbable mien. It was Nada who spoke first, however, addressing herself to Tino.

"You can't get—is it guarded?" she asked.

Her brother shook his head and turned to Cameron, who followed close behind, desiring him to break the news.

"No—not guarded, so far as we know. The platform has been destroyed—perhaps deliberately, or perhaps by a landslide —we can't tell. But there's more serious news."

"More serious?" cried the Donna. "Is Condylis there?"

Cameron looked quietly into her eyes, desiring to convey a silent warning. The men stood near, listening. He hadn't yet decided whether they should be told the most serious fact until a revelation was inevitable. The Donna, in an instant, divined his intention, and walked slowly away from a group sitting near, as if in casual conversation with Nada and Cameron.

"Donna—I know you'll not let what's happened dismay you. I hold myself to blame," he began, uneasily.

"You are withholding something, major. What is it?"

" The yacht—it's gone," he said simply.

She accepted his statement so calmly that at first he thought she could not have realised its significance, but her following remark told him she had not misunderstood.

" Then it was Bandioli who released Condylis," she said, half reflectively. " It's the first time I've repressed a suspicion—it'll be the last," she added, determinedly. " You mustn't reproach yourself, major. Besides, it's all useless now."

She turned her face away and looked towards the sea, while Nada, all the eagerness of her excitement banished from her face, sought Cameron's, as if hoping to find in it some remaining sign of deliverance. For this news meant the total ruin of their expedition. They were prisoners, held in this cove, where starvation would infallibly encroach upon them.

Under the first shock, the mind refused to visualise the details of such a ghastly end to their adventure. Condylis had disposed of them without firing a shot, without having their deaths visibly on his hands. So much, in his most merciful mood. He might even return with the yacht and——

But the Donna was not a woman to let imagination take the breath of action.

" Condylis has bought Bandioli," was all she said " I suppose I didn't promise him enough. You see now, major, why I took such drastic steps to get an honest man in my yacht—and bring him to his death."

" Death!—we're not at that point yet, Donna," protested Cameron.

She gave an uneasy, sad laugh, and her steady dark eyes met his, an expression of pity dwelling in them.

" I know of nothing we can do—except wait, miserably. Oh! any end would have been better than this ! " she cried, with a sudden bitterness sounding in her voice. And for the first time Cameron witnessed a display of some kind of motherly instinct, in the manner in which she placed her arm protectively around the girl at her side.

"Mother, there's one hope," said the youth. "I can swim round."

"Where?"

"To the old harbour. There's a path leads up the mountain from behind the cottages. Once I get beyond them I'll get to the Castello by way of the gorge. I might be able to repair the platform from above."

The Donna was silent a moment, and Nada answered for her.

"It's impossible," she said. "You couldn't land unseen. You'd be shot."

"I'll try it," replied Tino. "Mother—it's our only hope," he urged. "I'm going now—we mustn't lose a minute!"

He turned to Cameron, who was watching the struggle enacted in the mother's face. She knew well enough the heavy odds against success.

"Major," said Tino, "go with Luigi and the men as far up the steps as you can. If I succeed you'll hear me call by noon. If not—well——" He broke off, shrugged his shoulders, and then added quietly: "It might as well come that way as this. Mother, you agree?" he asked, turning to her.

Cameron saw the Donna mastering the denial that rose within her. There was no tremor of the voice, no trembling of the mouth, no betraying emotion when she answered him.

"Yes, I agree—at once, Tino."

And then, to Cameron's surprise, she suddenly took the boy in her arms, held him a few moments in silence, kissing his cheeks, his brow, his hair. When Tino went to his sister, Cameron turned away. Nada was of frailer stuff, for all her high spirits. He heard the girl sobbing distractedly; and then Tino's voice addressed him:

"Good-bye, sir—at noon, we'll say."

"Wait!" commanded Cameron. He had made a swift decision. This lad must not go alone, carrying all the risk of their delivery. "I'm coming, too—we may not both get through, but one might."

Immediately the three of them, the Donna, Nada and Tino, were opposed to it. They depended too much on his courage and resource. The men without him might turn difficult. He did not know the coast and the lie of the land behind the Castello. The swim was a very long one—was he an expert?

"No—but I'm good for three miles in this water," he answered, breaking down their objections one by one. "The men are all right under Luigi. Supposing Tino gets through, that track may be more than one man's job. No, Donna, I'm going! Will you wait here, while I go over to Luigi?—we must take him into our confidence. We'd better not tell the men yet. He can get them all up the track as far as possible. If we don't signal by two o'clock, then he must get them all down again—and explain."

He left them then, and went across to Luigi, who was busily checking the few supplies they had landed, and drew him to one side. As Cameron anticipated, he, too, wanted to join the swimming expedition.

"I could swim round the island, m'sieur! Let me go, and you stay with the Donna."

"It's settled, Luigi—I'm placing them in your care. You understand clearly what you're to do?"

"Exactly, m'sieur," answered the lieutenant, aware that further pleading was futile. "And, m'sieur——"

He hesitated, his serious eyes roving over the company of men smoking and chatting in groups as they sat about. Then, as if he regretted his intention, he was silent.

"You were asking——?" said Cameron.

Luigi gave a short forced laugh, and avoided his companion's eyes, but he did not complete the broken sentence.

"You were asking——?" persisted Cameron.

Luigi faced him then, his hands playing nervously over the leather bandolier he wore across one shoulder.

"M'sieur—when the worst comes—if so, I had thought——"

But again he hesitated, and Cameron, following his glance, saw that it shifted from the men, over towards three figures standing by the shore, to the Donna and her children.

"Go on, Luigi—yes, if it should," said Cameron, comprehending the unspoken fear.

"When all our hope's gone, and the men get restive," answered Luigi, slowly. Then, abruptly breaking off, as if he could not speak the thought in his mind: "Death would be better than that, m'sieur!" he cried, passionately.

The two men looked at each other in silence. This was a thing neither could sanction, yet each felt its necessity.

"We may come back, Luigi—or Condylis may—all kinds of things might happen before that. If not—why——"

He hesitated, unable to give words to the act in Luigi's mind.

"Pardon me, m'sieur, but I know—I know you love her," said the Italian, quietly, and added, in a voice so low that he was almost inaudible, "I, too, m'sieur—but with no right."

The pathos in his confession checked Cameron's sudden resentment against the fellow's assertion. So Luigi had seen, for all his restraint and the affected indifference with which he had disguised his true feelings towards Nada. The girl herself did not know, should never know. Yet this other lover, with faultless intuition, had divined it all. In that moment, when Cameron felt the truth of his love challenged, he suddenly drew very near to the volatile young adventurer, for whom, hitherto, he had felt an amused contempt.

Cameron looked him straight in the face, a full confession in his eyes as he met the Italian's.

"Luigi,—you have as much right as I," he said.

The young fellow smiled, sadly.

"No," he corrected, "none at all, m'sieur—that is plain."

"How?"

Luigi looked down at his boots, those spotless top-boots, in which the heart of a child delighted. But it was a man's voice, charged with suffering, that answered:

"I have no sign, no word—no moment of kindness, even. She sees and hears but one—you, m'sieur."

Cameron did not speak. There was nothing he could say. Useless to tell this fellow that his own passion could have no gratification, that his career, his country, his own personal setting, all made the thought impossible. Nada in England, Nada under the restraint of conventions and traditions that would make her as miserable as a caged eagle—the idea was futile. And it was not in him to use her blind adoration for a temporary satisfaction of his senses. His relationship to the Donna, to Tino, to this enterprise, made that impossible—even had he the will.

He was no saint; and her appeal, all unconsciously heightened by her natural grace, hammered at the senses until his head swam with the peril of her approach. She trafficked dangerously with the forces of which she had so little comprehension, because, as yet, she had gone unscathed. Her haughtiness, her reproof, her disdain, were as inflammable to the desiring heart as were her dancing eyes, her smiles, her deliberate approach to intimacies and confessions; as this poor Luigi, Latin of Latins, knew all too well, consistently scorned and snubbed.

Luigi was the first to break the silence of understanding that had grown between them in this moment.

"She does not know, m'sieur. She has dressed like that, she thinks she is one of them—but I can see their eyes. Men are men, m'sieur. These fellows would not be here—I should not be here—if we didn't expect Chance to throw us a few prizes in the lottery. She's safe enough now; but if things fail—if hunger comes—why——"

He broke off, and laughed discordantly.

Cameron put a hand on his shoulder.

"I must go. You'll do what you think best—in that extremity, Luigi. Keep the men away from the rocks out there; they'd better not learn yet that the ship's deserted us. If we don't hail you by two o'clock, leave a sentry posted and camp down here for the night. How long will the rations last?"

" Till to-morrow night, m'sieur. The boat with the supplies hasn't come."

" It won't. It would be wise to keep a sharp look-out at the end of the cove. I don't expect Condylis will come—he can let Bandioli do all he wants—still, it's better to be prepared. Good-bye, Luigi."

The hands of the two men met in a long grip. Whether they met again was a lottery, but this crisis had brought them to a swift and complete understanding.

Cameron rejoined the Donna. Tino was waiting impatiently for him. Whatever that strange woman felt at parting with her son and the man whom she had drawn into this adventure, no sign showed in her face. But Nada, of a substance less stern, despite the mould, clung first to Tino, and then, as Cameron bade her good-bye, suddenly burst into tears. In an impulse that sought to comfort her, he lifted her face and kissed the perfect white brow, with its black straight hair and arched eyebrows. He saw her lashes were wet with tears, her lovely red mouth trembled. She made no response to his farewell.

With a swift step he set off with Tino towards the ridge of rocks running out from the cove.

The sun was now hot and the calm water sparkled like a floor strewn with diamonds. There was no horizon rimming that world where sea and sky rose indivisibly up to the blue vault of the cloudless day.

Arrived at the uttermost point, Tino, who had leapt like a cat over the jagged rocks, turned to his companion.

" We'd better strip here," he said. " We'll have to leave some of our things."

" You won't swim in them? "

" It would drag us too much," answered the youth. " Here's some cord. I'm making a bundle of my trousers, shirt and shoes. You can tie it on my back. They'll soon dry when we land."

" And our revolvers? "

"I've thought of that, m'sieur. Give me your cartridges."

Cameron emptied his revolver, and also gave him his spare cartridges.

"I'm putting them in this bottle—the water can't get in. Stuff the revolver in your trousers."

They were soon stripped, Cameron robust and white against the slim, tawny body of the youth. But he saw at a glance that for all Tino's slightness there was untiring strength in his agile limbs. He would need all his own maturer vigour to keep pace with this young panther.

"Ready?" asked Tino, when they had strung one another's bundles behind their backs.

"You lead," answered Cameron.

The youth lowered himself in, diving being impossible owing to the bundle hanging from a cord passed round his throat. Cameron watched him strike out, and followed. He was relieved to find the sea warm. It would make the long swim before them less exhausting.

Ten minutes later they were well off the shore, Tino taking a parallel course once they had cleared the isolated rocks marking the sharp indentations of the coast. Steadily they swam, side by side, breaking the still, clear surface of an almost motionless sea.

CHAPTER XVII

I

COLONEL CONDYLIS was particularly grateful that his own swimming feat had been undertaken under cover of darkness.

It was not that he could not swim—in his day he had been as active in the water as in the saddle—but he was grateful to have avoided the observance of so undignified a return to the island where he was master. Once again his extraordinary luck had saved him. True, he cursed volubly against the trick that had been played on him. Even as he landed on the jetty steps, exhausted with the weight of his wet clothes, his thoughts were not of his own uncomfortable condition, nor of his deliverer following closely behind and now dragging his wet body up the first of the jetty steps. They were directed, now his safety was assured, to the man on that yacht who had so nearly made him an ignominious prisoner. Glib, smooth-faced liar that he was!—Condylis almost regretted his escape from him, since it meant postponing the pleasant hour of reckoning. Still, the postponement would prove well worth it. A kind Fate had sent him a creature like Bandioli to his rescue, and though the price had been excessive, he was not the man to study economy when his supremacy was at stake.

Condylis's revengeful thoughts as he clambered up the jetty steps were suddenly checked by a hullabaloo that broke out from the guard by the machine-gun. The fact that he had already been dozing necessitated a prompt and noisy alarm to demonstrate that he was now much awake.

"Shut up, you fool!" shouted Condylis, in a condition that demanded a secret advent. "It's me—Condylis, d'you hear? Shut up!"

"Signore! signore!" stuttered the amazed man, now dimly discerning a bedraggled, sodden mass that had the voice, if not the aspect, of the Governor of Sagusto. More footsteps made him turn nervously. Kosrev, the Russian, without boots or breeches, like the Colonel, strode forward, the wet tails of his red shirt clinging about his heavy thighs.

"We've returned from a dinner-party on that ship—d'you hear?" stormed Condylis. "And if you set any value on your life you'll not say a word about how we returned. And give me your boots and trousers. You can walk up with this fellow and get them back at the house."

Without a word of protest, the guard parted with his trousers and boots. Condylis got into them, after taking off his shirt and wringing it out. Fortunately the night was warm. In silence, after Condylis was clothed, they set off, down the harbour, along the street where that same morning that scoundrelly Englishman had walked. It was almost deserted, for Sagusto began the day early and retired early. They went on through the silent piazza, and up to the closed door of the house.

Condylis knocked lightly, and the negro within, keeping watch for his master's return, opened immediately.

His jaw dropped when he saw the apparition so strangely like and yet unlike his resplendent master, who had departed that evening, a worthy testimony to so much polishing and pressing. Now he looked on a head whose locks were plastered down upon a scowling brow, and into eyes that furiously met his own. Jacketless, in dirty old trousers and clumsy boots, Condylis walked in, saying no word. The other men followed, and a brief altercation made him aware of his two companions, stopped by the negro.

" Let them in! " he said. " One of them's lodging here, the other wants the things I'm wearing. Find that fellow some clothes! " Then, turning to the man from the ship who had been his gaoler: " You, what's your name? "

" Kosrev. What's to become of me? " he whined, in a Fiume-dialect Italian he had acquired during his sojourn there.

" Where do you come from? "

" Nijiniski Novogorod."

" *Dio mio !* You don't think I'm going to send you back there, do you? You can stay here for the night and go back to the ship in the morning."

The Russian stared at him, wondering just how mad was this bullying man.

" My ship ! I can't ever go back there—they'd shoot me! "

" No loss much; it's less risk than going to Niviny—whatever-you-call-it, eh? " sneered Condylis, glaring at the shivering man. Thirty, perhaps, and a mongrel—written all over him.

" You can go back in the morning—it's my ship now ! "

Without another word he went off, disappearing through a door in the lower gallery.

His statement to the Russian had not been without foundation, but a certain native caution in Condylis made him regret being quite so free with his information. He never counted his chickens until they were cooped. But by morning they would be pretty well cooped, when Bandioli had landed them in that inaccessible cove. It was lucky he had had the stairway to the Castello blown away, for there was no other spot so securely isolated. It would save him much time and trouble, also a great responsibility. He suffered from no excessive estimate of the value of life, but to shoot two women and a couple of dozen men in cold blood, even if they provoked one by resistance, was not a job for which he had much stomach. Luckily he had got rid of anything in the nature of a pitched battle, which might not have been a certain success, since these grumbling scallywags on the island were not to be trusted.

It was a sad fact that the best fighters and toughest characters on Sagusto were either locked up or had had their backs well lacerated at the flogging-post. This terrorism had been forced on him in self-defence. But the stoutest among the people had come into open conflict with him. Of late they had tried escaping from the island, and the armed guard was needed as much for shooting anybody who attempted to swim off to a passing vessel, fortunately rare, as for warning anyone who might approach without authorisation. The coming of the Donna and that damned Englishman might have started a rising on the island.

Well, he was rid of them now. They would be safely dumped in that cove. Time would do the rest. But as he took no chances with any of the eternities so far as he could control them, he resolved to send a guard up to the Castello, to keep a look-out along the coast.

The heavy boots he wore made a great noise as he tramped

along the corridor, past the drawing-room. He was just wondering whether Donna Gonzalos had gone up to bed, or had ever come down from it—she often spent the day there, swallowing Asti and aspirins alternately, for imaginary relief from imaginary ills—when a sudden opening of the door flooded the passage with light. It trapped him in a merciless blaze.

"*Santo Dios!*" exclaimed the Donna, a dramatic figure in crimson silk, with a scarlet azalea in her rich black hair. "Enrico! Where have you been?" she screamed, and then broke into unrestrained laughter.

He pushed her away from the door and marched angrily into the drawing-room.

"To a fancy-dress ball, of course!" he answered, furious. A yapping Pekinese, affrighted, that had slipped off a cushion, received a kick that sent it yapping away in a higher key.

"Close that door!" he thundered.

A little sobered by his anger, the Donna closed the door and stood by it, watching him striding up and down in front of the fireplace, filled with hibiscus and hydrangea.

"Come here!" he commanded.

But the Donna did not move. Instead, she gave her black lace fan a little defiant flicker.

"Your mood seems about as ugly as your attire," she answered, tauntingly. "Even a dog shakes himself before coming ashore!"

He glared at her, and saw that she was not to be frightened.

"You wanted to go and dine with that charming young Englishman. I wish you had—instead of me!" he said.

"What's happened? Has he thrown you overboard?"

Condylis looked at her murderously. She was the most stiletto-tongued woman he had ever encountered in all his journeys through the four quarters of the globe. For some reason her venom gave him a kind of inverted pleasure. So at this remark he laughed, in the same mood as that in which he would have throttled her.

" He's nothing but an assassin—a silken assassin in your eyes, dear Donna ! " said Condylis, sarcastically, squeezing the water out of his hair. He took a spiteful delight in picking up the Donna's Mexican shawl with which to rub his head as he spoke.

" When I got on board he showed me down into his cabin—for a drink. Once in, he turned the key on me."

" But why? What for? " asked Donna Gonzalos.

" Suppose he wanted me out of the way, with you so amorously in the offing," replied Condylis, laconically. " Actually, he's Donna Soudaikos's hired soldier-boy."

" That woman—here ! in the yacht? "

" The same, my dear Emilia—with her twenty cut-throats shipped at Pola. They would have made short work of you—or perhaps leisured work," drawled Condylis, with a sensual leer, " for the nice young Englishman might have reserved you."

His malicious smile was suddenly checked by something that hurtled past, crashing on the wall behind him. He regained his composure quickly and looked down at the scattered pieces of a vase on the tiger rug.

" My dear Emilia, one day you'll have an accident and hit me. You won't get another try then. I like to be kind to my women-folk, but there's an end to my softness."

Donna Gonzalos, breathing hard with her exertion, fanned herself busily, still by the door.

" Won't you sit down and listen to the tale of my delivery into your arms? " he asked, mockingly. It was the only way he could deal with her.

She threw him a defiant look, and then deliberately crossed the room towards him and sat on the settee, gazing up at his soddened figure as if taking pleasure in his discomfort. What-ever her faults, she didn't know the first letter in the alphabet of fear.

" Although I know you've a fine contempt for my intellect, Emilia, it's served me well enough this time. God knows what they intended doing with me. Whatever it was, your situation would have gone. Believe me, that Englishman, for all his attentions at lunch——"

"Oh, stop that! It doesn't follow because a man isn't a boor in his manners, he's merely——"

She did not finish the sentence, and shrugged her bare shoulders, the beautiful snowy shoulders that she kept so well uncovered.

"That Englishman," continued Condylis, "has been very clever. He comes ashore as a tourist, from his *Three Castles*—gets himself invited to lunch——"

"I suppose you asked him to stay?" interjected the Donna.

Condylis scowled and continued:

"Invited himself to lunch—ingratiated himself with you, and with me, and lured me to his ship."

"Whisky, wasn't it, Enrico?"

"It seems he's been picked up by our Donna in Venice or somewhere, and was on board the *Lucciola* when she put into Pola for that cargo of cut-throats. He's a slick beggar. Our fellows have been looking all over the Adriatic for that boat, and she's here, in the bay."

"Here?"

"*The Three Castles* is the *Lucciola*; he's merely changed her name with a pot of paint and flown the British flag."

"How'd you learn that?" asked Donna Gonzalos, lighting a cigarette and watching him alertly. Like herself, she never knew when he was lying.

"They've a skipper aboard—Bandioli. When they'd got me nicely locked up he paid me an unofficial visit. It seems he comes from Ancona and knows what we've got here. Every man's a price, especially cash down. I offered him a hundred thousand lire to deliver his crew over to me. That wasn't so simple, as he pointed out. A wily devil, Emilia. So he suggested dumping that little private army and its hired general, and then dealing with his crew, which isn't particular. To-night he's dumping them."

Condylis laughed sardonically at the trick now being played on his unsuspecting rivals.

"Where's he dumping them?" asked the Donna.

"Where they won't trouble us again, my dear," answered Condylis. "I must go and change. Are you coming?"

"You're not—you're not drowning them?" said the Donna.

There was something in the manner of that young Englishman that would not die out of her mind. His voice, his eyes, so lacking in the furtive cunning she found in those of the men she knew, and his courtesy, so different in its nature, without an objective, unlike the feline courtesy of these Southerns, set him apart.

"There's enough of us got wet to-night," grinned Condylis, pausing near the door. "Where's Mahassein?"

"Out, I think. And the Donna—what are you doing with her?"

"She'll tread her own soil once more, my dear—thanks to the kind creature I am to all womenfolk!"

But the laughter in his voice made the listening woman's heart beat quicker. He would murder anyone and laugh like that. She had heard it in that courtyard, above the sickening whistle of a lash and the moans of a half-insensible victim. There were other tales, told in the village—exaggerated, doubtless, and yet not beyond his capability.

"The ship's coming back in the morning. We'll inspect it then, my dear. I wouldn't like to disappoint your desire to see it—though I fear the nice young Englishman won't be there to do the honours."

He slammed the door behind him, a sneer on his face as he went. Donna Gonzalos got up wearily from the settee, picked up the timorous Pekinese, and surveyed herself in the long glass in the recess by the fireplace.

There were times when she longed to leave this place. But where should she go, and how would she fare? Women of a cautiously withheld fifty years, plying her calling, had not the zest or blind faith of youth in the procuring of tomorrow's daily bread. She had, in a degree, luxury and ease here. Her soul was steeped in sloth, amid other weaknesses. She had a cat's craving for sleep and warmth. On this island she had no one to contend with, to keep her watchful of encroaching rivals. Condylis had tired of her, but she ignored his hints steadily. With each month she became more firmly established. No, Sagusto, despite Condylis in some moods, had become a haven. And in all the world she had never found that before. She was tired and sadly aware that her arts had always trafficked in a fickle market. There had been one man—— But men like that never lived long, she reflected; they were snatched up from this world's weariness and corruption.

She kissed the Pekinese, muttered a few endearing words, went to the window and looked out on the moonlit night. It was warm and starry, with a milky drift hooping the grey vault. On the hills the cypress stood black and sharp, as if cut out of jet. Below, she could hear the chorused, incessant croaking of frogs; afar, a cold glimmer betrayed the sea.

The lovely tranquillity of the night goaded the unrest in her heart. She was a bad woman as the world accounted bad women, and yet within her rose a sense of injustice, of wrong meted out to her beyond all proportion to her deserts. Another chance, another turn in her days of youth, and it could all have been so different.

That young Englishman, when he found his woman, his mate —her destiny at his hands would be so different from her own. Her faults had been of her making, God knew well enough, but her desires had always been a little above her faults, and always they had been mocked by Fate.

The calm, the displayed glory and peace of this Southern night covering a scene marred by man's deeds! What had Condylis done to those people in the ship? To what doom were they sailing over the moonlit sea? If it had been possible, effective, she would have screamed a warning through that night, across the sleeping valley, even if the man overhead had come down and choked the mortal breath in her. There were moments when, in the consciousness of her evil existence, she almost longed for a violent, self-sacrificing end.

With a sigh she closed the windows, put down the dog on his favourite cushion for the night, turned out the lamp, and left the drawing-room. It was lighted only by a shaft of white moonlight falling across the snarling head of the tiger-skin.

II

Condylis was up at dawn, and immediately aroused Mahassein, to whom he related the events of the previous evening. That young man evinced a proper if simulated surprise. He had never quite accepted the tourist explanation. Tourists were quite unknown at Sagusto, which was uncharted on most maps, and so inaccessible that no one voluntarily sought it out. Mahassein's suspicions had been aroused, however, by the singular fact that Mr. Cameron had landed unaccompanied by anyone— and most notably without a female companion. Tourists, wealthy ones like he purported to be, did not sail alone on private yachts.

But it had never occurred to Mahassein that this genial Englishman had any connection with Donna Soudaikos. He had not the air of a man who had relations of a business or other kind with strange ladies. Like most of the English Mahassein had met, this one was rather serious-minded, devoid of temperament. His encounter with the Donna Emilia, watched with some surprise on his part, had revealed an exquisite courtesy and a capacity for making a good impression. But the Donna infallibly awoke the gallant dormant in every man. And there the matter had ended, to the Donna's disgust.

Mr. Cameron had been a mystery. If Mahassein had known he was Donna Soudaikos's agent, he might have made a bold proposal. Now, as he listened to Condylis describing his escape and the trap prepared by that scoundrel in command of *The*

Three Castles, his mind actively sought a counterplan. For he was ready to acclaim the downfall of Condylis, to assist it, if he could do so with safety. The abuse of the last six months, the terror his violence evoked at times in the heart of the Armenian, made him desperate.

He had proposed going on board with Cameron because he knew, sooner or later, as the hated agent of a hated tyrant, one of the islander's knives would be plunged into his body. There had been four covert attempts on their lives in the past month, which had goaded Condylis to fresh cruelties against these cowed victims of his rapacity. The men were dying in the mines every week, underpaid, underfed, and over-worked. A revolt brought a merciless flogging, a form of punishment suggested by that mediæval survival in the courtyard. Two runaways, who had seized a fishing-boat the week previous, were now sentenced to a merciless flogging. Every day the terrified priest summoned up courage to protest against some outrage. Condylis had threatened to wall him up in his church unless he kept to his own business of baptising, marrying, and burying.

"Hurry out!" shouted Condylis, as he turned to leave Mahassein's bedroom. "The ship'll be here any moment now, and we'll board her at once."

"Is that safe?" asked the Armenian, slipping into his riding-breeches and top-boots. "He might kidnap us—or hold us to ransom."

Condylis laughed and leered knowingly.

"He'll play no tricks with me; and the hundred thousand lire stays on shore—for him to fetch."

"Have we got it?"

"No, only half; but he doesn't know that—he'll get something else in part payment."

Condylis laughed heartily, some secret thought provoking his mirth.

"And he'll get the ship and its contents. What more can the fellow want?" he added.

Mahassein pulled on his shirt, his mind working as he talked.

"But he might pick up his party again if you don't keep your word," suggested the Armenian, watching his chief cautiously.

"And risk being clapped into chains by Cameron and his men? You're an utter fool, Mahassein. That Bandioli knows which side his bread's buttered—half the hundred thousand down, a rich cargo, and a ship thrown in—it isn't everybody's chance."

"What do you mean—a rich cargo?"

"Exactly what I say—I'm a man of my word, aren't I?" cried Condylis, throwing out his chest. "But you'll know that later. Come along! Find that fellow Kosrev; we'll take him back with us. The first thing you've got to do is to send Savrin and a couple of fellows to blow up the Yana bridge."

"The bridge?"

"Yes, blow it up at once—I'm taking no risks."

The door slammed behind Condylis. Mahassein stooped to lace his breeches. There could be only one reason for blowing up the bridge across the gorge—the possibility of someone getting into the deserted Castello. But no one could get in—not from this end of the island. Nor from the other, for Condylis had had the platform joining the steps blown away a month ago. Yet this order showed he was taking no risks. Why this unnecessary precaution?

Suddenly he found the clue. Had this Bandioli disposed of Cameron's party in the cove on the north shore? The thought was a horrible one—they were to be starved to death! There was no way out—he knew that cove well, and its inaccessibility —save by boat. A good swimmer, an excellent swimmer, knowing the tides, might gain the coast three miles higher up, by the old harbour, but Condylis had a guard living there.

Mahassein broke into a sweat at the thought. That woman and her daughter, her son, and Cameron, were to be deliberately starved to death!

They were not his friends, they were his official enemies, so

F

long as he was in the service of Condylis.   But he was no villain
at heart, and this scheme for their end revolted him.   He would
be powerless to help, and he dare not suggest to Condylis any
moderation in their treatment.

There was a tap on the door, and in answer to his response it
opened, and the stable-boy, accompanied by an unshaven,
starved creature, entered.

"This is the man, signore," he said.

Mahassein looked from the boy to the man, whom he had
never seen before.   He was fair, bullet-headed, with a peasant's
simple blue eyes.

"Who are you?" he asked in French, and receiving nothing
but a stare, repeated the question in Italian.

"I am Kosrev, signore, from the *Lucciola*," he answered.

Mahassein looked at him, puzzled for the moment, then
suddenly he realised this was the guard who had released Condylis
and swum ashore with him.

"Thanks, Yanko, I'll look after him," said Mahassein to the
boy, who cleaned his boots and groomed his horse.   He had
earned the lad's gratitude by checking a merciless lashing given
at Condylis's order for some trivial neglect.

The boy shuffled out, Mahassein watching him go.   He had
dark blue eyes, yet it was not his eyes that the Armenian saw,
but his sister's, of whom he reminded him.   Yanko's sister had
made life tolerable on this island, sprightly little witch that she
was.

"Come along with me—the Colonel's waiting," said Mahassein to the Russian.   He noticed the fellow was trembling
either with cold or fear.   On his way down he wondered again
about the rich cargo.

CHAPTER XVIII

SHORTLY after seven o'clock, as the harbour of Sagusto lay bright in the risen sun, Bandioli anchored *The Three Castles* within hail of the jetty, and thus brought to a successful close an excellent night's work. He had disposed of that objectionable Englishman, of the owner of the ship, and of three boatloads of desperadoes. There remained for him the ship itself, a crew that daren't disobey, and now, the collection of ready money for the service he had rendered Condylis.

Scarcely had he anchored, when he saw a boat put off from the jetty, and as the ladder was lowered it came alongside. Condylis sprang up, accompanied by Kosrev and a stranger. The two men greeted each other curtly, and went below, leaving Mahassein above deck. The Russian disappeared aft, a miserable object, who crept about as though he feared a bullet in his heart at any moment : a not inappropriate end, reflected Mahassein.

Below, when Bandioli had locked the door of the salon, into which he had shown Condylis, the two men sat down.

" So this is the Donna's little abode, eh? " said Condylis, surveying the room where only a few hours ago the two women had made their preparations for the landing. It had already been searched by the skipper, who had discovered a small jewel cabinet holding half a dozen valuable rings, but, to his chagrin, not the pearls the Donna usually wore.

" Did you find anything? " asked Condylis, when the other man made no response.

" Yes—some clothes, and her cheque-book."

" Where is it? You'd better let me have that—in case we meet," he added, with a wry smile.

" It's no use without the signature," said Bandioli, taking a cheque-book out of his pocket, " and you don't know how much she's got in."

Condylis looked at it. It was drawable on a bank in Trieste.

He put it in his own pocket.   Then he leaned forward, smoothing the red-baize cloth with his ringed hands.

"Now listen, Bandioli—I've a little scheme to put to you.   I can't pay you one hundred thousand lire outright—I haven't got it——"

"Then why did you——"

"Listen.   I say you'll get more before you've finished.   I'm a man of my word.   Now this is what I want you to do."

For half an hour the two men were closeted together.   It must have been a very satisfactory discussion, for when they appeared on deck again Mahassein observed they were on the most cordial terms with each other.   So cordial that, when Condylis told him Bandioli was coming back to lunch with them, he felt no surprise.   They were a pair of well-matched scoundrels.   When Bandioli left the ship with them, his younger brother, the second officer, took charge, with a revolver in his belt.   A promise of double pay had wiped out the last scruples belonging to that heterogeneous crew.

They lunched at twelve, and the Donna, as lavish with her smiles as her perfume, appeared, elaborately gowned and languorous in voice and gesture.   She had the merit of always responding to company.   Her mercurial nature expanded like a sunflower beneath the warming rays of masculine attention.

Bandioli found her enchanting, and she found Bandioli pliant, to a degree that flattered her.   Once, indeed, she had to check him discreetly, lest Condylis should say outright what she knew he would say afterwards.   Mahassein, arriving late from his task of sending out men to blow up the Yana bridge, found her preening herself in the salon, to which she had withdrawn, Bandioli bobbing about her like a captive balloon.   Condylis carelessly watched the pair as he puffed at his cigar.   He drew Mahassein aside, and was questioning him about his arrangements for the destruction of the bridge, when Bandioli's voice broke in upon them.

" I've just asked the Donna if you and she won't dine with me to-night? " he called, from his place at her side on the settee.

Condylis frowned, slowly knocked the ash off his cigar, and hesitated before replying.

" I was invited to dine there last night, you know, but——" he began grimly, with a sly twinkle in his eye.

A roar of laughter from Bandioli and the Donna greeted this remark.

" That settles it, dear Enrico ! " exclaimed the Donna. " I go with you, to protect you. If you'd taken me last night I'd have scented danger, despite Captain Bandioli's cleverness." She cast a flattering smile at the skipper.

Bandioli rose, and kissed the Donna's white hand, not with the grace of Mr. Cameron, who had brought more youthful tribute, but with a masculine surrender that was not lost on her.

" To-night, then. I'll send the boat at seven. *A rivederci !* " he said, and as he pronounced the words he was careful that his eyes expressed an unquenchable longing for the swift approach of that hour. The Donna lay back, and watched from the rim of her fan Bandioli and his host leave the room. Then, suddenly aware that she was not alone, she looked up swiftly at Mahassein, observing her as he stood with his back to the fireplace. They were old enemies, since they had never been old lovers.

" And what is it interests you? " she asked, archly.

" A rich cargo," he answered, enigmatically.

She looked at him, but his face told her nothing.

" I don't follow you," she replied, coldly.

" I wouldn't like you to, Donna," he answered calmly.

The Donna glared at him for a space, then, kicking out the flounces of her silk skirt, and shutting her fan with a snap, swept angrily from the room. The Pekinese followed, tinkling oddly after his mistress.

There were times when Condylis could be almost charming in his ponderous, deliberate manner. This evening was one of them, reflected the Donna, as she finished her dressing and stood surveying herself in the unbreakable Venetian mirror. Twice he had been into the room to look at her. Once he had suggested a paler rose in her hair, again that she should wear her pearls— a spoil from a Venezuelan victory, in those brighter days when men had been ready to commit suicide for her. Not that she had ever let them; it was better that they should live and give. These pearls represented, in that sense, a life preserved. With the consciousness that they stood between her and the menace of age and destitution, she had clung to them through all the vicissitudes of fortune.

"Emilia, I've never seen a throat that could carry pearls like yours—it shames their lustre," he said approaching her.

"Flatterer!" she laughed, and let him give her a playful bite on the ear. It wiped out the memory of other bites, less playful. "And the tiara?" she asked, lifting up a diamond and tortoise-shell headdress.

"No, not with the pearls—it lessens their effect," he answered.

She put it down again, susceptible to his flattery. It had cost him five thousand lire in a moment of weakness, in those early days of their meeting, at Sebenico. The pearls alone were worth fifty thousand lire. They were sufficient extravagance.

"Emilia—if you are too attentive to Bandioli I shall be jealous!" he whispered, ardour in his voice, as he watched her screw on her heavy earrings. Her shoulders were superb. He picked up a crimson shawl and draped them in it, and she threw him a happy laugh as he followed her out of the room.

At the jetty they found the boat ready, and were rowed across in the reddening dusk. At the top of the accommodation-ladder, Bandioli, suave, and for once remarkably immaculate in a white drill suit, received them. In the last light of the day he conducted them round the deck.

It was an evening of enchanting calm. The upper sky was cerulean, flecked here and there with wisps of pink clouds catching their colour from the deepening hues of the sunset. Along the western horizon, above the sea's rim, so that the sun burned crimson between dark bars, a narrow black cloud hung threateningly. Sagusto, sunk in the encroaching shadow, was edged with gold along the crest of its mountains, peak and cliff fading into the gathering night in which a few stars began their vigil. Around the ship there was not a sound. The smooth flood, emerald in the light and grey in the shadow, seemed no longer a sea, but a lake upon which the yacht rested like a dreaming swan.

"Shall we go below?" suggested Bandioli, when they had been up on the bridge and admired the trim equipment of the ship. He led the way down.

"I'll show you where they locked me in, Emilia," said Condylis, turning off to the left. "Look!"

He flung open the door of a small cabin whose porthole opened to the west, and the Donna entered.

"I came in like this, and sat down there. Then a tap came— tap, Bandioli!" called Condylis.

Bandioli, outside in the corridor, closed the door and tapped.

"Just like that," explained Condylis. "Cameron went across to the door, opening it, and a fellow there—where Bandioli is now—whispered something—pre-arranged, of course. Cameron said, 'Oh, excuse me!' and went out—so!"

Condylis crossed the cabin, went out, and closed the door behind him, in demonstration. The Donna, sitting in the carpet chair, heard the key turn in the lock. How neat it had been! She could not withhold her secret admiration of Mr. Cameron. No wonder he had trapped Enrico!

She was about to tell him so, but he did not come in. She sat a few moments. What was he doing? There was not a sound. A little impatient, she got up and went to the door. The handle did not yield to her abrupt turn.

"Enrico!" she called. "Enrico!"

There was no answer, no sound of any kind. What a stupid

joke! With a clenched hand, she hammered imperatively at the door.

"Enrico! Let me out! Do you hear, Enrico? At once!"

She heard her cry die down into the silence. And then, suddenly, she gave a scream. With all the strength of her fear and fury she picked up the carpet chair and beat frantically on the door.

She repeated her attacks until, an hour later, *The Three Castles* was more than eight knots from Sagusto.

CHAPTER XIX

BY three in the afternoon, Lieutenant Luigi, waiting with his men near the broken platform, had lost hope. It was an hour past the appointed time and still no hail had come from the rocks above. With ten of his men he had waited there through the morning and the noon, in the pitiless glare of the sun, from which they could find no shelter on the exposed face of the cliff. With a great effort he had persuaded the Donna and Nada to remain below, where some of the men prepared a midday meal, that had been brought up to the watchers. Even now he was reluctant to go. What could have happened to Cameron and Tino? If he went down to the cove he would raise terrible apprehension in the minds of the two women, yet if he sent no word they would make the ascent to find out what had happened.

Soon after three o'clock Luigi had made up his mind to leave, a couple of men keeping watch in case the signal came through, when the sentry ahead suddenly shouted. They saw him waving his arms excitedly in their direction. Immediately the lieutenant was on his feet. Accompanied by three of the men who had been resting near him, he ran up the rough track to the place where their outpost stood.

"A rope, signore! Look, a rope!" cried the sentry, pointing excitedly to the cliff overhanging his head.

Luigi looked up. He was right, a rope was being lowered from an invisible source. The lieutenant, now as excited as the men around him, shouted, for it was still beyond his reach. He could see it had been knotted into loops, evidently to offer footholds.

No cry came back in answer to his own, but the rope was being steadily lowered. Sometimes it caught on the higher crags, when a violent shaking from its invisible end loosened it and sent it dangling down clear of all obstacles.

At last, with eager hands, the lieutenant could seize it. He gave it a fierce jerk, and was immediately answered by another from above.

"Shall I go up?" asked a little fellow, eagerly looking at his lieutenant.

"No, wait," replied Luigi; "perhaps someone's coming down."

As he spoke there was a cry from above them, and Luigi recognised Tino's voice.

"We're here! Are you coming down?" asked the lieutenant.

"Yes, hold the rope taut!" came the voice above.

The party held the rope and felt the strain being put on it by someone descending. A minute later, over a projecting crag, a figure appeared, cautiously seeking the foot-loops. It was Tino, descending upon them.

He was breathless when he reached the path where they awaited him, and sank exhausted to the ground. Luigi, stooping over his collapsed figure, suddenly drew back with a cry of alarm. The lad was covered with blood, on his shirt, his breeches, his arms and neck.

"Signor Tino!—Tino!—what's the matter? Where's the major?" he cried, raising the youth. He saw him open his eyes, stare wildly for a second, and then collapse again, his face burying itself on Luigi's shoulder. His limp body would have fallen to the ground had not Luigi rigidly held him.

" He's fainted ! " he said, with a glance at the lad's inert head. " Quick, your flask ! "

One of the men helped to lay him down, and forced some rum between his bloodless lips. The shirt was sodden on the right side with blood.

" Look for the wound," commanded the lieutenant.

Eager hands stripped off the shirt, but on his body they could find no mark. Quick fingers unloosened the belt at his waist. The stomach and thighs had no wounds on them. Where had the blood come from? It was fresh and the shirt was wet with it.

They were quietly examining him when Tino opened his eyes.

" That you, Luigi ? " he asked, faintly. " Quick, the Castello —up the rope ! There's no one."

His voice died again with faintness.

" I'm not hurt—there's nothing—it's the major."

" Where is he ? " asked Luigi. The boy could sit up now. He had been dazed by a shock of some kind, and was utterly exhausted.

" Luigi—quick ! " implored Tino, seizing the young man's hand—" they're after us ! Cameron's hurt, down by the bridge. They shot him in the loin. I carried him, but couldn't go on. They're not at the Castello yet—if you're quick ! He's down by the bridge. Go !—now !—now ! "

He lay back exhausted, and Luigi got up from his knees, giving quick orders. One man was despatched to fetch the party below, one was left with Tino.

" Are you ready ? " said Luigi to the remainder. " When I'm up, I'll signal—come quickly."

He swung himself up the rope, passed from sight over the crag, and a few minutes later a violent shaking of the rope told the men below he had arrived. One by one they mounted. When the last of them had gone, Tino struggled to his feet.

"Where are you going, signore?" asked the remaining soldier, a stolid little Serbian.

"Up there—we're wanted—come!" he cried, but he staggered as he went towards the rope, and clutched at it to prevent himself falling.

"You can't—not yet, signore," said the man, taking him, not roughly, from the rope to which he clung.

"Oh, I must! I must! Major Cameron—the major—they'll get—do you hear?—they'll get him!" cried Tino, in the hysteria of despair and anger at his weakness. Tears filled his eyes, and he sank, exhausted, on to the path. It was monstrous —at this moment of all moments he could do nothing! He beat his hands on the ground in a frenzy of impotence.

"Signore, signore," pleaded the little man, kneeling at his side, and offering him the flask, which he pushed roughly aside. "They'll be here from the cove soon," he said, assuringly.

But the lad seemed not to hear, and sat, a disconsolate figure, his back bowed, his face buried in his hands, as if in an attempt to shut out some fearful sight.

They found him so half an hour later, when, panting with their exertions, the remainder of the landing-party arrived. One by one they scaled the rope and disappeared. As the last one waited his turn a cry made Tino look up. It was Nada, bending over him, one arm stretched protectively across his shoulders.

"Tino—what is it?—tell me. You are hurt?" she cried.

"No—the major, Nada—I've deserted him!" he said, dully, not looking up.

"Where?" she asked, in sudden fear, and then, "Oh, but you haven't—not deserted him—you couldn't. Tino, you couldn't!"

He laughed grimly at her words.

"Where's mother?" he asked, quietly.

"Coming now."

"We must go on, Nada, we must—we——"

"She's here," cried Nada, as the Donna came in sight. The dog at her side, catching sight of his master, joyously skirmished around.

"Tino—you aren't hurt?" cried the Donna, as she saw him.

He looked up at her, and then painfully rose to his feet, swaying slightly as his sister held him.

"No, mother—I would to God I were!—The major!—oh, mother, the major——"

She saw he was on the verge of tears, overwrought with some ordeal through which he had just passed, and she tried to comfort him.

"Not now, Tino—tell me later," she urged.

But he shook his head violently and looked at her, wild-eyed. "We must go on—at once! He may be taken—murdered!"

"Where is he?" asked the Donna.

And then, standing between them, half supported by them, he poured forth his story, often on the point of breakdown.

They had made their swim without mishap, but arrived so exhausted, owing to ill-luck with the changing current off the old harbour, that they had barely strength to draw themselves up the shingle. For some time they rested in a small cove to the south of the harbour, where they dried their clothes and, later, dressed. With extreme caution they made their way over the rocks towards the small bay in which the harbour was situated. Then they had climbed the rock face and were able to look down upon the harbour and the half-dozen hovels that fronted the unused jetty. It was fortunate they were so high, for below them, lounging against the old sea-wall, was a man, armed. He was so placed that their landing in the bay would have been seen immediately.

They had kept, then, to the rocks and slowly worked their way over the great masses of fallen cliff towards the back of the huts, where the maize-fields were spread across the valley, on either side of the Yana. There were a few peasants working in the fields, but they were easily avoided, and after an hour's fatiguing work they had gained the goat path, known to Tino, which led upwards through the foothills to the old cart track ascending the east face of the mountain. Soon after this they were sufficiently high above the valley to overlook the hills on the far side, and to see Sagusto and the sweep of its bay in the distance.

" We got careless then, I suppose—thinking the worst was over. We took to the track, keeping a sharp look-out. It must have been nearly noon when we came to the bridge. You can imagine our relief to see it there, still intact. But we were very cautious while approaching. The place was quite deserted, and I saw there had been no recent tracks made in the road to the bridge. We waited then, p'r'aps ten minutes, hidden behind the olives, watching the place, to make sure there was no one about, and then we decided to make a dash for it."

He paused to recover breath, and continued:

" We crossed all right—you know how the track goes up from the bridge on the other side, towards the south wall of the Castello. Well, we were half up it, delighted with our luck, when, without any warning, there was a rifle-crack. I stopped dead and looked behind, and there was the major, in a heap on the ground.

" You can imagine what a shock it was—that sudden shot in the dead silence. I rushed back to him, and before I reached him he got up, holding his hand so, mother——"

The lad put his left hand over his loin, in illustration.

"They got him there, and he couldn't walk, the shock had toppled him over. I lifted him up and ran into the cover of the olive-groves. They were potting at us fiercely then, from across the gorge, I think. He was in awful agony and bleeding terribly. He begged me to leave, but I wouldn't. After a rest I carried him on again—up through the woods this time, for I daren't risk the track. It was terrible work, his weight and the rough going —and I had to put him down again. You see, I knew they'd be down at the bridge in half an hour. I was risking everything

on getting up to the Castello.   If it was empty, I knew we could
fasten ourselves in."

"And you did it?" asked Nada, wiping the blood from his
arms with her handkerchief.

The lad shook his head sadly, and looked at her, misery in his
eyes.

"No, I didn't, Nada—I couldn't! He was so heavy and we
were already exhausted. And he bled so dreadfully. Not a
murmur from him. I thought he'd fainted once, he was so
quiet. I felt his blood soaking through to me all the time—
look!"

He pointed to the reddened shirt the men had stripped off him.

"Where is he?" asked the Donna, trying vainly to conceal
her anxiety.

"He begged me to leave him, and when I wouldn't he said
I'd have the death of all of you on my shoulders—they'd find us,
and get up to the Castello first. He couldn't move, he was in
such agony; but he never left off imploring me to leave him.
I saw he was right, and we decided the best thing was for him to
hide, so that we could sally forth later and fetch him. I got him
into the thickest part of the wood—in a hollow by some old
roots—and left him. Mother, I left him, but you know I didn't
—I didn't——"

He could not finish his words, and broke down, holding his
head between his hands, rocking in the misery of his mind.

"He was right, Tino," said the Donna, soothingly. "You
did right to obey him."

"But if he's found—if he's found, mother!" repeated the
distracted boy.

Then, mastering his emotion, he finished his story. He had
gained the Castello, quite deserted, and after bolting the courtyard door, had faced the task of reaching the broken platform.
He had found a long rope in one of the outhouses. In his weak
state it was impossible to repair the platform, so he had decided
to lower himself from above. The door in the north wall was

locked, and for a time he was completely baffled in his attempts to get out. Finally, he had squeezed through a lancet window in the west bastion, and from there had gained the path leading to the steps down the cliff.

Tino scrambled to his feet when he had finished his account. He was better now, he said, and his strength was returning. With it came his fighting spirit. He would not confess it, but his first sight of blood—that warm, unceasing flow from his companion—had unnerved him more than the danger through which he had passed.

" Mother—I must go on ! " he urged. " You must wait with Nada. Luigi doesn't know the place. I must get out to the major."

" You're not fit," answered the Donna, anxiously.

He tightened the belt about his waist, fierce with determination, and without another word went to the rope and began climbing. Before he passed from their sight he waved to them cheerfully.

But when he had gained the top he felt a pull on the rope, and looked down. To his amazement he saw Nada already half-way up, progressing steadily, loop by loop.

CHAPTER XX

I

LUIGI and his men lost no time in penetrating the Castello. Fortunately the walls to the north were low, and by going up over one another's shoulders they gained the crenellated rampart, and from it, by an internal staircase, the inner courtyard, round which the old part of the Castello had been built. But they had to exercise wariness. Even if Condylis's men had not yet reached it, there might be all manner of traps laid for them. Moreover, inside the Castello the narrow stone passages were ill-lit, and to their unfamiliar feet the steps and turns were difficult to traverse.

The place appeared completely deserted. They went through the kitchens—barren, enormous rooms that would have garrisoned a small army. Then, by a flagged corridor, lit on either side by deep slotted windows, they gained what appeared to be the grand salon. It was paved with Verona marble and had a painted Cinquecento ceiling from which hung an enormous wrought-iron chandelier, with half-spent candles. The fireplace, enclosing a dog grate, was magnificently escutcheoned with the arms of past owners. It had been the great hall of ceremonial receptions at one time, when Greek had given place to Saracen, and Saracen to Venetian, in the restless record of this stronghold.

But they could not wait to examine the place, and Luigi strode on through the dim hall towards the massive doors at the south end. They were locked. Baffled, they retraced their steps to the passage.

"The house runs west and east from here. You take that wing, I'll take this," called Luigi to his sergeant.

Another corridor, a flight of steps down to a lower level, and he found himself in front of mahogany doors, gilt-inlaid and panelled. They opened, revealing a long, narrow room that was obviously the refectory, with its barren tables. A rafted compass ceiling rose from the marble corbels. The far end of the room opened into one of the corner towers.

The view that met their eyes was superb. Beyond, on the horizon, rose the rocky, barren shoulder of Sagusto's great mountain. Its lower slopes were pine-clad, dropping to a dark and thickly-wooded ravine. Spanning this ravine, a slender bridge, its arch entirely unsupported from rock ledge to rock ledge, shone in the afternoon sun, its light stonework contrasting with the dark ground of the woods behind it. A track ran up from it towards the Castello, lost and re-discovered in its winding up the steep ascent.

Luigi saw at a glance that in the old days the place must have been impregnable. The Castello commanded the ravine, the bridge, and the track winding like a white ribbon, zigzag fashion, up the opposite mountain-side. The pinnacle upon which the Castello had been built, its massive bastions going deep down into the jaws of the rock like a molar tooth, was almost isolated. It was protected on the south by the deep ravine at whose base the Yana rushed tumultuously over its boulders, and on all other sides by the sea, a thousand feet below.

" The next floor now ! " cried the lieutenant.

In the corridor they converged on the men who had explored the east wing, which terminated in a similar tower. Together they mounted the shallow steps of the grand staircase to the upper storey. The centre of the staircase was carpeted. The place had an air of having been adapted to modern use, but there was a grimness in its massive strength that no refinements could disperse. Bedrooms ran along the upper floor, without particular interest, but out of one of them, through an old walnut door, they gained a spiral staircase, narrow and dark. It ran up the turret, and, panting, they emerged on the open roof. Around them rose the battlements, between whose crenellations they surveyed the olive woods, the ravine, and the sea, almost surrounding the rocky peninsula on which the castle perched. Through this machicolated platform they could see the precipitous walls of their stronghold.

Luigi placed a guard there, to cover the approach to the bridge, and descended again. In the great hall he heard voices. They were those of Tino and Nada, calling out for them. The youth had fully recovered, and ran towards Luigi.

" The others are coming ! I want a sortie-party at once—for Major Cameron," he cried. " Not more than four—I'm going down to the wood where I left him."

" I'll come," said the lieutenant.

He gave quick orders to his sergeant. Two men stepped forward to join the party.

"Leave a look-out on the Lion Tower—it covers the bridge," said Tino.

"The Lion Tower?" asked Luigi.

"Yes—the east tower—I'll show you."

"I've done it; we are ready, signore."

It took them a quarter of an hour to work their way out by the gardens, towards the ravine. They dare not risk the cart-track. It was too exposed, and visible from the mountain-side opposite. Their way led through the courtyard, by the long line of stables built against the enormous wall on the east, and then through a thick wood of chestnuts to a goat-path erratically threading the steep hillside.

Nada, watching through the windows of the refectory, saw the party scouting down, and finally lost their trail. Half an hour passed, but they did not come. Meanwhile the shadow of the late afternoon advanced up the mountain-side. Inside the Castello the men were busy under the directions of the Donna. A fire was started in the kitchen, the cupboards were explored, the whole place rapidly assumed its ancient rôle of a castle besieged. The place had been left unmolested, and a discovery of stores in the butler's pantry filled them with cheerfulness. Starvation might not be their end.

"Mother!" cried Nada, bursting in upon her, as she superintended the checking of the larders' contents, brought out and stacked on the floor of the great kitchen, "Tino hasn't come back—he's been gone nearly an hour, in search of the major!"

"We must wait," replied the Donna, calmly. "It will be hard work bringing him in."

"If he's safe," said Nada. Then, with a sudden fierceness, "Tino should not have left him!"

The Donna looked at her daughter steadily, waiting until one of the men, carrying a sack of flour, had left the kitchen.

"Nada, you are crazy—love-crazy!" she said, sharply.

The girl stared at her mother, surprised into speechlessness.

" Do you think I haven't seen? " said the Donna. " Is this a time for letting your heart turn your head? What more could Tino have done?—but I won't discuss it. Don't let me hear another word. There's enough to contend with. Go and do something! "

She turned coldly from her daughter, and continued her work. Nada watched her in silence. Sometimes her mother was a strangely inhuman creature, sometimes she had a fierceness that frightened her.

Half an hour later an excited man rushed up the staircase shouting, " They're back! they're back! "

With a fluttering heart, Nada ran down the staircase to the level of the courtyard, her cheeks flushed with expectation, a flood of tenderness filling her whole being towards this man who was risking his life for them.

It was Tino she saw first, then Luigi and two of the men. In a moment her glance comprehended all. Her heart seemed to stop. She went up to her brother with blanched lips.

He was dishevelled and haggard with fatigue, but this was nothing compared with the misery of his eyes, his voice, as he put out his hands towards her.

" Nada! Nada!—we can't find him—they've got him! " he cried, in a breaking voice, holding her close, as if he would draw comfort from her presence.

" Got him? " she asked, hoarsely. " How do you know? Have you seen them? Tino, Tino! tell me! He isn't dead? "

She clutched at the open neck of his shirt, her frail fingers holding it in the sickness of despair.

He did not answer at once, but looked from her to Luigi, standing silent at their side, understanding all, and sorrowful for her sorrow.

Tino slowly drew out of his pocket a handkerchief, stained with dull brown patches.

" We found this—I gave him it when I left him. It's told us something."

He paused, and with a sudden passionate demand she shook him with her tense hands.

" What does it tell you? " she cried, wildly.   " The truth—I want the truth !   Do you hear? "

He put an arm round her, in an effort to soothe her, but she stood back, with quivering face and head erect.

" We found it down by the bridge—not up in the grove, Nada.   It means they must have found him and taken him——"

A shrill cry cut across his words, and in a voice hoarse with passion :

" You deserted him !   That's why they've got him !   And you've come back—you've come back without him !   Why didn't you follow?   Why?   Why?   Then I will ! " she cried.

With a last glance, almost malevolent in its wild anguish, she turned from him, and rushed back to the door through which she had come out to them.

The men stood bewildered, Luigi amazed, aghast, at the cruelty of her words.   And then, in the stricken silence, he heard the boy's voice at his side, in passionate, agonised protest.

" *Mon dieu !*   what does she say—what does she say?   I didn't leave him !   Luigi, I didn't leave him—I didn't !   *Mon dieu !*——"

His cry was choked in his throat.   Quivering and exhausted, Luigi caught him just as he swayed in the onrush of unconsciousness.

II

An hour later Luigi found time to look in the room where Tino lay deliriously crying out his denial as he tossed from side to side.   They took it in turns to watch at his bedside, since they were all busy with preparations for the night and the defence of the Castello.   It was with thankfulness Luigi observed that Nada did not come near the delirious boy.   He said nothing to the Donna about the scene in the courtyard, and had warned the two men.

" The strain's exhausted him, Donna," said Luigi, as she

stooped anxiously over her son. "That long swim, and carrying the major——"

As he spoke a dull, heavy sound broke on their ears. Alert, they looked at each other in silence. The sound had come from outside, not from within. It was an ominous sound, and had died away slowly into the still air.

"Whatever is it?" asked the Donna.

Baffled, they listened, but it was not repeated. Only the unhappy muttering of the sick boy came to their ears. "I didn't, I tell you, I didn't!" he reiterated, endlessly, protestingly.

"I'll go down, Donna, and find out what it is—it's outside, I'm sure," said Luigi.

He left her in the darkening room. Through the window she could see the sunset touching each crag with its lurid glow, the shadows in the fold of the mountain deepening to purple. How often she had seen this last radiance of the day falling in beauty on the lovely heights! She loved Sagusto with a passion that made death here more desirable than life elsewhere. It was in her blood, her heritage, and nothing should drive her from it. These might prove the last hours of possession, since the menace grew so close with every moment; but she cherished them.

At the sound of footsteps she looked up from the chair in which she sat, to see the shadowy form of Luigi in the doorway. Something on his half-discerned face told her that he had grave news. She rose quietly and went towards him.

"What is it?" she asked with marvellous calm.

"The bridge—they've blown it up!" answered the young man.

Her eyes met his, steadily, with no light of fear or dismay. She saw what he thought and voiced it unhesitatingly.

"That means they'll not attack—and we can't. They're going to try starvation," she said.

"I didn't—oh, I tell you I didn't! Mon dieu! He implored me to go—he implored me!" came the restless voice across the dark room.

"How long can we—— Have we food?" asked Luigi. He felt the sweat break out on his brow. Action he never feared, but this waiting, waiting. . . .

"Three days; at most—four. That means a week, with hunger," answered the Donna.

"*I didn't. God knows, I didn't desert him! Nada! Nada!*" the voice rose in a scream.

The Donna crossed to the bed.

"Tino—we know, Tino. You were brave. Rest. Nada knows that," she said, soothingly.

Something swept by the lieutenant hesitating in the doorway, and gained the bedside, prancing fussily. It was Kim, joyously discovering his master.

"Down, Kim!—take him away, Luigi," said the Donna, capturing the Dalmatian by his collar.

Luigi took the dog, leading him out.

"Donna, the meal is ready. Shall I send someone up?"

"Yes, I'll come. Send Nada."

He hesitated, but it was a command. Perhaps the Donna knew best. He went out, towing the reluctant dog.

Below, in the refectory, they had got ready some kind of meal. The long table was lighted with candles, whose pale flames contrasted weirdly with the rich glow of the sunset beyond the high, narrow windows. They were observing no ceremony and little precedence. The men who were free of duty lounged by the fire-grate. Luigi, coming in from a fruitless search for Nada, saw they were hungry. He spoke to the sergeant, ordering him to begin, and went back to the Donna. The girl had probably hidden herself in one of the rooms, abandoned to her tears, or ashamed of her preposterous outburst. But he said nothing to the Donna, except that he could not find her.

"Won't you come down, Donna?—I'll stay, or send a man up," he asked.

"No, you go, Luigi. I'll wait until Nada comes. I'm not hungry and I can eat afterwards."

He went down and joined the men at the table.

"I believe that dog's had nothing to drink all day!" he exclaimed, seeing Kim hovering round, expectantly, his tongue lolling. "Give him some water, Reno."

The man filled a bowl and put it down for the dog, who lapped it eagerly.

"Poor old Kim!" cried Luigi, throwing the hound a slice of his polenta, which it snapped voraciously, tail wagging.

The men talked noisily. Luigi sat eating steadily, his mind busy on their defence, their supplies, Nada, Tino, and Cameron's disappearance. It had been a full, momentous day.

A howl, dismal, strident, made them all start. It came from the dog, by the fireplace. They turned, and what they saw held them in horrible fascination. The dog leapt, twisted, and spun round several times, in wild, eccentric spasms. Then, moaning, it curved its spine, tottered, fell, and stretched suddenly rigid, as a last tremor shook its tortured body.

Luigi sprang to his feet, breaking their hypnotic trance of horror, and ran to the dog. It was dead, with glazed eyes wide open in staring terror. Luigi turned to the table.

"That water! Has anyone drunk it?" he cried.

No one answered. In absolute silence one of the men took up the big jug and emptied it upon the floor.

Luigi found the Donna, sitting erect beside her son's bed.

"He is calmer," she said, as he entered. "He's sleeping heavily now."

Luigi approached and looked down on the flushed face of the youth.

"Donna, you must go and eat. Leave me with him," he said.

Without a word she rose, and he saw she was very weary at the end of this long, trying day. Yet one more blow she must suffer, he could not hide it from her.

"The water, Donna—is the well the only supply?" he asked.

She looked at him a moment before replying. Something in his voice warned her.

" Yes—why do you ask? "

" It is poisoned, Donna," he replied, simply.

She looked at him again, and then without a sign, without a word, left the room.

CHAPTER XXI

I

CAMERON, exhausted by the loss of blood from the bullet-wound in his loin, lay on his side without moving, in the hollow where Tino had placed him. He was protected from discovery by a slight knoll in front, in the sparse olive wood in which they had so desperately sought shelter on the exposed hillside. It was a miracle that they had escaped so well, and in sticking to him so heroically the lad had risked his life with reckless indifference to the bullets spattering over and around. The wild, inaccurate shooting from across the ravine might have proved fatal to either of them had Chance directed a vital shot. Cameron's disablement had stirred Tino to superhuman strength in his determination to get him to some kind of cover. Even then he had had a desperate, obstinate argument with the lad before he would go on alone.

" The lives of all those down at the cove depend on you now—don't you see that? " he had insisted.

" But, m'sieur—you can't be left! " retorted Tino.

" Your mother—Nada—do you intend sacrificing them for me? Go! Perhaps they won't find me."

The boy looked at him in anguish, hesitated, but was finally conquered by the determination in Cameron's face. Making him as easy as he could, Tino stood up, reluctant and dismayed.

They heard the crack of rifles away on the opposite hillside. Suddenly the boy fell to his knees, took Cameron's hand and pressed it between his own.

"May God protect you, m'sieur!" he cried, brokenly. Then he rose to his feet, and went quickly.

Cameron's anxiety now turned from his own plight to that of his companion. The lad was utterly exhausted, and nerve-racked from his first experience under fire. He had stuck to him, carrying a dead weight an incredible distance up the hillside, stumbling over the rough ground, ever seeking cover from the marksmen across the ravine. He had still to reach that hilltop safely and face whatever awaited him at the Castello. It might be guarded, he might be plunging towards his death. And the Castello gained, he had still to effect communication with the watchers from the cove.

Could the lad do it? Their swim had exhausted them, even before these later adventures. He owed his life to this mere boy, to his heroism in sticking to him under that wild, raking rifle-fire. Where were those fellows now? The firing had ceased, and in the hot, still afternoon there was no sound save of the cicadas. Raising himself, the pain shooting through his loin reminded him of his wound. The handkerchief he had over it to staunch the flow of blood was soaked. If it didn't stop——

A snapping of twigs made him alert through his faintness. Had they crossed the bridge? Were they searching for him? But there was no further sound. He heard a mountain bee hover about and pass. Half an hour must have gone. Perhaps Tino had gained the Castello. It would be quite an hour before help came, if at all.

Suddenly there was a cry, and three men, so swiftly appearing that they seemed to have sprung out of the ground, closed in on where he lay, their rifles centred on him.

Cameron could not understand a word they shouted at him, and faint, he scarcely realised whether they were friends or enemies, until they had seized him with an unmistakable fierceness. In his pain he cried out, and as they lifted him he felt the ground sink away, and he toppled forwards.

It was dusk when he seemed to come out of a sleep of exhaustion, with a throbbing head and parched throat. Around him the woods and crags had reddened in a falling sun that rested its vast disk on the rim of the burnished sea, which slowly began to swallow it.

Turning his head, he became aware of a man crouching near, smoking peacefully, a rifle across his bended knees. Someone had placed him on a bed of fern leaves. For a few moments he could not recollect how or why he came to be there, but a swift pain in his aching side recalled his wound. Then this man was a guard over him!

Cautiously peering round, he saw he had been moved from the olive grove. Weary, he closed his eyes and lay back. The dusk was taking the colour from the sky, and the night grew over him. Tino, where was he? And the Donna and Nada? Nada, with her dark eyes and bacchanal air—the wild, swift creature of these hills.

A sound came to his ears. The man started to his feet. Rescue?

But the hope was dashed. Three men appeared with a rustic litter, swung from a pole between two donkeys. They lifted him in, and jerkily started down the mountain-side, now clothed in darkness. Each jog from the donkeys caused him agony, but he almost forgot it in the chagrin that he was a prisoner, helpless in the hands of that blackguard Condylis.

At midnight they halted before a high gateway. It opened, and they passed in. A few minutes later he was lifted in the litter, carried across a yard, through a door, and dumped like a sack on what appeared to be a straw-covered floor. He heard a door slam, a bar shot across, and was alone in the absolute darkness.

He must have slept then, for when he opened his eyes the grey light of dawn filtered through the high window and the chinks of the door. The room was barren but clean, with white-washed walls. Despite his pain, Cameron dragged himself across towards the door, cautiously peering through one of the chinks. Slowly the glimpse he gained cleared in his sight, and with it came a strange dim recollection. In the centre of a cobbled yard stood a post, with queer iron loops on either side, about the height of a man's head. Somehow that post was familiar, unpleasantly familiar to him.

And then, like a rush of light across his mind, came a clear recollection. It was the flogging-post he had seen one morning —could it be only two days ago?—in the stable yard of Condylis's house!

II

Colonel Condylis, smoking on his loggia after breakfast, surveyed the morning landscape with an air of complete well-being. Yet it was not the beauty of the scene, of lemon and orange groves, of vine pergolas, maize-fields, and red-roofed houses clustering along the bright hillside, that filled him with self-satisfaction. It was the fortuitous events of the last forty-eight hours, which had shown him that his luck was still a very dependable asset. He had escaped from the wily Englishman's clutches, and he had rid himself of that tiresome Donna Gonzalos, without costing him a scene or even a moment's unpleasantness. Moreover, in doing so he had thereby, in virtue of the intrinsic value of her jewellery, halved his payment to that scallywag Bandioli, who had sailed off in glee with a ship, a woman, and fifty thousand lire.

As for the Donna Soudaikos and party, they had sought their own fate. Time and Nature would do the rest, relieving him of any unpleasant responsibility. They had got on the island; they might get off it, if they could. It was not his affair.

Finally, to complete his triumph, the man to whom he owed his humiliation, and the threat of a complete disaster, had fallen into his hands. It was this good fortune that presented a problem requiring thought.

" Ah, Mahassein!—you've seen him? " he cried, swinging round as the Armenian came out on to the terrace. " What do you make of him? "

In the many rôles of his not ancient past Mahassein had been a medical student at Bologna. Condylis had sent him, therefore, to examine the prisoner.

" It is nothing serious—a bullet's traversed the loin. I can't find it, it's only a flesh wound, and he should be right in a day or two—it's weakness chiefly."

Condylis halted thoughtfully and looked at Mahassein from under his heavy brow.

" I suppose I can't flog him—yet? " he asked.

The Armenian started, and the effect pleased Condylis. He liked terrorising this whippet of a man.

" *Dio mio!*—you won't do that? " cried Mahassein, protestingly.

" Why not?—I should really stand him up against that wall and shoot him, this morning."

" I wouldn't do that—he's English—there's the English Government."

Condylis was quite aware of it, to his chagrin, but he enjoyed the alarm shown by Mahassein.

" Who asked him to come to Sagusto? And what about his little dinner-party? However, as you say, he's a damned Englishman. I'll give him his life, but I'll take some of his skin."

Pleased with his ferocity, he puffed hard at his cigar, blowing it in his assistant's face.

" It's getting him off here that's the problem. I wish they'd shot him in the undergrowth. A nuisance that ship's gone; it would have served. Emilia wanted to meet him. Bandioli loved him."

He laughed appreciatively at his own wit.

" It'll be dangerous to let him go—he'll talk," observed Mahassein. " In fact, I don't see how we'll keep this business quiet, anyhow."

"There's much you can't see, Mahassein, and it isn't your business to," sneered Condylis. "I've thought it out. He'll have to sign a promise never to come back, and make the Donna and company sign it too. Then we'll ship the lot with the next ore cargo."

Mahassein stared at his chief in astonishment.

"You're not going to let 'em starve up there?" he stammered.

"To death?—no. What do you think I am—a murderer?"

Mahassein was silent. He knew well enough what had been Condylis's intention. If Cameron had been there, or killed, they would have been left to their fate. Cameron's capture had saved them. Condylis dare not accept the direct responsibility of his death.

"I'll let 'em get hungry enough to sign anything. If they want any further encouragement we'll have a little exhibition in the stable yard," said Condylis, smiling slyly.

"In the stable yard?" repeated Mahassein, wonderingly.

"Yes—they might be glad to save Cameron's skin, if not their own," explained Condylis.

Mahassein drew back as if he had been struck. This man had a diabolical ingenuity. His resource again and again paralysed all thoughts of revolt in Mahassein's nauseated mind. There was no outwitting this man. Only a suicidal fool would cross him.

"That appeals to you, eh?" asked Condylis, facetiously. "Governments can write notes, but they can't stop a man from having had a flogging—when his own friends wouldn't help!"

He laughed boisterously, enjoying his own ingenuity.

"So get him well, and feed him up, Mahassein. I'll see him myself this afternoon. You've got the place strongly guarded?"

Mahassein nodded. His heart was sick within him.

"You'd better let him see those two men coming up from the mines this afternoon. It'll give him some idea of how we do it. Don't wait for me, I'm not going until I've seen Zapoulos.

He wants more sentries, down the gorge, in case they try to cross it now the bridge's gone. Let him have 'em."

" I can't."

" Why not? "

" We've not enough men we can trust," said Mahassein. " We daren't take more from the mines—we aren't safe now."

" Fiddlesticks! " snapped Condylis, pulling up short in his walk and frowning at the Armenian. " You encourage 'em with your scared face! Look as if you'd shoot first and think after! That's the way to deal with them. Good morning! "

He dismissed Mahassein and walked into the house.

CHAPTER XXII

I

By noon Cameron was greatly refreshed. Mahassein had washed and dressed his wound with great care. He had taken the precaution of cauterising it, but was quite satisfied that the bullet had made a harmless traverse of the flesh. During his attendance Cameron had tried to draw him into talk, but he remained reticent, in contrast with his garrulity on their former meeting.

The morning wore on, and with the coming and going of Mahassein, who had also brought him something to eat and drink, he had obtained through the open door a fuller view of his prison. His room opened into the courtyard, as he surmised. In the old days the buildings running round it had housed the guard of the Captain of the People, who had dwelt in the house. The masonry was mediæval and solid. Escape over the high walls was impossible, even had he been fit. The only exit was through an arch, running the depth of the buildings, and gated

t the inner end with an iron grill. From the other end, which
ie could not see from his chamber, he heard sounds of heavy
doors swung back. Doubtless there was a guard posted there.

The courtyard, and the rooms surrounding it, seemed to
have been converted to stabling uses. From time to time he
heard horses led out and brought in. How long would Condylis
keep him here? And what did he intend doing with him?
He wondered what had happened at the cove, and whether
Tino had succeeded in reaching the Castello and joining the
track.

It must have been noon—his wrist watch had not gone since
his long swim the previous morning—when he heard someone
unlocking his door. The sunlight flooded in, and a figure,
slight, in ragged green shorts, stood blocking the bright daylight.
Then he came forward bearing a tray. As he drew near
Cameron recognised his visitor. It was the boy in the courtyard
to whom he had thrown the cigarettes one morning. Did the
lad recognise him?

Without speaking, he set down the tray, and then went outside again, bringing in a small table and a chair Evidently this
was to remain his prison, thought Cameron.

With a smile the lad came forward to help him up from the
straw on which he lay, but Cameron did not need any assistance
and hobbled to the table. The boy stood near, arranging the
earthenware dishes. As he did so he spoke in a half whisper.

"Signore, I shall bring you food again to-night, at six.
Here's a key that unlocks the door. After I leave you for the
night——"

He broke off, and made a noise with the dishes. They heard
footsteps go by, and die away.

"After I've gone, you'll hear a cart come into the yard. It
brings hay. When it's unloaded it'll back up against this door.
Slip out and into the back, and get under the covers. Keep
there! you'll be driven out."

The boy passed a key under the tray, listened, and turned to

go. Cameron caught him by the arm. He was too astonished
to grasp the full meaning of this astounding message.

" Who's cart—who is it? " he asked, excitedly.

The boy frowned, warningly.

" A friend—from the farm," he answered, quickly.

Before Cameron could ask another word, the lad had gone.

He sat back in the chair, trembling in his weakness and excitement. The key lay coldly in his hand—it stood for reality in
that surprising moment. Swiftly he slipped it into his breeches
pocket. The door was slammed, the key turned, and a bolt
was shot home, ostentatiously. The room was in shadow
again. He began to eat. His appetite had returned, with this
hope.

A friend. But who? None of his party could know where
he was, even if they had discovered his capture. It must be
someone here, in the house itself or in Sagusto, who was coming
to his aid.

Then, swiftly, the mystery was solved. Mahassein! Mahassein had told the boy. He was a timorous beggar, but
cunning. He was terrified of Condylis, and was safeguarding
himself. His taciturnity this morning was now explained.

Cameron began to wonder where he would be taken. The
boy had spoken of a farm. Mahassein had accomplices. It not
only gave him hope for himself, but for all of his party. Condylis had enemies within his gates.

He finished his lunch, and lay down again. After a time the
door was unlocked, and he sat up, expecting the boy. But,
instead, a man walked in, leaving two others standing by the
door. At once Cameron recognised him. It was Condylis.

" Don't get up," he said, with mock courtesy, seating himself
in the chair, a hand on each knee, as he beamed at his captive.
" So we meet again, Mr. Cameron—but you're my guest, this
time. The trapper trapped, eh? "

He leaned back, a grin on his dark face, and rubbed his hands
along his thighs.

"Sagusto seems to attract you," he continued. "Well, it's not a bad place, as you'll find. It's a pity you've left your camera behind, for I've arranged an entertainment this afternoon—a piece of pure mediævalism. I remember you told me you liked the mediæval."

He turned his head, calling the two men by name. They came in.

"Take the signore outside—and put him on this chair," he said, rising.

"I can walk," retorted Cameron.

"Ah! splendid! Mahassein's an able fellow, Mr. Cameron." Cameron ignored him and followed the two men.

Outside, the blaze of sunlight, filling the courtyard dazzled him in his transition from the dark room. The men placed the chair by the door and he sank into it dizzily. What was Condylis's game now? As the question rose in his mind it was answered by something he saw, and his heart almost stopped within him.

There, at the flogging-post, were two men, their wrists locked in the manacles over their heads. They were stripped to the waist, the muscles of their bronzed shoulders contracted with the strain of their position. On either side of them, with sullen, repulsive faces, stood their executioners, whips in hand, awaiting the word.

"These two fellows, Mr. Cameron, were as anxious to get off the island as you were to get on. The Court—myself—has sentenced them to fifty lashes."

He gave the word. Cameron closed his eyes in sick disgust.

II

As promised, the boy entered with the last meal at six o'clock. He said nothing and would have gone without a word had not Cameron stopped him. The boy spoke only Italian, and his accent was peculiar. Cameron, to make sure he had understood correctly, questioned him. The lad answered reluctantly. He

G

seemed full of alarm, and glanced apprehensively towards the door as he spoke.

" And your name? " asked Cameron, finally.

" Yanko," said the boy, smiling for the first time.

" I shan't forget you, Yanko—if I get through."

" *Grazie*, signore," answered the boy softly, and glided out.

Cameron ate mechanically. He was listening acutely for sounds in the yard. Ten minutes passed. He felt the key in his pocket. The boy had omitted bolting the door on the outside. If someone passed and noticed! He could do nothing then.

Half an hour later he heard the clatter of hoofs over the cobbles. They were heavy ones. They drew near, passed, and died away. All was still. Then, from time to time he could hear the stir of the horses, down the courtyard somewhere. They would be unloading now. Who were they?

Cameron felt the sweat break out on his brow, but his hands were icy. He was faint and in an agony of apprehension lest he should not hold out. The scene this afternoon—— He closed his eyes, and clung to the table by which he sat. It was almost dark within the room.

At last! They were moving again. He heard the clattering as the horses were turned, the rumble of wheels as they backed. It drew nearer, nearer—was outside his door.

With a supreme effort he steadied himself, rose and crossed the floor, key in hand. The lock turned easily, silently. He opened the door slightly, to find the back of the cart barring the doorway. Slipping out, he pulled the door to, and locked it in feverish deliberation. Then, with a last effort that left him exhausted, he climbed the cart, and tumbled in over the backboard. As he covered himself with the sacking on the floor he had a fleeting glimpse of the carter's back.

Without as much as a side glance, the driver started the horses, and the cart moved off, clattering across the courtyard towards the gate. By the rumbling echo Cameron knew they were passing under the archway to the outer gate. Would the sentry stop them? Cameron lay with held breath. But the cart went on, from under the arch. The cessation of noise, the soft thudding that followed, told him they had gained a gravel road.

He made no movement and no one spoke. Once, after they had been going some ten or fifteen minutes, in his anxiety and curiosity he could not resist peering from under the sacking up at the driver on the seat. The man sat slightly bowed, a Tuscan straw sun-hat thrust down almost to his shoulders. By his back, covered with a faded blue shirt, Cameron judged him to be a young man. But he was otherwise invisible, and not once, in the course of a journey that lasted an hour, and led up through the foothills beyond the village, did he turn to look at his passenger, or even to assure himself that he was there.

At last the cart stopped, under the roof of an open shed. Cameron heard the driver jump down, walk round the cart and unfasten the latchets of the backboard. The sacking was roughly pulled away from him and he sat up. It was so dark that he could hardly see his deliverer.

" You can get down," said a young voice.

Cameron started with surprise. The words were spoken in French. And then he knew who it was for certain.

" Mahassein ! " he cried, joyfully, tumbling out of the cart and catching hold of his rescuer.

There was a laugh, a silvery laugh, unmistakable this time.

" Nada ! " he breathed, incredulously. With a swift movement he swept the hat from her head, and she stood revealed.

" Mahassein, m'sieur !—do I look like Mahassein? " she laughed.

" Nada, you amaze me. My dear child——"

But the next moment, swept together by their common joy and danger, they were in each other's arms, and all their questions were forgotten in that moment of rapture.

He heard her story as they sat in the poor little homestead where they were waited upon by an old man and his wife, so old that one was stone deaf, the other nearly bent double. Nada began by explaining how, angry at Tino's desertion,—

"Desertion!" had cried Cameron, and he would not let her proceed until she had heard the full tribute to her brother's heroism.

"I was just mad—you mattered more than the whole island," said Nada, when he finished. "I was horror-stricken at the thought of you there, on that hillside, wounded. Poor Tino!— he must have seen I was crazy with anxiety."

"Well, go on, Nada. Thank God, he got back safely to you all—and then?"

She had left the Castello in the waning light and hurried recklessly down the hillside. Halfway, in her wild folly, she had almost stumbled upon the men carrying him. She followed cautiously then, down the steep, across the bridge, and up the other side. "I'd not been over many minutes when it blew up—they must have left a time-fuse in it to prevent being followed."

She realised then she could not get back to the Castello. Desperate, and aware of the futility of making any attempt at rescue, she had shadowed the bearing party up the mountain, over the moor, and finally, dropping with exhaustion, along the five-mile track leading to the plain and the village below. On the outskirts of Sagusto, aided by the night, she had crept closer. At last she saw the bearers of the litter containing their prisoner turn in at the courtyard, now converted into a stable-yard for Condylis.

"At least I knew where you were—it was something. I thought of this cottage, and arrived here at midnight. This old woman was a servant, she nursed Tino. I knew she could be trusted. Early this morning I went out and watched the gate of the yard."

"But, Nada—the risk!" cried Cameron.

"Oh yes—but not so great, really. These breeches and the big sun-hat disguise me completely. Well, I saw a boy go in and out with horses, I followed him into one of the fields, and got into conversation with him. He gave me a terrible fright. 'You are Signorina Soudaikos,' he said, all at once, staring at me. It was useless to deny. 'You are a friend of the gentleman?' he asked. I saw my one chance was to tell him everything. M'sieur, that——"

"Denis, please!—my name's Denis," he corrected. The old woman had gone away. He put his hand over hers, holding it. She answered its pressure, smiling.

"Denis, that boy was wonderful! For some reason he was your friend."

Cameron nodded. A smile, cigarettes, that had been all.

"He told me where you were—said he could get to you. Then he suggested a plan. A cart was going to-morrow, taking hay——"

"To-morrow, Nada?" queried Cameron.

"Yes—to-morrow. That was his idea. Why couldn't the cart go to-day, with a driver who would help? For a while I didn't see his ruse, and he had to explain. The boy left nothing unthought of. Well, you know what followed. He managed to take in your meals, and find a spare key. I got a cart here and a load of hay, and lumbered up to the gate. The boy—Yanko—met me up the road, and sat at my side. When the fellow at the gate questioned us, Yanko answered him. He knew the sentry, and we went straight in."

Nada related then all that she had heard in the countryside and the rumours from the village. There might be a revolt at any moment. It only required a leader. They would rise to a man if the Donna and Tino came. Their first task must be to set them free in the Castello.

"But how, Nada?—the bridge has gone. They can't get that way or from the cove," asked Cameron.

"I've thought of that. But there's a way, Denis. Old Zano here has a cousin who's a fisherman up at the old harbour. He will arrange for us to be picked up to-morrow, after nightfall, a mile to the south. We can reach the cove, take half a dozen of our men on board, together with mother and Tino, and bring them back. Then the boat can return for the others."

In her eagerness Nada did not see the doubt in Cameron's face as he listened.

"But, Nada, why leave the safety of the Castello? What could we do here?" he asked.

"Do?" she repeated, a little impatiently. "Denis! What can we do there—except starve? There's probably no food left by now. We can fight here. The whole village would rise."

She met his doubts, objections, questions, and finally she convinced him. Better to die fighting in an attempt that had some possibility of success, than to await the horrors of the end threatening them up at the Castello. Their situation was now so desperate that further attempts to avoid open conflict were useless. The true Condylis had been revealed to him that day. There was no pity, no mercy in the man.

They talked until nearly midnight, when the old man and woman made preparations for them to sleep. There was only the one room, with its wide slab grate on which a log fire had burnt itself out. They made a couch for Cameron, with some newly-shorn fleeces in a corner of the room. Nada lay on a mattress by the fireplace. The old couple occupied the bed let into a recess on the back wall. Some hens roosted under the table. A dog and a cat slept amicably in an overturned barrel.

But Cameron did not sleep for a long while. He was too excited with the events of the day, with the plans for the morrow. And his wound ached. If only he could last out. Fortunately, he could rest all the next day until they set out for the rendezvous on the shore.

Outside, the moon raced up a sky filled with scudding clouds, covering and uncovering its bright face, sending alternate light and darkness into the room where they lay. Once, in a moonlit interval, he sat up in the silence, his eyes wandering from object to object standing forth, hard and clear, in the white light. In his survey his glance fell upon the head of the girl sleeping near him. It was aureoled in its black tresses, now loosed and reflecting the silver light. Her face, with black lashes and eyebrows emphasising the beauty of its ivory contour, showed only one spot of colour—her mouth, pursed and crimson like an early rosebud. Despite the pain, he leaned over towards her, and would have touched her mouth with his, in tribute to her thoughtless beauty, but he feared to wake her. Instead, he let his lips linger on the softness of her hair, and robbed the moonlight of its long caress.

CHAPTER XXIII

I

To Cameron the next day seemed interminable in its dreary length. They moved him early into a store loft in the gable, deeming it wise to take precautions. Condylis must have discovered the escape by now, and would perhaps have the country-side scoured by his men. The farm was an hour's ride from the village, but even so it might be visited when nearer search had proved fruitless.

Despite his appeal, Nada had departed, and Cameron's one hope lay in her astonishing disguise. The riding-breeches and boots, together with the old blue shirt and the obscuring Tuscan straw, obliterated all traces of the woman. She had made the disguise more thorough by staining and dirtying her face and hands. She would have passed under close observation as a peasant from the hill farms. Despite Cameron's eager questions, she revealed few of her intentions, promising to be back by noon, when she hoped to have completed all arrangements for the evening. She left, accompanied by old Zano. They drove before them a flock of goats, completing the disguise and giving a purpose to their apparent wandering.

True to her promise, Nada returned at noon. Cameron saw by her face that all had gone well.

" There's trouble brewing down in the village—the revolt may come any moment," she told him. " The place is humming like a bee-hive. They say Condylis quarrelled with Mahassein over your escape, and wanted the guard shooting. Mahassein protested, and he's locked up! Yanko hasn't been near—I thought he'd better not go down there. He's coming with the horses at eight."

" But, Nada—where've you learnt all this? " asked Cameron, as she related her morning's work. " You haven't been in the village? "

" Yes—oh, I was quite safe! I went to the church and found the Pappa. He didn't know me until I told him who I was. The poor old man cried like a child over me. He'd heard that we'd all been blown up in the Castello."

She paused a moment, and Cameron saw her fear at once.

" Nada, you don't believe it—you don't think it's true? " he asked, the fear rising in his heart, as she stood so pale before him.

" I don't know—oh, I can't think, Denis!—it couldn't be, it couldn't be! " she cried, in the agony of her fear.

He took her in his arms, and felt the trembling of her body against his.

" The Pappa says there'll be an outburst, and it'll be terrible. He hears it all around, the village is smouldering. Two men were flogged yesterday, mercilessly——"

" I saw it—it was ghastly! " said Cameron.

" You saw it? Denis, you said nothing about that! " cried the girl.

" Why should I? we have enough to face. But the Pappa, Nada? "

"He remembered you—I told him everything. He thinks we might have a chance if we don't come too late."

"Too late! What does he mean?"

"Before they burn the place. They are like wild beasts down at the mine. Once the guard is mastered he thinks they'll stop at nothing. They'll murder Condylis, him, us," she explained.

"Us?" he echoed.

"They don't understand. Why should they, Denis? My mother, the Pappa, Condylis—we're all alike to them—in authority, oppressors. They'll not reason, once they begin. The Pappa wants us to come soon—before the storm bursts. They would flock to us, then, if they saw we opposed Condylis. We must take the mines first, and then march on the village."

In her talk there was an eagerness that made him wonder if she fully realised the danger and magnitude of their task.

"Nada, you know what this means—fighting, bloodshed, perhaps futility? Condylis will stop at nothing."

She threw back her head, determination in her eyes, in the passion of her answer.

"I know—and nothing matters."

"Nothing matters—Nada, what do you mean?" he queried.

"In Love there is no Death, Denis. That's all that matters. Don't you understand?"

But he made no answer, and the flame of her eyes died away beneath the tenderness of his own.

II

At eight o'clock, Yanko arrived with the horses. They had decided it would be safer not to ride, but to take out the cart again, Nada and Yanko sitting on the driving-seat, and Cameron resting behind on the straw-covered cart bottom. The rapidly falling dusk, heavy as they entered a ravine leading up out of the valley, shrouded them from observation. After an hour's steady going they had reached the coast. Here the cart was left in

Yanko's charge. He was to wait until they came back, which
might be midnight or later. The rest of the journey down to
the beach was made on foot. Nada had wanted Cameron to
remain behind, but he would not hear of it. She had already
faced enough danger alone. After his long rest at the farm he
felt his strength returning.

They found the man with the sailing-boat, drawn up in the
corner of one of the huge rocks littering the rough shore.
Nada greeted him. He was a young fellow, burnt with the
Adriatic suns, a Slav, judging from his broad, blunt features and
grey eyes. He spoke little, busy with raising the sail, after they
had rowed out from the shore.

" How long will it take to the Castello? " asked Nada, when
the sail had caught the night breeze and they began to run
steadily before it.

" An hour, signorina—if the wind holds," said the man.

He sat in the stern, quietly smoking as he kept the tiller.
They ran noiselessly over the calm water, now silvered with the
risen moon. On their port side the great hills of the island lay
sleeping like mammoth animals. Not a light could be seen
along that rock-bound shore, not even when they passed the
old harbour.

Cameron and Nada, sitting in the bow, hardly spoke to each
other through that hour. The night was warm and starlit, and
the loveliness of it sank down into their hearts, bequeathing
something of its great calm. They were happy as they had
never been happy before, despite what lay before them and all
the stress of events gone by. Cameron was no longer troubled
by a disturbing sense, such as he had known whenever she had
drawn near him, as if he had feared she would surprise him into
some betrayal of his suppressed desire for her. He thought of
that first night on the yacht, after he had accepted the task, when
she had come and stood so quietly at his side under the great
sail. He had experienced a vague unrest from that hour, an
inhibition, a conflict with some force combating his will. Now

he knew it had been vain.   Like other men, he was destined for
this happiness.   He resolved to take it boldly, since Fortune had
smiled so richly upon him.

He looked at her, alluringly boyish in her masculine clothes,
and she, seeing his face as she lay, resting her head on his shoulder
smiled back in wordless happiness.   So the hour passed, the
headland was gained, and they bore on the port tack towards
the cove.   A little skilful sailing, and the man brought his boat
right under the bluff of the precipice.   The entrance to the
cove was somewhere near.   He put out his oars, Nada, standing
up in the bow, directing him.   Presently they found the channel,
and the boat shot in, grounding at the place where they had
landed in the dawn two mornings ago.

To Cameron it seemed like an age.

They had wondered whether they would run any risk from
surprising a guard left down in the cove, but no challenge came
out of the night.

" There's no one here," said Cameron, examining the small
shore enclosed by two rocks.   " Tell him to wait, Nada."

She spoke to the man in a language Cameron could not follow.
The Slav produced an old lantern from his locker for their use.

" We shan't need it," said Cameron, " and it might alarm
them."

" It will be dark out of the moonlight when we turn the
bluff," replied Nada.   " We'll take it, even if we don't use it."

With a last word to the boatman, who had made himself
comfortable in the stern, they set off up the steps.

It was a night of enchantment, in which they would have
lingered and delighted had they not been occupied by their
mission.   The sea lay like a silver pool below the rocks, carrying
their black heads into the shining wash around them.   After
the heat of day, the cool air bore and intensified the aromatic
scents of the subtropical growth.   The crevices were luminous
with fire-flies.   In half an hour they came to the break in the
track, and a fear that had sprung up in their minds was allayed.

" It's there, Nada—look ! " cried Cameron.

Like a black thread the slender rope hung down the over-hanging cliff.   If it had been drawn up they would have been frustrated in their attempt to reach the Castello.   For that reason the lantern had been put in the boat.   If the rope had been missing they would have tried swinging a light out at sea, to attract attention in the Castello, but it would have been hazardous, and perhaps misunderstood.

Cameron called, and his voice died down in the night.   No answer came from above.   Fastening the lantern at his waist, he began the ascent, loop over loop.   Nada, watching anxiously, followed when he signalled his arrival on the upper ledge. Together they stood a moment, looking around, and then tackled the final ascent.

When they emerged at the top, on open ground, the Castello lay before them like a dwelling in fairyland, bastioned, battle-mented, the moonlight glinting white upon its narrow windows. Not a light shone in them, visible from the ground.

They advanced through the rock gardens, every inch known to Nada in happier days.   To their surprise the gate to the outer courtyard stood open.   They passed through to it.   It was silent, impressive with great shadows and moonlight cutting a pattern across its slabs.

" Shout ! " said Nada, in a voice that was awed by this silence.

Cameron shouted, and heard his call echoed back from the high walls.

" We mustn't surprise the guard," he cautioned, and as they crossed the courtyard to the main door, he repeated his cry.

The door at the top of the steps was closed, but when Cameron turned the handle, it opened, admitting them into cavernous darkness.   Again he shouted, and heard his cry echo along the hall.

" Light the lantern," said Nada.   " They must be in the lower rooms on the front."

The lantern threw a yellow pool of light about their feet,

increasing the immensity of the gloom through which they moved. In the main hall they paused, hearing nothing but the echo of their steps. They opened the door into the salon. It was moonlit, the light flooding in through the high windows, their colours patterning the marble floor.

"Denis—where are they?" whispered Nada, in a trembling voice.

"Are there any other rooms where they could be?" he asked.

"The refectory—this way. They might be there."

She led the way, and he followed, their steps sounding on the marble pavement. Nada threw open a door, and Cameron, behind her, looked down a long hall, with a central table, and chairs on either side. There was nothing but moonlight and silence.

Then Nada saw something, and started back with a cry, clinging to Cameron.

"What is it?" he asked, peering into the great chamber.

"Denis—look there!"

He followed the line of her quivering hand, raising his lantern as he went forward. Suddenly, with an involuntary cry, he stopped. There, shining up at him, with a ghastly green glare reflected in its set eyeballs, was a dog, stretched full length in the *rigor mortis* of a violent death.

III

They had to rouse the boatman, who was slumbering in the stern. Without a word he rowed them out from the cove, raised his sail, and began the return tack, out past the grim headland, blacker now the moon had sunk behind it.

Cameron never forgot that journey over the calm sea, along the shore of the unlit island. All the beauty had gone from the night, in their eyes. That silent, empty castle had struck a chill of fear and mystery into their hearts. Where had they all gone, and how?

Had Condylis reached them? That was not possible—the

bridge was destroyed. There was no sign of a struggle within. The place was entirely deserted, with not a trace of their occupation, except that ghastly corpse of the poor dog. It was hardly possible that they had attempted the crossing by the mountain head, or down by the gorge. It was too dangerous, and Condylis's men would be watching. And even so, it was incredible they would all attempt it, leaving not a soul behind. The only means of evacuating the Castello was by the cove. Since they had no boats, that, too, was impossible.

For Nada the shock and disappointment had been profound. Her courage, buoyant so long, had failed her at last, and she collapsed in Cameron's arms, sobbing like a child.

When they reached the shore again, at the spot where they had embarked, she was calmer, and as they walked up the beach towards the pinewood where Yanko waited with the cart, she talked to him of fresh plans, of her surmises upon their disappearance. Perhaps they had obtained a boat, perhaps they were attacking the harbour.

Cameron encouraged her to talk, it took her mind away from their disappointment. He had no belief in the boat theory, and when she asked him if he thought it possible that Bandioli had returned, he shook his head.

" Scoundrels never go back to their victims, Nada—besides, Condylis could prevent that," he commented.

What little hope he had, vanished whenever he thought of the dog, lying poisoned in that empty hall. It was a symbol of foul play.

The cart rambled on. Nada sat with him inside it this time, leaving Yanko to drive. They had left the high ravine and were descending the foothills towards the valley in which Sagusto lay. Once, Cameron looked over the sides of the cart, and saw the lights of the village, clustered at the foot of the valley and spreading out in a chain along the hillside, until they grew more scattered and, finally, solitary. The drying by the fire had revived Cameron's gold wrist watch, and looking at it closely in the faint moonlight, he saw it was nearly eleven. Their return from the cove had been earlier than anticipated. They rode on in silence, no longer in the mood for talk.   Then, all at once, they started up, alert. Yanko had pulled in the horses with a jerk, and sat upright on the driving-seat.   Next, he stood up, looking ahead.

"What is it?" cried Nada, in alarm, fearing they had been discovered.

The boy turned excitedly.

"Signorina—the sky! Look!"

He pointed towards the valley. They scrambled to their feet, and followed the direction in which he pointed. And then they saw something that made their hearts beat quicker. Away there, over Sagusto, a lurid glow spread in the sky. It grew and shrank waveringly, momentarily lighting the hillside behind, then dying down.

"What is it?—a rick fire?" asked Cameron.

"No, signore—there are no farms there," answered the boy, staring hard. "That's on the edge of the village—up the hill. They're all vineyards there."

They watched, and suddenly the glow spread again.

"Look, signore!" cried Yanko, as a tongue of flame leapt devouringly skywards, and fell back, finding nothing to sustain it.

They watched fascinated. A shower of sparks rising after another sudden glow told of something that had collapsed.

"What can it be, Yanko?" asked Nada.

The boy did not answer for a moment, watching the glow, that waxed and waned fitfully.

"I don't know, signorina—but it is near the village, if it isn't in it.   Something at the top end."

The glow had gone at last.   The sky lost its lurid reflection. The far hillside faded, grey and indistinct in the night.

"Drive on, Yanko," said Nada.

The boy waited a few moments, as if disappointed not to see a further outburst, and then, seating himself, started the horses.

CHAPTER XXIV

THEIR sleep was troubled that night.   From his place Cameron
heard Nada stirring restlessly.   She, poor child, was overwrought
with anxiety.   The disappearance of the Donna and her party
from the Castello filled their minds with fruitless speculation.
Cameron went over and over the facts, seeking for some clue,
some kind of solution.   He had purposely scoffed at Nada's
suggestion of foul play by Condylis.   Was it possible he had
lured them out by some means?   But even that did not explain
the death of Kim.   It was a sinister fact—and suggested other
horrors, to which the appalling silence of that deserted castle
contributed.

Cameron wondered what step could be taken next.   Sooner
or later the whole island would be searched, and he and Nada
be discovered.   These old people were running a great risk,
which could not go on indefinitely.   The idea occurred to him
of going boldly to Condylis, threatening him with retribution
from outside, and making such terms as he could for the safety
of Nada.   But he soon dismissed it, knowing well its futility.
Condylis wasn't a man to yield to threats that had little possibility of fulfilment.   Even so, the mysterious fate of his companions went unsolved.   If Condylis had captured them in
some way he would be unapproachable.

So through the night he lay pondering, planning.   Finally,
in sheer fatigue, he fell asleep, nothing decided, no loophole
discovered.

He awoke abruptly, as if starting out of a nightmare, to find
the old man shaking him roughly by the shoulder.   The half-
light of early dawn filtered through the window and fell coldly
upon the disorder of the farm kitchen in which they lay.
Cameron sat up, and looked drowsily at the old fellow, who,
half-dressed, was speaking to him excitedly.   Unable to understand a word of the man's speech, he looked towards Nada, but

she was sleeping soundly. Then it was that he saw the door
was wide open and someone was there, waiting. Alarm gripped
his heart in the moment. They had been discovered! With
another look at Nada he rose and went to the door, and the
fear dropped from him at the sight of the boy, Yanko, bare-
legged and breathless, standing there.

"Signore!" he cried, excitedly, as Cameron came out.
"The colonel is dead—he was killed last night!"

The boy trembled with the wonder of his news. He was
panting, as if he had been running hard.

"Dead—Condylis?" repeated Cameron, unbelievingly.

"Yes, signore. They burned him—that was the fire we
saw!"

The boy poured forth his story, so fast that Cameron could
not follow it. It was in vain he kept restraining him. In his
eagerness, Yanko turned to the old man, explaining, elaborating,
his hands as busy as his tongue.

Leaving them, Cameron aroused Nada, who woke with a
start.

"Nada—it's me! Come—here's Yanko. He says Condylis
is dead, in the fire last night!" he explained.

He saw her stare at him, as if he were a figure in a dream.
Then she threw back the rugs, shook her tumbled hair and got
up quickly. She caught the sound of Yanko's voice. At a
sign from Cameron, the boy came in, the old man hovering
behind.

"What is it, Yanko?—how do you know?" cried
Nada.

"Signorina, I've come all the way—running. He's dead,
signorina! They burned him last night! That blaze we saw,
that was Marenki's winepress. They chased him there, across
the fields when he escaped from the house. They surrounded
it, signorina, and they killed the guards, but the colonel got
away, over the roof and out to the fields. Mahassein was with
him—they got him first!"

" Mahassein—where is he? " asked Cameron, following this much.

" Dead, signore!—they shot him as he ran with the colonel, but they missed *il pescecane!* "

" Who? " queried Cameron.

" That's a nickname, the dog-fish, for Condylis," explained Nada. " Go on, Yanko—but they found him? "

" Yes, signorina," cried the boy, joyfully. " He barricaded himself in Marenki's press-house, and they couldn't get in—so they burned it. He was roasted alive! Alive! signorina—they heard his shrieks! Santa Maria, he is in hell now! "

The lad's voice rose in shrill delight. Never had he carried such news. He smiled, searching their faces for approval of his great news.

" How did it begin?—tell the signorina," cried the old man, who had now pulled his wife out of bed, wrapping an old coat around her, as she hobbled forward.

" I don't know—down at the mines, I think. They flogged two men yesterday. One of them killed a guard and took his gun. That started it. All the miners went with stones and threw them at the house. Then they broke through and killed more guards, and the others ran. They've taken all the furniture and burnt it. And, signorina, there's nothing left of him, nothing! The Pappa went up to the presshouse and cursed the cinders, while they searched for him. *Evvero*—there's nothing left, and the Pappa's cursed it! "

The boy talked, breathlessly, telling his wonderful story. The old woman, seeing his legs were all wet with the dewy meadows through which he had come, began to wipe him down with motherly care, but he danced away from her.

" Signorina—you will go down with the signore? " he cried. " I'll get the horses—it is safe now. The *polizia* have come— they've heard the Pappa's prayers."

" The police—whatever does the boy mean? " asked Cameron of Nada. " What police, Yanko? " he said, turning to the lad.

" The *polizia* and *carabinieri* with rifles—the Pappa prayed for
your safety and they came in the night, in a battleship!"

Nada and Cameron looked at each other. The boy was
being carried away in his excitement.

" Yanko—did you see them?" asked Nada, severely.

The boy met her eyes, unabashed.

" Oh no, signorina—Mario told me, and I——"

Cameron glanced significantly at Nada. Then, putting his
hands on the boy's shoulders, he faced him squarely.

" Yanko—our lives may depend on what you tell us. You
are not lying?"

Immediately, by the hurt expression in the lad's eyes, he knew
he had spoken the truth.

" I'm sorry, Yanko," said Cameron. " I believe you."

Nada questioned him then, but could not shake his story.
Condylis and Mahassein were dead. He had seen the cinders
of the presshouse which the Pappa had cursed. And Mario, his
great friend Mario, whose mother cleaned the house of the
Pappa, as well as the church, had seen the *polizia* and the *carabinieri*, who had come in answer to the Pappa's prayers for the
safety of the Donna, the Signora Nada, the signorino her brother,
and the signore inglese.

" The boy's right, Denis—it must be an Italian ship that's
put in to the harbour," said Nada, convinced by Yanko's
unwavering story. " We must go—at once!"

She turned to the boy, who watched her face eagerly.

" Get the horses and the cart, Yanko—we'll come."

The boy hurried out. It was fully light now. In the east
a flush of rose broke over the hills, whose feet lay swathed in the
fleecy mist. Within the kitchen they ate and drank coffee as
they completed their dressing. A momentous day had begun.

CHAPTER XXV

TWICE in that ride down to Sagusto Nada had to restrain the boy. He drove the horses mercilessly. The cart seemed in danger of being knocked to pieces by the pace at which it was bumped over the rough track. But as soon as the protest had passed, Yanko, as if obsessed by a demon, seized the horses again. Cameron and Nada, bumped about on the floor of the cart, saw that all attempts to check Yanko's eager spirit were vain, and let him have his will.

"I can't think that battleship story's true," said Cameron. "It's secondhand evidence. Yanko hasn't seen it, and I've not much belief in Pappa's prayers. But it's probable that Condylis has met his end—and I don't feel sorry."

"I hope Yanko's wrong—if that's an Italian battleship it's the end of us."

There was a note of despair in Nada's voice that made Cameron regard her intently.

"The end?" he queried, puzzled by her remark.

"Once the Italians put foot on Sagusto they'll stay, on any pretext—and here's one good enough. Mother risked everything to avoid that!"

He recalled, then, the Donna's fears of annexation on that first night aboard the *Lucciola*, and her inflexible determination not to invoke the help of Italy or Yugo-Slavia.

"It's probably only some boat that's called—or the ore boat back from Sebenico," suggested Cameron, in an attempt to allay Nada's fears.

A little later, something flashing across his mind caused him to sit silently pondering.

"What is it, Denis?—you've thought of something?" cried Nada, watching his intense absorption.

He did not answer for a few moments, but when he looked at her he knew evasion was impossible.

" There's something ! " she repeated.

" Yes—I wonder it didn't occur to us before," he admitted. " This explains their disappearance from the Castello."

" The battleship?—you think it's taken——"

" It may be a battleship, or a ship of some kind that called at the cove."

" But how would it know? " asked Nada, breathlessly. He saw the blood flush her cheeks in the excitement of the thought.

" They may have attracted it in passing—they could signal from the Castello. It would be a chance."

The girl caught eagerly at his hand, holding it, her eyes bright with a sudden hope.

" They're alive, Denis—it's a battleship! Yanko is right! " she cried.

But he kept a sober tone in his voice as he answered, aware of the bitterness of dashed hopes.

" My dear—we can't be sure, but we shall know soon."

The cart rattled on, the journey seemed interminable. All at once they were interrupted by Yanko, who turned on his seat.

" Signore, we'll see the ship in a minute. We'll see the harbour round the corner."

He whipped up his horses again, bumping the cart wildly over the holes and boulders of the rough mountain road. They were nearing the valley. A hundred yards more, and they had turned the corner of the hill and saw Sagusto below them. With quickened hearts they looked towards the harbour, expectant, believing, unbelieving.

Disappointment swept over them. The harbour and bay were invisible beneath an early morning sea mist.

" It's there, signore—though we can't see! " called Yanko, more positive than ever.

Cameron and Nada did not answer. The boy drove on. They were nearing the outskirts of the village now. The sun, not yet on the houses, caught the campanile of the church in a loop of gold light, with its twin bells visible in the upper arches.

The last five minutes of that drive seemed an age. They were in a street now, obstructed by goats going to be milked on the very doorsteps of the customers. Suddenly, Cameron gave a shout that made even Yanko start.

" Stop ! " he yelled at the boy, leaping to his feet.

For Cameron had seen something that sent the blood coursing through his veins. There, on the corner of the street, standing with the butt of his gun grounded between his feet, was a figure that dispelled all Cameron's doubt. It was a man in the uniform of a blue-jacket, his wide trousers tucked into brown canvas half-leggings, his round white-topped cap tilted over one eye. At that amazing moment he stood for everything that was dearest to Cameron—home, country, sanity.

" Hi ! Jack ! " he yelled.

The sailor started as if he had been struck. He swung round in the direction of the cart and saw a man lowering himself hastily out of it. The words, the accent, were English. He went up to Cameron, and with a wonderfully recovered composure, saluted and addressed him.

" Are you Major Cameron, sir ? If so, we're looking for you."

" I am ! " replied Cameron, reading " H.M.S. *Milton* " on the cap-band.

" There's a search party just gone up that lane, sir—I'll fetch 'em," he cried, darting off.

Cameron went back to the cart.

" The boy's right, Nada," he said, excitedly, lifting her down in her bewilderment. " It's a battleship—British ! "

" The signore knows I speak the truth ! " cried Yanko, triumphantly, looking down on Cameron from his seat.

" Yanko, you do—and it's golden too ! " he laughed, giving the boy's brown leg a slap.

They heard the tramping of feet, and towards them came four blue-jackets, armed. With them, in a reefer, white ducks and half-Wellingtons, was a midshipman. He saluted smartly as he came up, with a cheery smile.

"Major Cameron? Good morning, sir."

They shook hands. It might have been the Esplanade at Cowes instead of a street in Sagusto. A dozen doors had opened, a swarm of half-clad natives blocking them.

"We've six parties searching for you, sir," said the midshipman, and then, seeing the youth at Cameron's side, he stared a moment, conscious of something singular about this breeched and shirted figure.

"This is Ma'm'selle Soudaikos," explained Cameron.

The young officer saluted briskly, and swallowed his amazement.

"Ma'm'selle, we're hunting for you also!" he said.

Nada turned to Cameron, not understanding.

"Ma'm'selle doesn't speak English. Have you the Donna on board?" asked Cameron.

"All the party, sir. We took them off last night."

"From the Castello—when?"

"In the second dog-watch, sir. We had an awful job with the old lady——" He cast a nervous side-glance at Mademoiselle Soudaikos, to see if she understood, and, assured,— "Couldn't get her to move," he continued. "Swore she didn't want any help, and the whole of 'em nearly crazy with thirst! You'll come to the ship, sir? We'll escort you. This place is in a queer state. They've been murdering one another overnight—five dead in a house off the Square, and a Greek colonel-something chased and burned alive. But p'r'aps you know all about it? When the Admiral heard, he——"

"The Admiral—who?" asked Cameron, quickly.

"Sir Reginald Durose—he's flying his flag on the *Milton*, sir. He transferred from his yacht——"

"Good Lord!" interrupted Cameron, in his surprise. "You don't say you've got Cartwright and Meredith on board?"

"Yes, sir, they're here, and anxious about you. Mr. Cartwright had a stiff job with the old Donna on a rope ladder. But she's like a lamb this morning."

He gave an order to his men to march ahead. Cameron told Yanko to follow with the cart, and explained where they were going to Nada, who had stood silent at his side.

The midshipman looked nervously at her. It was difficult to believe she could be that fierce old Donna's daughter.

" I say, sir, I suppose she really doesn't know what I've been saying? " he asked, apprehensively.

" No, but Ma'm'selle will talk French with you."

" She won't, sir—mine's too awful! " he answered, defensively. " Phew! just look at this crowd gathering. Shall we move?—I'll get on the other side of the lady, I think."

Down at the harbour they found a picket boat, and were rowed out to the ship. She was a light cruiser, of about twenty thousand tons, with her for'ard guns stretched out like elephants' trunks over the fore-deck. A white awning sheltered her aft, where the ensign fluttered above her veranda hull. A beautiful creature she was, in her spotless coat of slaty-grey, docile upon the blue water.

At the top of the accommodation-ladder they were met by the Admiral's secretary.

" Sir Reginald's below, sir," he said, addressing Cameron, and looking covertly at the girl in the riding-breeches.

" This is Mademoiselle Soudaikos," explained Cameron. " Donna Soudaikos is here, I'm told? "

" Below, sir, with the Admiral. This way, please."

He led them across the deck and down a companion-way. A few moments later they were ushered into the wardroom, where Sir Reginald, the Donna, and Cameron's two friends, Cartwright and Meredith, came towards them with cries of welcome.

CHAPTER XXVI

THEY were a long time exchanging news, and it was not finished when the bugle sounded for lunch. The Admiral had a story almost as exciting as Cameron's. Just off Bari they had sighted a foreign-looking ship, flying the British ensign.

"That didn't make us suspicious, though naturally we looked at her closely. It was the name on her stern that drew us—you never saw such lettering! We hailed her, but got no reply, and I'm blessed if she didn't suddenly change her flag—for a Greek one. We worried her then, suspicious at once, and ordered her to stand by. An impertinence, I suppose, for we weren't a ton heavier—you know the *Rover*."

"The yacht! Then you weren't on this ship?" asked Cameron.

"Oh dear, no!" answered Sir Reginald. "Meredith and Jack, here, were with me on our way to Brindisi—the trip you declined. Well, the next act reads like a novel."

The Admiral glanced down the luncheon table—"We're finished? Then, ladies and gentlemen, let's go to the veranda. We'll have coffee there, steward."

With cigars and coffee, with breaks in the narrative in order that it might be translated to the two ladies, Sir Reginald related the part played by the *Rover*. They had found chaos on board *The Three Castles*. Her skipper had been killed, stabbed in the back by a virago who swore she had been assaulted in her cabin. She told an incredible tale about being kidnapped and stripped of her jewels. But it seemed to find corroboration from half a dozen hands who stepped up. They made it understood that the ship, really the *Lucciola*, had been stolen, after deserting its owner, a Greek lady, who, with twenty soldiers, under the command of an Englishman, was trying to get back her property, an island called Sagusto, off the Dalmatian coast.

The virago, who swore she was a Donna Gonzalos, bore out the story, with much in addition concerning the blackest of villains, named Condylis.

"We pricked up our ears when the Englishman came into the story. His name was Cameron, she said. Even then we didn't connect you—we thought you were back in England. The dead skipper's brother was obviously lying when we questioned him. The crew refused to sail under him. So we decided to send the ship under escort to the Italian authorities at Bari, and let them deal with the Donna. I called up the *Milton* for duty—she was cruising near Ragusa. Just before she reported, your trunks were discovered. We knew then who the Englishman was! When the *Milton* came, we transferred to her, sent *The Three Castles* to Bari, and with two of her crew to pilot us to the cove, sailed north for Sagusto.

"You know the rest. Now your story, Cameron. There's been a revolution, I hear. We saw a blaze as we were anchoring, but had no idea what was happening. We were worried about you and this young lady, who seemed to have vanished. But we couldn't land in the night, even had we known what to do or where to go—so we sent off a shore party as soon as it was light. We heard then what had happened to Condylis, and we sent out search parties to find you both. That's our story—now yours!"

Briefly Cameron narrated the events of the two days—his capture, Nada's rescue, their mission to the Castello, ending in such despair.

"You must have missed us by about two hours. We landed at the cove at dusk, and left about eight o'clock," said Sir Reginald. He rose, and turning to the Donna, addressed her:

"Donna, you must have much to say to each other. My secretary's been out here three times for me—will you excuse me?" With a bow he went.

Cameron looked at Nada. There was one thing he had not

told the Donna.   He seized the opportunity boldly, the moment
he had taken her aside.

Marvellous woman!   At the end she gave him that quiet
smile, unperturbed, as ever she had been, whether facing ruin,
starvation, death—or a prospective son-in-law.   It was Tino
who made all the noise when he was allowed to know, that
evening.   The ship's doctor saw a remarkable advance in his
condition the same hour.

Two days later, towards four in the hot afternoon, as the
gunnery lieutenant dozed in a hammock chair placed in the
shade of a gun-turret, he heard a rich cockney voice say to an
invisible companion:

" 'E's cleaning 'is things nah!   'E's in the guard for that
splicin' of the major-bloke to the Greek gel! "

" Not 'ere? " protested another voice.

" No!   in that church there—by the ole Greek papper with
the whiskers and black funnel 'at."

" Lor!   Are we goin' a honey-moonin', then? "

" Not as I've 'eard.   We're off on Wednesday.   The *Rover's*
coming up to take 'em to Venice."

The lieutenant jumped up and went off to seek his friend.   If
they were going on Wednesday, as overheard, their shooting
trip with that blithe Lieutenant Luigi was off.   It was simply
amazing how the lower deck always got the news first!

CHAPTER XXVII

IF anyone, on that last day spent by Cameron in Venice, had
ventured to prophesy that, within one week, he would be kidnapped, have entered the service of a mysterious lady, have
landed on a strange island, in command of her hired soldiers,

been wounded, imprisoned, and rescued by the mysterious lady's beautiful daughter, and married to her—he would justifiably have called the fellow mad. But Cameron had since learned that fiction can never hope to be as fantastic as fact, and that the most imaginative writer is a trite historian in the realm of life.

Standing by the rail of the yacht beating its placid way from the island fading in the dusk, Cameron knew, in this hour of his sadness, he might never again be so happy. It lay there, Sagusto, mysteriously linked with his destiny, merged in the tide of the oncoming night. Over its mountains, penetrating the storm-dark clouds, the cold stars glittered. In warm contrast, the yellow lights of the harbour and village shone through the purple veil fallen upon the waveless sea. So had some Roman, some Saracen, or Venetian adventurer seen it and left it, those centuries back, in success or defeat.

But even as he looked, knowing a few minutes would take it from his vision, and the bold headline, with its castle, be lost in the impenetrable night, he wondered if any had ever left it, in all its vicissitudes through Time, moved by gratitude as he was moved, because of the richness it had brought into his life.

Three-bells rang softly through the ship. For a moment he had a feeling that he was standing fearfully alone. The farewells, the sunset, the night, his so swift past, his so inscrutable future, filled him with the fear of solitariness, increased now by the hostage he had taken against it. He lived henceforth in two lives, his own and hers. Even now it was her sorrow he felt, knowing she had just left his side so quietly, to let her tears —unhappy, happy tears—fall in solitude, lest he should wonder or fear that she might doubt. Never again, until one of them put out on that last sea, through the great darkness, need tears flow for such cause as these now flowing.

Perhaps now he might go to her, the sacred moment of her sorrow past, her homeland left. He bared his wrist, to check with those soft bells his watch, and remembered then that an island boy wore it as one might wear a king's reward.

He turned from the sea and the night. A warm glow filled the companion-way, hospitable in the greyness around. Cameron went towards it, closing and opening a chapter in the book of Life.

THE END